Prairie Academy

Joann Ellen Sisco

Book # 1 of the
CARLILE CORNERS
Series

Signalman Publishing Kissimmee, Florida

Prairie Academy
by Joann Ellen Sisco

Signalman Publishing
www.signalmanpublishing.com
email: info@signalmanpublishing.com
Kissimmee, Florida

Publisher's Note:
This is a work of fiction. Names, characters, places, and incidents are either the product of the author's imagination or are used fictitiously, and any resemblance to actual persons, living or dead, business establishments, events, or locales is entirely coincidental.

Cover design by Rob Cheney

ISBN: 978-1-940145-11-2

Other books by Joann Ellen Sisco

Carlile Corners Series:

Blossoms in the Grass

The Shaping of Shady Ridge

Cookies, Hats, and Hankies

Under the Haystack

War Eagle River Series:

Twixt the Road and the River

My Sister My Friend

Like an Eagle

The Mighty Cedar

Turn Left Off Main

Three Times A Mama

Hilltop House

Mill on the War Eagle

FROM NEW YORK TO THE PRAIRIE

Josie saw the flames in plenty of time to jump from the bed and disappear through her second floor window, but she did not move. She stiffened with fear, but still she did not move. Her legs had no feeling. She was tired of running, anyway. If the hungry flames wanted her... well, they could just have her. She was not going to run anymore.

A deep breath, and then a tiny voice. "Josie? I think..."

A sleepy reflex action caused Josie's right arm to reach out, surround and draw toward her the tiny girl on the bed beside her. She felt a light-fingered touch, like butterfly wings, patting insistently against her face.

A voice. It said, "Josie? I think... I...," then a sudden flood of liquid warmth spread over Josie's face, neck and chest, coating her night dress with a sudden, sodden weight of wetness. There followed a scream of dismay in the four-year-old voice. "I didn't... mean to! I didn't do it!"

One thing about it, though, was Josie's first thought, the flames that had surrounded her, paralyzing and brilliant, were successfully drowned out by the regurgitated remains of her young cousin's supper.

Feet on the braided rug, hand seeking through the darkness for a match and the candle. By now, small Esther's voice had aroused the entire household. Aunt Nettie's face, still blank with sleep, appeared at the door, vague in the soft light of the candle.

Josie told her, "Auntie, go back to bed. I can take care of her. At least, her fever broke."

In an exhausted weariness, the little girl's mother turned back to her own bed while sleep still claimed her. The offer of help was too tempting to refuse.

Interestingly, the child's own clothes were untouched, and only minor spots had hit the bed. Stripping off her own clothing, Josie wrapped herself in whatever was handy and made her way to the kitchen and the wash pan of water that occupied the stand beside the tin pail of water.

Within minutes she was swabbed down enough to continue the night, though there would be no sleep for 17-year-old Josie. The scream of the night birds and the screech of crickets spread a blanket of sound over the prairie of the Oklahoma Territory. Circled within her arm the little girl breathed softly while Josie's own thoughts raced each other in their effort to make sense of her life up to now.

Four short months ago she lived in a lovely house in the center of New York City, snug within the safety of her father, a successful lawyer, and her mother, who was ready to guide her into every facet of life required of a young lady of her age and station. Just next year, there would be the party announcing her coming of age. After that, there would be... well, one thing would lead to another in their proper succession. Her parents would see to that.

It had been Christmas Eve... presents... decorated tree... cheery flame for toasting marshmallows and chestnuts. A quiet family night with her 7-year-old brother beside her excitedly trying to guess the contents of the presents marked for him. Tomorrow the festivities with friends would begin.

Later that night, the candles had been carefully extinguished after the fireplace had been banked for the night. Her parents retired across the hall to their bedroom, and Josie had playfully pushed her brother up the steps ahead of her... away from his stack of coveted presents.

It had been hardly moments later that she began to dream of... what? A smell that seemed familiar... but out of place. What...?

Fear, alive and palpable, flung her from her bed and into her robe. The cold of the bedroom was being invaded with warm air and smoke. She flung up a window and stared out onto the snowy yard, now sparkling lively with red reflections from the downstairs windows. Leaning out, she saw the flames.

Instinct pushed her through her door into the hall, and she met a billow of acrid smoke boiling up from the kitchen. Thoughts raced... if the kitchen was aflame, the living room and her parents' bedroom would already be in ruin. Slippered feet scrambled through the smoke into her brother's room. A relieved breath, he was safe.

"Josh! Up!" and putting action to her words, she yanked on the first part of him she reached... being a pajama-clad arm. His body thudded onto the rug, seat first, and she jerked him up. Flinging up a window, she prepared to push him through, but was stopped by the thought of the picket fence so close to the house. Too close for safety. Sharp picket ends. Dangerous!

"COME!" she demanded and dragged him by the arm, his bottom scooting on the floor. Into her room, she banged the door closed, wrapped a small comforter around his shoulders and pushed him to the window, hardly realizing that he was still asleep and muttering his irritation.

"Jump! You got to jump!"

"No! Go away!" He grabbed the sides of the window and held on, trying to return to the bedroom. Josie scooped his feet off the floor and set them on the windowsill.

"Now, jump!"

He either couldn't or wouldn't, but remained balancing himself 15 feet above the snowy yard. A tongue of flame had crawled over the fleece of her bedroom carpet and now reached for the edge of the floor length curtain.

"Josh! You got to jump!" she screamed in desperation. But, as the flame leaped up the length of the lace of the curtain, she knew he couldn't move. Holding to the window frame, she planted a foot against his back and shoved with all her strength. He must not fall through flame in his fleecy nightclothes.

The small boy woke up on the way down, emitting a horrified scream just before landing face down in the soft, fresh snow. Josie grabbed up a quilt and threw it after him, watching as it floated down on the brisk December breeze.

Out of the window went another quilt and an armload of shoes from her closet. As an after thought from looking at her slippered feet, she flung out the entire contents of her sock and underwear drawer.

Pulling her robe around her she stepped onto the windowsill and launched herself into space.She landed mostly on a quilt, and searched frantically for Joshua, while being amazed at the number of assembled neighbors, their coats pulled on hurriedly over pajamas, searching anxiously for survivors and staring with horror as the flame filled the windows of the burning house.

Josie, now snug in bed with the tiny girl pressed against her, shivered and tried to stop the scenery from passing... once more... through her mind. Sometimes it stopped at the moment of her impact with the snowy yard, but usually she was forced to live through the next days.

A neighbor with boys who were Joshua's friends took possession of him and his sprained ankle. Josie sorted through the snow and found two shoes, not mates, and watched... mind paralyzed... as events took place.

The fire truck could do nothing but keep the carriage shed from burning, and before daylight her father's law partner appeared seemingly from nowhere.

Wrapped in a quilt, she was settled into a carriage and taken away. Her mind sought for an answer to whatever seemed to be happening, and could not be happening, but as she stared into the cup of steaming tea before her, she knew that it had already happened.

Dad and Mother, gone without a word. House a mass of flames, and a yard full of people. And now Mr. Blaine, her father's law partner, stood with arms hanging tensely down, as though searching for something to do. Sharon Blaine, his wife and Josie's mother's best friend, sat beside her, a kind hand on Josie's robed arm, seeking a way to give comfort.

"Honey...? Darling girl, don't let yourself think. Not yet. Tomorrow is soon enough. Your brother is safe, and only because of your bravery." Her hand reached for the teacup and lifted it toward Josie's face. "You really must sip a bit because it will help you."

Josie pulled her thoughts together. If it would help, she must try, because she needed all the help she... but there was no help for her parents... gone. So final and so sudden. So gone! With her hand she covered her dry eyes and sighed. Flames! They wouldn't go away!

The soft voice again. "Darling...? Josie, sweetheart, your mother would want you to take care of yourself. You must take a drink, and take a bit of medicine. Right now, Sweetheart. It will help... I promise." The soft voice pleadingly insistent.

Josie obediently lifted the cup. The warm tea, sweetened and creamed, flowed comfortingly through her smoke-parched throat. Without conscious thought, she picked up the small, white pill and washed it down with more tea. But it was as though the tea created more tears, and Mrs. Blaine held and patted her, and finally the exhausted girl could allow herself to be put to bed.

And now, outside the window, a rooster flapped a warning with his wings and lifted his beak skyward for his morning crow. Josie's mind snapped to the present. Immediately after the rooster crow would be the impatient moo of the cows, begging to be separated from their heavy bags of milk and be put out to pasture. And there it was... a chorus of mooing and baaing, and the morning had started.

Then came breakfast. Five cousins, their parents, Josh and herself. Eggs, meat, potatoes, gravy and a multitude of biscuits. Eat. No time to think, and that would truly be a blessing.

* * *

In New York City, Elias Blaine had waited two days, thinking, and now could wait no longer. There were things to be done, and the girl who had been so carefully reared must now make decisions that would affect the rest of her life. And that of her brother.

There was money to take care of her and her brother, and Mr. Blaine was the trustee and guardian of their welfare, just as this girl's father had been named guardian for his own sons. There had been specific instructions. If at all possible, she was to go to her mother's sister, who was homesteading in the Oklahoma Territory. It was his wish that she should stay there until she was twenty-one.

She would be given an allowance for her expenses and board at the house of her uncle and aunt... and there were a lot of other words that did not yet register on the girl's frightened mind.

There was now a mail route, of sorts, in the territory, but it was still sporadic and undependable. More reliably, a Teletype message was clicked out at the Santa Fe depot at Oklahoma Station, which had been newly named Oklahoma City. The message was forwarded, as instructed, to the settlement of Argyle, twenty miles to the west, and further sent to Carlile's Corner, a community mail repository. There it would be held until some member of the family happened by to pick it up.

A message not being expected by the family of Matthew Wilson, it took the teletype almost two weeks to reach him but even that was considered good timing, compared to a couple of years ago.

The message was read with horror. Parents gone. Two orphans would be coming their way, if at all possible.

"Of course they must come. But after what they are used to, the change will be a shock," and Aunt Nettie waved her hand around at the crowded room. "Bein' no time to build onto the house, they'll just have to take us the way we are." It would mean two more persons on the crowded bench at the table... another nail in the wall for hanging dresses.

She continued. "'Course, being almost summer the boys are already sleeping in the hayloft, and that boy'll want to be with them. Then, that'll give us till fall, to... what? Oh, well, we'll do what we have to do. There'd be no way I'd let my sister's children stay with someone else when they got family to come to."

Back in New York, there was shopping to do, and Josie firmed her chin and smilingly agreed to whatever Mrs. Blaine suggested. "Honey, I look at these dresses and wonder... it would be good to know how it is out where you're going..."

Josie understood. "Maybe plainer things? Solid shoes? If I need something else, maybe you could send it...?"

"Oh, Darling Girl, you are so like your mother... so sensible."

Boys were easy. Shirts, trousers, jacket and hat. Three pairs of shoes, a dozen pairs of socks. Two huge trunks packed. Were there schools there? Josh had just started, and his father would want... well, with everything changed, who could guess what their father would want? A sigh. What to do?

"Josephine, honey, what do you think?" but Josie couldn't think.

The message came back from the territory, "Yes. Come as soon as possible. Take train to Oklahoma Station. Hire a coach to Argyle and you'll be met."

"Josie, you have grown cousins there, haven't you. I think you must be met at the train depot. I don't know if it's safe for a girl your age...?"

The answer came back. "Can meet at train depot Oklahoma City. Advise day."

* * *

Back in New York. Elias Blaine had searched his brain for what must be told this girl in his care. "I have one more thing, Josie, and I hesitated to ask you about it. In the instructions, your Dad said I was to ask you if you remembered the post you and he put up in the rosebush patch, the one you put a birdhouse on. Does that mean anything to you?"

Josie stared with wide eyes at the question. Unbidden tears flooded into them, and sobs shook her shoulders.

"Oh, honey, I didn't mean anything. We'll forget it for now."

The girl looked up with red eyes, and shook her head. "No, we can't. He said if something happened to him, we should dig up the birdhouse post. I don't really remember much, but I know he dug around the post several times. It shouldn't be too hard to get up."

Together the man and the girl walked past the blackened heap of debris, following the picket fence to the winter-dead rose garden. The birdhouse post still stood. Scoop after scoop of dirt, and the hole became deeper. Then the clink of metal against metal, and a tightly closed steel bucket appeared. A lid was easily pried up. Inside were three pint jars packed with coins, their gold shining brightly from within.

"Hmmmmm, well that answers one question. I was prepared to advance you money until I could get your Dad's affairs in order, but it seems he's taken care of that himself."

The girl stared at the jars. "I saw one jar being buried, but I forgot about it. I didn't ever think something... could..."

"Don't think of it, Honey. I wish you didn't have to make grown up decisions, but there's another one we have to talk about. This ground where the house was... it's very valuable, and could be worth a lot more in a few years. We can sell it now and put away the money, or we can keep it for a while, just in case you or Joshua would want it later. It will be for you to decide, but we can wait a few months if you like."

She looked into his sad face, trying to think what her dad would do. There was no answer there. Of course not! If her dad was making the decision, he would re-build here, but then the decision would not be hers.

"Mr. Blaine, my Dad wants me to go to Oklahoma Territory. That's where my family is. I'm thinking if we need to buy land in the future it will be there. I just can't think of anything else."

The man nodded, satisfied. "Then we will sell. You made a good answer." Brushing the dirt clods off the bucket, he moved toward the carriage. "There's one other thing, and I need to ask you."

"What is it?" She sighed and faced him, squaring her shoulders bravely.

They climbed aboard, and the matched carriage horses clomped along the brick street. "Josephine, this is a big question. We need to think carefully. The family where your brother is staying is a good family of excellent reputation. The one thing they don't have much of is money. They have contacted me with an offer.

"They say that it would be their pleasure to keep your brother until you get settled, maybe for a year or two, and they would make sure he got to the school where your dad wanted him to go. The school is already expecting him, and I think his entrance fee is paid. Now, this family has agreed to keep him and put him in school if you can agree to pay the additional fee to let his friend go to the same school."

Josie stared ahead. The bricks of the street disappeared under the feet of the horses as their hooves clomped along. What were the words she had just heard?

The lawyer continued. "There would be certain advantages, to be sure. I believe they were thinking to be kind, as you are suddenly faced with a lot of decisions, and Joshua is so young. I'm afraid, though, that you'll need to decide quickly."

Josie sat up straight and tall, and drew in a deep breath. "Does it seem to them that I can't take care of my brother? He's the only family I have and I was the one who saved him from the fire. I almost got myself burned trying to get him out the window but I love him and he's my brother. How could anyone think I would go off to another country and leave him behind? What would he think of me later, and what would I think of myself? I don't want to see those people, ever, because I would surely say mean things, and they have been very good this whole month. Can I send them some money to take care of what Josh has cost them, and have you tell them I will take my brother with me when I leave?"

The man turned to her with a small smile. "I would have bet that was what you would say. You did the right thing, of course, and we can leave them some money. Fortunately, money will not be an immediate problem to you. I'll say this, you look a lot like your mother, but from your actions, you are certainly your father's daughter."

Then the impact of what she had just said descended on her. "Wait. What I said was mean and hateful and they were so kind. They took Josh without a hesitation and took care of his ankle. Is there any way... I mean, is it possible to pay for the other boy's first year at that school...?"

Mr. Blaine patted the clenched fists in her lap. "I believe there would be, and I'll take care of it."

Out in the Oklahoma Territory, Nettie Wilson spread out the letters from her sister that she had received over the last few years and carefully saved. "I've been trying to get a picture of what that poor girl is going through, and I'm encouraged. From things Nora says in her letters, she's her father's daughter. After those two failures and when it seemed Josie would be an only child, her dad hired that tutor so she could be taught the same as a boy. Nora laughed and said the only available schools for girls taught music and painting, and a little fancy sewing, and that her dad wasn't having that for his daughter. Josie learned numbers and history and how to say all the right words. Nora said she thought he would have her reading the law if there was someone to agree to teach her!"

Matt Wilson nodded with understanding. They'd been through all that before. "What'll we do with that boy? There ain't a school of any kind within ten miles of here. You doin' what you can, that ain't no kind of an education for a New York boy."

"Yeah, well..."

* * *

It was on the train that Josephine Wheeler experienced the first dream. Josh had shed tears, but the weight of it all had not yet settled on the seven-year-old boy. The noisy, smoking engine, and the grinding of the driver wheels excited him. She had put him in charge of the huge lunch basket, hoping to settle him down, but he was alternately standing, sitting, crawling, and staring out the window.

Josephine felt that she had not had a night's sleep for weeks, and here she was going... to... who knew where? She would meet the family who were strangers. It had been seven, maybe eight, years ago and she had been a child when she last saw them. Now she felt like she was at least a hundred and fifty years old and the memory was dim.

Lawyer Blaine, Uncle Elias, as she was encouraged to call him, as they would have business together for several years, had helped a lot. One of the trunks was layered with the gold coins and given a false bottom. It was also packed with items she would not need for a while, and was sent on ahead, heavily insured. The other one was checked into the Santa Fe baggage car, and was currently trundling along behind them.

No more decisions for a while. There was nothing she could do now to make matters better or worse. Several coins were sewed into her petticoat, and into Josh's trouser pockets. There was enough food in the hamper to last a week, even for a boy with a bottomless stomach.

Threatening dire punishment if he bothered anyone or attempted to leave the car, she leaned back into the comfortable seat and shut her eyes. The vibration of the car and the grind of the gears in the massive drivers lulled her, and the chatter of her brother reassured her that he was still nearby.

Thoughts wandered, trying in vain to connect themselves. The train trip was, to her life, like a period and paragraph of a story. One thought was finished and another one was to begin. At that point, no comprehension or decision was required of her, because she had no part in writing this story. The painful drag of the last six weeks had left her exhausted and the sound of the train carried her thoughts away.

They were still east of the wide Mississippi River. Her tutor had told her a lot about it, all the commerce and travel, and how valuable the mighty river was to the country. It would be interesting to see it.

She adjusted the back of the seat lower, fluffed the cushions and wriggled her shoulders into a comfortable hollow. She erased her mind. If she had made bad decisions, it was too late to do anything about them now. If there were horrors ahead, it was too soon to cry. There would be much time later.....

* * *

Soft bed. Quiet bedroom. Things she loved nearby, and favorite books standing on their edges, waiting to be re-read. Tomorrow would another day of her pleasant life. Then she smelled the smoke.

At first, it curiously tickled her nose in an enticing way. Then the familiar sickening smell and the terror! Flames! JOSHUA! She tried to push up from her bed, but her feet tangled into the legs of the train seat before her.

"JOSHUA!" She couldn't hear her own voice so she screamed louder. She had to wake him but something was holding her in her bed. She tried to kick it away and bumped her leg. The pain made her scream. Louder! LOUDER! Drawing in her breath, she forced out the sound. "JOSHUA!"

Something patted her face and made sounds but she impatiently pushed it away. She had to get up! Then strong hands pushed her against her bed, and the smell of smoke became overpowering. The hands were too strong, and she lay back and prepared to meet the flames.

Now a soft voice. "Honey! Dear, you must wake up!" Josie forced her eyes open and stared into the soft wrinkles and the snowy white hair. Smell of violets. Soft hands held hers.

Behind the soft lady stood the bald and whiskered source of the smoke, still mouthing the fat cigar. Anxiously patting her arm were the seven-year-old hands she knew so well, face pale from fright and with a scared and worried look on his familiar face.

Looking around. "Oh, I had a bad dream. I'm so sorry to disturb everyone." But, Joshua spoke up to defend her, facing the man and the old lady. "Our house burned down and my sister got scared. We almost burned up!"

It had been a bad introduction to her fellow passengers, but after that she was well known up and down the length of the train.

Colorado, 1895

It was on his fiftieth birthday, though he was not aware of it, and the man stretched out in the feeble Colorado sun to dry out his wet and weary feet. The dampness of the mine and perspiration of his feet were a constant threat of disease, and he was sure he could feel mold growing between his toes. Very likely it was a fact.

Even with two pairs of shoes, letting one pair dry out while wearing the other, there was no answer to the dampness but perhaps three pairs would have been better. It was something to think on. There were lots of things to think on while probing the depth of the Colorado dirt in hope, always in hope, that a yellow nugget would show itself. Digby had never lacked things to think on, and it had been this way for years. He had lived here, alone, as one season had melded into another and the years went by.

Lately, he had been thinking on closing up shop at the mine and going down to the flat land to spend his last years, and would likely have continued to think on it for the next ten to twenty years if something had not happened.

It was wondrously strange that a subject that could have occupied two decades of thought, could be settled in a single moment by something no bigger than a lady's arm.

The warm sun on his feet, the grazing teeth of his two animals, the drying of the mold between his toes coupled with the increased weariness made by the pick, shovel and rake, had pulled on his eyelids and made him forget the advice he continuously gave himself. He did not hear the small prairie rattler as it advanced, raised its head and waved its forked tongue as it queried the pinkish shape of the object before him. It could possibly be edible, and a nip with his deadly fangs would decide. With a dart of his head, he fastened onto the toe closest to him and prepared to wait.

The man jerked awake, griped the pistol that was always near his hand, aimed and squeezed, and the body of the small rattler lay in bloody pieces and suddenly had no more need to search for something to eat. As for the man, the flame within his smallest toe immediately expanded to a bright hot furnace, and he knew that an instant decision was crucial.

Ax. Reach for it. Lift it. Remove the poison flame before it spread. With strong arms he lifted the ax and sized up his target. Paused a second to reconsider, but knew he had no choice. A deep breath and a downward plunge of the weapon.

A second or maybe two seconds. Still there was time to regret that even his big toe could not be saved. Big toes were a help in walking, but he could already feel the poison blood being drawn into it.

Crash. Instantly, the rattler, his closed fangs and the end of his right foot were no longer attached to his leg, and for a moment he watched in fascination as his blood gushed onto the new, green grass.

Ripping his shirt from his arms, he wound it around and around the cut, enclosing the unbearable pain while stemming the flow of scarlet. As he stared, the faded plaid of his worn shirt turned to a dull red.

The image of his grazing animals floated toward the sky and the slope of the land tilted on edge as he sank back to the ground. The dog looked on with concern. A warm swath across Digby's face and a soft furry collar around the neck were the last things the man felt before blessed numbness engulfed him.

As consciousness returned, the burning stab of pain startled his eyes wide open to the singing of birds overhead and the glare of the morning sun. He was completely dew-wet except where his legs were covered warmly with a tanned deer hide. He was chilled from the cold Colorado night except for his right side, against which his wooly sheep dog was pressed.

First thought... he must have lived through the night. Second thought... what to do next? Third thought... thinking was too difficult. He closed his eyes to sink back again into the pain. The dog's tongue across his ear brought him back to his thoughts. His body had lived the night through, therefore he owed it a chance to continue living.

Pain! He could do something about that if he could just get back into the mine. He had the dried leaves of the native datura plant. His Kiowa neighbors had told him how the plant could be used to bear his pain, but too much of the plant could take over his body as well.

How much to use? First he must get it. Standing and walking was out of the question. Crawl. Turn over. Hands and knees must be made to move. Now begin. Dried blood held the shirt-bandage firmly. Turn off the mind. Move forward and do not stop.

He crawled through the mine entrance, the dog encouraging every forward inch. A lengthy pause brought the warm tongue across his face.

Medicine bag, made from the skin taken from the leg of a bear and drawn tightly on both ends.

Small jar of crumbled plant leaf residue. He'd never had occasion to use it. How much comfort would the plant give him before it claimed his life? Have to try and see.

Shaking a scant teaspoonful into his tin cup, he poured in a little water and stirred with his finger. Drink it down. Dried crumbled leaves with the water. Filling the cup from his water jug he chased it with two cups of the cold liquid. He felt the water's coldness as it coursed through his fevered body.

Bed. Crawl to the inviting stack of skins accumulated from his hunting. Keep crawling toward it. Moving the water jug before him, he reached the skins and rolled himself onto them. There was thinking to be done.

If he was alive to see the sunrise again, he would now go down the mountain. Then what? He would take...? What would he take with him? What did he have of value...?

The familiar ceiling of the mine entrance spun slowly above him before it sucked him into its vortex, winding his mind back through the years of his life.

What was his name before it had been changed? This thought struck a void, so it moved on. He was brought here. His remembered Pa had been as tall as a tree, so Digby, himself, must have been very young. He must have had a Ma, but there was no mental picture. In later years he had overheard Pa say to someone that he was stuck with this one, meaning the boy, but he made sure there'd be no more. How had he done that? He did not say.

He must have lived somewhere, because he had a memory of houses and people. Dim, but absolute. After that, he remembered travel. Holding tightly to the saddle horn as the animal beneath him followed along on a lead held by Pa on the other animal. What was the other animal?

Stops along the way. Come nightfall, a barn with hay for the horses. A manger for himself, and his Pa gone. Pa's voice promising someone that he would pick up his kid come daylight, but now he had to go to work. Whatever was the "work" Pa did, Digby was never able to determine. Later, he decided it must have been card games, or maybe theft, because they never stayed twice at the same place.

He didn't know how old he was when Pa put him on the horse and they headed out, with Pa singing wild songs as they rode. "Hey, sprout, you and me, we hit us a soft streak! Luck changed and we changed with it. From now on, my name is Striker. And you? You're gonna be Digby, 'cause you got a life' a pick and shovel work ahead'a you. Me? I'm gonna strike it rich in a gold mine."

Whatever the name that was originally assigned to the boy, along with the image of a mother, faded into the new images he saw every day. He and his Pa rode, stopped to hunt, ate what they shot and kept moving west. Occasionally, when passing a lone cabin, a brace of fresh shot game could be traded for a loaf of bread or left over biscuits, both items considered to be delicacies to the travelers.

A panorama of mixed up scenes and patchwork experiences crowded through Digby's mind, until a shot of pain startled him into the present. He had moved his foot and bumped against... what?

He stared about him, pulling his senses together to make a whole thought. He was... in a cave? No, a mine. Why was he here? It was...? Home? Sunshine flowed through the distant opening, and bird sounds came from somewhere, but he was alone. Why...?

A weak lassitude flowed over him like warm butter on a hot stone. He must have food. Where...? Remembering the deer jerky, he pictured where the container would be. He projected his movement toward it. His weakened brain struggled over every obstacle between himself and what he needed to survive.

A shadow appeared at the opening. On silent pads, the dog advanced. What was he called...? Yes, his mind contrived, the animal's name was Tangle. Tangle...? Yes. He heard a sound and it was his own voice speaking to the dog.

With hurried steps and waving tail plume, the animal came forward with something in his mouth. Fur. Limp. Legs and head drooping. The dog placed his catch on Digby's bed and nudged it toward the man's neck.

Warm. Fresh caught. Nourishing. A normal and automatic motion by the man produced a knife in his hand. From a pocket...?

Pushing himself into a sitting position, he sliced a haunch from the cottontail rabbit and drew back the skin. Another slice and the warm, rosy flesh was in his mouth. Chewing. Another bite. Just the taste and knowledge of the warm raw meat now produced its own strength. He would live a little longer. Maybe.

As the dog watched, Digby consumed most of the rabbit and pushed the remainder aside. The dog promptly took the scraps and left the mine.

Clearer thoughts were forming. Something must be done about the foot. But, what...? Bear grease. There was always bear grease for everything. A fat bear provided a lot of grease, and a lot of meat if one could stand the gamy flavor.

Walking stick...? Just inside the mine entrance it stood, leaning against the wall. Could he walk with a stick? Would what was left of his foot actually hold him up? It was time to see.

Crawling the distance, he gripped the stick and stood, using only his left foot. Gingerly, he lowered the wounded member, screaming with pain as the bulky wrapping touched the ground.

Using the stick for balance, he moved in short hops to gather supplies. Water. Bear grease. Clean cloth. Strips of skin cut for many purposes. A hobble back to the bed.

Next trip. Medicine bag. Hollowed-out rock with bear grease and wick. Would need a light handy. The new fangled go-fer matches safe in their waterproof wrapping.

He was beginning to feel the strengthening effects of the food. Smart dog, that Tangle. Was he the fifth, or maybe the sixth dog with that name? Didn't matter. The very young Digby had seen their current dog scuffle with another one, and called it a Tangle. Name had stuck for decades and several dogs. Good name.

He settled, exhausted, on the fur of the bed and thought. What else? He should get what he needed while he was moving. His gun? Where was it...? Nodding in answer to his mental question, he knew it would be outside where he had used it. Had to have it. When he finally put his hand on the familiar metal of the weapon, he felt he had never gone on such a long journey from the cave, and now he must go back, but he would do it. In his situation, a man without a gun was nothing.

Back on his bed, he surveyed the bandage. Should he take a bit of the datura to help him through this operation? Maybe... No! He might take too much and not be able to finish what had to be done.

He peeled back layer after layer of the hastily wrapped shirt, cringing at the pain. The last layer was somewhat stuck, and bled slightly when separated, but when he looked at the exposed wound he gagged and looked away. Torn flesh. Exposed bones. Oozing blood.

Firming his mind and breathing deeply, he drizzled water over the injury. He knew he could not stand to blot it dry, so he waited and forced his mind to other thoughts. When it was dry, he spread the fresh cloth open and layered a liberal amount of the bear grease over it. So far, so good....

Clenching his teeth, he picked up the heavily greased cloth by its corners and draped it over the raw flesh. Hmmm, it did not hurt as bad as he was prepared for. In fact, the warmth of the grease almost seemed comforting after the sting of the colder air. Now was the time for the datura. A tiny sprinkle, much less than before. Mix in water. Follow with two cups of water. Job done.

Now, there was more thinking to do. He would go to the flat land as he had intended all along. He would not be able to sit astride an animal, so he must make ready the travois sled. Such a wonderful discovery he had borrowed from his Kiowa neighbors for bringing in heavy meat carcasses, surely it would carry him behind the strong jenny. It was at that point that he lapsed into an exhausted sleep.

Later, and more thinking.

Worthless would carry everything in the two roomy saddlebags that hung over each side of her back. Getting ready would be the big problem. Hopping was hardly the answer, and using a stick, even if he could stand it, left only one hand.

Crutch! Of course! There would be a proper formation somewhere within the grove of aspen saplings. Somehow he would need to cut down a tree. A small one. Could he chop sitting down? If he had to, he could do anything. Actually, after the ordeal of removing the rattler poison, chopping a sapling smaller than his wrist was hardly a trick at all. With his knife, he circled the branches above the forked "Y" until he could break them.

Crawling back to the mine, dragging the newly made crutch along beside him, he felt a renewed sense of accomplishment. An uplifting, actually. A long expected decision had now been made, and there were new things to experience, life would be...? Well, it would be what it would be, just as it had been all his life.

His eyes lighted on another answer. He didn't need a travois sled. He had a small, two-wheeled cart. When one of the horses was taken down by a mountain lion, his Pa had bought a cart to draw behind the remaining animal. They had needed it anyway for the things they brought back on their annual trip to Guthrie or Arkansas City.

Oklahoma City Station

The huffing engine on the Santa Fe railway screeched to a jerky stop as the clickity-clack of the drivers was shut down. Passengers were jerked forward, then left sitting silently at the Oklahoma City Railway shed.

The seventeen-year-old girl was breathless from apprehension, and the seven-year-old boy was just as breathless from excitement. Josephine Eleanor Wheeler forced her nerves into steadiness as she gathered her wrap, commanded her brother to do the same, hooked her carpet bag of necessities over her left arm, threaded the lunch basket over her brother's right arm, and held his left hand firmly in her right one. This was clearly not the time to risk losing him, after days with him on the rails.

Now, to locate her cousin. Who should she ask? What would be the proper thing to say? What if he wasn't there? Why couldn't it have been her uncle who came? A grownup, for goodness sake!

Down the metal steps and onto the smoky cinders. Stepping carefully, practically dragging Joshua who wanted to dash in every direction. Cousin? What would he look like? She had never seen him, and he hadn't seen her. Oh, why hadn't she stayed in civilized New York?

Elbows gouged her, baggage bumped her and excited voices closed in on her. And ahead a tall boy with a head full of red curly hair came hurrying toward her carrying a sign. What a sign! It screamed, "JOSEPHINE ELEANOR WHEELER"!

What was going on? Suddenly the face of the boy broke into a grin. 'You're Josie! Ma said to look for a pretty girl, and that'd be you. Ma's most often right about things."

Josie stared. Hmm, cousin? Well, no one said he had to be alone, so where was the adult? "You are...?"

"I'm Jefferson, and I come to get you. I already know where your other trunk is. They say we gotta wait on that porch till it comes off the baggage car. Man, oh man, I'm glad to see you! I've been waitin' a whole day and a half."

"Uh... where is the other one?"

"What other one?"

"The one that came with you. Like, an older one...?"

"Shucks, Cousin Josie, weren't no one come with me. Didn't need no one else, and they was all too busy to take off work for maybe three days. Pa made me come early to be sure I got here on time. Pa's like that. He don't take no chances on bein' late. I was lucky! I got to make the trip to get you. We got us the two seated buggy so's to have room for all your plunder."

Buggy? Where was the stagecoach? "Uh... I'm supposed to ride on the..."

"Law, Cousin Josie, I should'a told you. Ma got to thinkin' on them two trunks. She allowed they'd be big, and the stage'd not be able to load 'em on. Leastwise, both of 'em.' Said for me to head out from Argyle toward Oklahoma City with the double buggy and get 'em both. Things is too valuable out here to risk lettin' 'em come on after. Could get lost. We're gonna load up and take on out ahead'a the stage. We need to get goin' to be back in Argyle for the night. We done got us a room where they'll put us up."

Josie tried to digest what must be important information, but it seemed to be transmitted in a foreign language. Young Jefferson Wilson looked at the puzzled expression on his cousin's face and offered a wide smile of encouragement.

"Don't you worry none. I know just what to do. If you want to wait inside, bein' tired and all, I'll get us ready in no time."

Josie sighed and looked around. Apparently her life was now in the hands of a boy who looked like he should maybe be on holiday from his boarding school and just out for a lark. But there was no one else. He was all she had, and she sincerely hoped he knew what he was doing. She tightened her grip on her brother and pulled him into the ticket office.

Joshua begged and pled to go help their fascinating cousin, but Josie's grip never loosened.

It was only minutes, however, that the head full of red curls again appeared. "Got it ready! Right out the side door."

Still with a tight grip on her brother's arm, Josie followed the commanding voice... because she saw no other avenue to take. Sure as his word, he had brought around the "double buggy" with two huge trunks now loaded aboard the rear, their ends sticking out behind. So heavy they were, that it seemed they might lift the front wheels of the buggy off the ground, and perhaps even lift the horses.

"Here, Sprout, you jump in a'side'a me and let your sister have the back. She's likely had more'a you than she'd'a liked!" Young Joshua did not need a second invitation, but scrambled up the iron buggy step and settled himself on the front seat.

Jefferson held a hand toward Josie, and she saw she would need it if she was to climb the metal step and manage her carpet bag and skirts as well.

Soft, smooth leather seats and a padded back. A foot-rest in exactly the right place. With an unconscious sigh, she settled back. Her body demanded a rest, but her mind seethed with indecision. Two thoughts tangled themselves together. She could let this capable sounding voice relieve her of her need to think, but that would mean relinquishing her responsibilities to this curly haired "child" who seemed to be taking over her life. Which?

Josh bounced up and down, back and forth, eager to be on the way. The red curls were now in front of Josie, and the rein had tapped against the rumps of the horses. The wheels turned and the buggy moved forward.

"Reason we're hurryin' on ahead, we're wantin' to get over to Argyle 'afore dark. We got us lanterns, though, if we don't. Ma said you'd be tired, and I'd need to get us a bed for the night, 'afore comin' on in. Them roads out our way... they could give new folks a fright even in the daylight."

The trotting feet of the horses drummed rhythmically against the hard ground, and the contoured back of the seat pushed invitingly against her shoulders. With a practiced hand, she loosened the strings of her high-topped "young lady" shoes, and rested the carpet bag beside her feet.

The suddenness of her cousin's voice cut into her thoughts. "Here, Sprout, you take the lines. I plumb forgot something." Whereupon a pair of trousered legs appeared over the back of the seat in front of her, followed by a lanky body.

"Ma said for sure to make you comfortable. Here I was, forgettin'." Flipping up the seat next to her, he drew out a soft quilt, its colors fading but still cheerful. Under the quilt were two thick-stuffed pillows, which Jefferson punched with his strong knuckles so hard that two, small white feathers worked their way through the seam and floated out toward the Santa Fe Station, now a half a mile behind them.

Gently pulling her shoulder forward, he crammed the marshmallow-soft cushion behind her. Without a wasted motion, he grabbed corners of the quilt, with a jerk that separated the folds, and with a sweeping motion settled the coverlet over her lap and feet.

"Ma sure was right when she said I was to look for the prettiest girl, and it'd be you. Ma's most always right. And she said you was likely gonna be give out, and maybe you'd lean back and rest till we get to Argyle, and could be you'd be ready to sleep by then."

The softness of the cushion hugged her back and settled her weary shoulders and the coverlet was cozy. She could hardly lose Josh now, and the important trunks were tied securely behind her. Also, she was sure that nothing she could say would alter what "Ma" had told cousin Jefferson to do, so she closed her eyes.

The little hamlet of Argyle, named for the Scotsman who operated the stage coach station, was prepared for weary travelers. A large room for ladies and another for the fellows. They were free if you elected to sleep on the floor, but ten cents bought a fold-out cot originally designed for soldiers on maneuver. Three cots had been arranged.

Uncle Blaine's words seeped into her mind. "Now, when you stop at Argyle, make sure the leather trunk stays with you all the time. There could be those wanting to steal it, if only because it might contain nice clothes like you'll be wearing." She was so tired!

Still... "Jefferson, I need to take my trunk in the room with me."

Puzzled, he looked from one to the other. "Which one?"

"Actually, both of them. My guardian gave me instructions, and I have to do what he says or I break the law." Maybe that was a stretch, but it was all she could think of.

"Well, let me see..." and he disappeared, but was back in minutes. "They said alright, but it'll cost ten cents each for help to get them in the room, and another ten cents each 'cause they'll take up space that could'a been rented with a cot." He spread his hands, apologetically, as there was no understanding the greed of a Scotsman.

Josie wordlessly reached into the carpet bag and sorted out the prescribed amount. Right now, money was the least of concerns.

Sandwiches and cookies were for sale, as well as steaming hot tea that smelled strongly of peppermint. Her mom's bedtime peppermint. Tears came, unbidden and aggravating. Embroidered hanky wiped them away. Any grief felt by Josh was swept away by a handful of sugar cookies with his tea.

Jeff disappeared, but soon was back. “All fixed. You got trunks on each side’a your cot. And the Sprout is beside me so close I can’t loose ‘em. So you got no worry.”

Concerned frown. “He can’t stay with me?”

Puzzled frown. “Cousin Josie, Josh is a fellow. Ladies wouldn’t like a fellow in there where they slept.” Strange that his cousin hadn’t noticed!

The pillows and quilt from the buggy had been transferred to the cot, and the exhausted girl wanted nothing more than to stretch out and forget the world, but there was that other thing. Should she go ahead and open the leather trunk wide enough to get some of the money to put in the strong box... if there was one? Uncle Blaine had told her to store only a small part of her funds, so it would seem that she did not have a lot with her. He had been very specific.

“Now, Josephine,” (he always used her whole name if he was starting to say something serious) “I could, by law, take all your money and hold it here, and that’s what I would do if you were staying in New York. But the fact is, you may have unexpected needs and also, sending money is not particularly safe, as yet. We don’t really know how things are.” (Just like a lawyer, but she was used to lawyers)

“Ask, in Argyle, if they have a strong room. Being that it is a stage station, I’m sure they do. Then, you can truthfully say that you put your money in the strong box for safekeeping, and if you need something, you have to go there for the money. That way, you should be able to protect most of it by keeping it with you in your trunk. Also, I will say this. I would not do this for just any girl your age, but you are your father’s daughter so I trust you fully.”

So, as she arranged her pillows and spread her quilt, she quietly took the key from her neck and opened the lock. Gently easing up the lid, she put her carpet bag inside. Fumbling low in the trunk, she extracted a handful of coins and quietly tucked them into the bag. Easing down the lid, she locked it and returned the key to her neck.

Looking around nervously, she saw that she was being observed. The elderly lady settling onto her bed smiled approval. "Smart thing, honey, you lockin' up your bag. Us all bein' asleep, no tellin' what meanness could be goin' on. I can see you had good raisins'."

Josie tried to arrange a friendly smile. Raisins? Oh, raisings... like upbringing.

"Thank you, ma'am. Tired as I am, I'll likely sleep like the dead." That part was true.

Hours later. As a part of some dream she couldn't remember, there came the wafting aroma of coffee. Real coffee. Was she back at home in New York? No, the hard canvas cot she lay on reminded her. Still, it was coffee. Memory created a loved picture.

Her dad had offered her coffee before she even knew how old she was. It was rumored among the New York set that coffee before age 20 would ruin a girl's complexion, and that rumor alone was more than enough to influence most any girl to abstain. She grinned to herself as she remembered her Dad's observation. "Likely the cost of the stuff was more of a concern to her folks than the girl's complexion. The stuff is twice the cost of tea."

Quietly unlocking the leather trunk and removing her carpet bag, she dressed and packed away her nightwear. Where there was coffee, there were grownups awake. The one in charge seemed to be a Mac McCormick, and she shyly approached him.

"Mister? Sir? I got to ask something. My uncle" (she had to call him something and 'guardian' seemed strange) "told me that being a stage station, you'd likely have a strong room... maybe?"

"I do, young lady. You havin' somethin' you need kept safe?"

The girl nodded and produced her best smile. "Yes, sir. I'm visiting here for a few months, and my uncle said I was to rent a container for some things, so as not to be robbed." At that point she pointedly removed a silver bracelet and a locket chain from her neck.

Mac nodded. "Good advice. You wouldn't be thinkin' on puttin' a gun in the box, were you?"

Josie startled, wide eyed. "Am I having to say to you what I put in the box?"

"No, young lady. I just thought if you had a gun you was wantin' to stach for a while, likely you've be interested in sellin' it. Good cash money can be had for anything that shoots, now'a'days." With a wink and a grin, he suggested. "Girl pretty as you, maybe she ought'a be carryin' herself a shootin' iron. Likely she could even get herself stole!" With a wink he added, "The thing is, purty girls is scarcer around here than shootin' irons."

He led her into a small locked room that had metal boxes on a shelf, with each one chained to the wall and equipped with a padlock. He stood guard with his back toward her as she dropped the two pieces of jewelry into the box, along with 10 of the gold coins, wrapped in a handkerchief. Locking the padlock, she returned the box to the wall.

She paid one dollar for the use of the box for 6 months and was told that if she did not visit the box or pay the next rent, whatever was in the box would be forfeited. She nodded agreeably. Sounded reasonable.

Coffee. Its burning bitterness and rich flavor woke up her throat and confidence. She had now done everything Uncle Blaine had told her to do, except to tell her aunt and uncle that she had been given a sum of money, but it was to be kept in the strong room. The lawyer said so. And if she needed to spend some, she must get his permission, and if she needed more, he would send it.

All this precaution, he explained, was not that he didn't trust her, he just didn't trust any other person, and she was his responsibility. She was to tell no one about the false bottom in the leather trunk...

not her uncle or cousins... and not even her little brother. No one! Ever! And he was counting on her to remember that.

Cookies and buttered biscuits with jelly could be had besides the coffee and tea. Cousin Jefferson managed to put away quite a number of them before he hired help to get the trunks back on the buggy.

Home was close. Why, Carlile's Corners was maybe only an hour away when the road was in good shape, though no one had ever remembered when that was.

* * *

Nettie Wilson was getting nervous. She had talked half the night. "Good thing that girl won't be no cash money expense. Her dad takin' care'a that part ain't no more than I'd'a expected." Then, "I'm hopin' she won't come here with frills and lace, makin' Carmelita want what she can't have." And, "Reckon she knows how to sew? I could use some help with the darnin' on them socks."

After a pause, "Took that boy outta school and him hardly started. Lawyer said books would come. What kind, I wonder. Maybe Darrell could learn a little, but not if they're telling how to talk in French or Latin. I hardly got time to help Carmelita with lessons, and nothing for the other two. Days get shorter and shorter. Work don't never get done."

Her partner in the bed had just nodded off, and she thought of something else. "Then a place to sleep. Reckon we need to think agin on putting up a room for the boys, come winter cold. With three of 'em almost grown men, and Darrel and Joshua, there'd not even be floor room." Followed by a sigh. "That girl's a stranger. I laid eyes on her for a few days when she was ten. This'll take some getting' use to."

A sleepy reply pointed out, "Yeah, and that lass is comin' into a house full of seven strangers livin' in a strange land that don't hardly know her language. What happened wasn't because'a something she did. It was done to her in one terrible moment. I take note that you and me, we sound pretty much like the neighbors when it comes to words, and they'll likely be strange to her."

He had a point, and Nettie went to sleep considering her niece's side of the situation.

Down the Colorado Mountain

The deep-pocketed side saddle bags were fitted over the protesting shoulders of Worthless, and the small cart, wheels liberally treated with bear grease, was loaded with all other possessions, leaving hardly room for himself. Hepsibah stood patiently switching flies with her short tail.

Tangle sat on his haunches, his plume tail scooping a flat place in the dirt, watching and eagerly waiting. A trip. New smells. He panted with excitement.

The padded "Y" of the crutch was beginning to feel normal, and the man could move along much better now. Leaning over was still a trial, and standing for very long made his foot ache. Sometimes his toes... that weren't there... tingled so strongly he had to look down to re-convince himself that they actually were not there.

Last item to put aboard was the can. He clumped his way down the shaft that had refused to produce many yellow pebbles, and scooped into the loose stones and clay. The can that had once held tobacco now held the product of his entire life. Loose gold chunks. Would he still be able to use them as money? Well, that question was for another day. He sat himself on the back of the cart and with both hands he hoisted his leg aboard.

"Move it on out, Hep! Come on, Worthless." The older jenny moved into the trail and her daughter fell in behind. Tangle dashed from the front to the rear, leaping in frenzied excitement.

Freed of the concern of packing, Digby's thoughts drifted back. Strange how the medicine plant took away pain but left almost forgotten memories in the place of it. Details of his life that he had scarcely remembered had come flooding back. Some sad... some frightful... but all interesting to some degree.

Like the trouble finding the mine. Pa's voice. "Got that mine by a lucky throw'a the bones, and, by gingoes, it's mine and I'll find it if it's my last action." Young Digby had thought, at the time, that it very well might be.

Then they saw the sign, leaning and weather beaten, but still readable. *HOPE MINE*. Someone had scribbled above the first word, "Abandon". Was that a prophesy, Abandon Hope Mine? Yes and no. For a flatlander looking to get rich, it would be true. For old Striker and young Digby, it was to be a way of life. Actual finds were rare, and there were weeks of total, dismal nothing, but their needs were small, and the picked-over remains left by the previous owner were accumulated. Applying the pick to the red clay walls produced occasional nuggets and gave a purpose and meaning to their lives. There was always tomorrow, and it could be better. If not, they would still eat and sleep, and what more could the rich man do?

There were the trips to civilization. Newspapers were brought back and Digby learned to read with a little help from his father, but mostly by his diligence spawned by boredom. From his father he learned numbers... the one thing the man was good at.

Trips to civilization produced overalls, coats, shoes and sox. Sometimes nuggets were spent, but mostly furs were traded. They were the skins of the animals they ate, and of the animals that had tried to eat them, and they always found a market. A kerosene stove was a welcome addition to the cave, and a lantern for evening light.

Striker always got booze, for what else was a city for? On better trips, the bottles and jugs were brought back to the mine, but often it was just consumed on site. Gathering places for men remained open as long as someone was buying, but young Digby must spend his time with the animals so they would not be stolen.

He nodded, even now, in puzzlement that anything that made

you lose your brains should, probably, not be willingly consumed. Especially when it smelled so bad! Pa could go for weeks, maybe months without a drop... and it setting right there, handy, in the mine shaft. Then when he got started, it lasted for days and he was a different person. Sometimes he hacked at the dirt so furiously that Digby must continually muck out the tailings or his Pa would cover himself up and essentially dig his own grave.

Most times, though, he sang until he was hoarse, cut down trees, or went roaring into the mountains daring the animals to take him on. Once a tired bear, fat and ready to hibernate, was accosted by the drunken human. Digby had not been far behind his Pa, and had seen what was about to happen. He leveled the shotgun, but before he could get a good sighting, the senseless man had approached the bear and poked it in the nose with a doubled fist.

The aggravated animal took a swat with a set of 2 inch claws, just as he would have brushed a hive of bees from their honey tree. Catching the man just below his ear, he cracked the vertebrae with a loud snap. The man hesitated, trembled, and then fell. The bear, already fat and stuffed for the winter, sniffed at the worrisome creature on the ground, just as the shot rang out.

Falling, he sprawled with his neck draped over the neck of his victim, and together the two breathed their last.

Digby struggled with his Pa's remains back to the mine and buried him beside the tobacco can of golden pebbles. The fat bear he skinned and he cut away the meat he could use. The fat he had rendered.

Each of the bear's legs was skinned, and made into bags. All of the huge claws were removed as well as the teeth and were placed by an anthill for the industrious creatures to clean up. The thick, winter fur was stretched and scraped, and a small hole was cut in the center. He had always wanted to try this, because he had thought it would make a very warm poncho, especially fur side down.

The cleaned claws and teeth of the animal were traded to a Kiowa woman for the best winter coat he had ever owned. It was made of wolf fur, double with fur both inside and out. He liked to think that the coat was a gift from his Pa... a final sort of going-away present... or perhaps a gift for his coming of age. He had no time or ability to grieve for what could not be changed. He had a lot of experience at taking what came and making the best of it, as he had been doing it all his life. He did, however, wonder exactly how old he was.

On his next trip to the flat land, he looked for a person about his age, and asked him how old he was. It seemed to make the young man angry, and he demanded to know what business it was of his. Digby's thoughts moved quickly as he commented, "You look so strong like you could do most anything you wanted to do, that I just wondered." Pacified, the young man had said he was fifteen. So, at that moment, Digby became fifteen.

It was interesting about small rivers. In the mountains, the streams gathered and headed straight down hill. On encountering a rocky ledge in the way, they simply pooled until they spilled over, created a waterfall, and then they proceeded once more on their way.

In the flat land, though, they meandered along, almost aimlessly. Encountering a prairie dog mound, they might be turned and aimed another direction. Twists, circles and ox bows were created. Just one of those interesting things to contemplate, now that he had made his break with the mountain.

Another thing... one that hovered irritatingly just outside his consciousness... was what would he do with the rest of his life. There was the foot. Part of it. It still ached abominably when he stood for periods of time. He would never walk normally without a crutch, and the use of a crutch made him essentially one-handed.

What sort of a job could he do...where would he live... and where would he start to find out? What skills did he have other than sifting through the red dirt and pebbles for the coveted yellow? Summer would not be a problem, now that he had the oiled canvas he could stretch over a low tree limb to create shade or dryness. But winter?

Another situation... there was no vacant land anymore. The resident Kiowa tribe were very tolerant of short term squatters, but he felt that permanent roots of some sort should be put down. Somewhere. Thought should be given to the fact of getting older.

Most homesteads could use help but had little or no money to pay for it. Perhaps a barter of goods and services? Work for a dry bed? That might be the best road to take.

What could he offer? Not plowing...nor harvesting. Not horse breaking or cattle herding. He became very good at laying stone while he made the walls of his home of 30 years, building it within the Hope Mine. The problem was, he could hardly gather or carry the stone anymore.

He had no desire to acquire land of his own, and all of central Oklahoma Territory had been chopped up into quarter sections and these had been assigned in the 'land run' several years ago. There were a few homesteaders who had to give up and go back east because of a variety of circumstances. He had just been told of one.

It seemed the new baby had taken the life of its mother when it was born. Father and several children were heading east as soon as he could get his things together. This he had learned by asking around in the settlement of Argyle. Old man McCormick, from the stage line, had directed him to the place, though Digby was hardly interested. He did, however, have to start somewhere.

He looked out over the partly cleared land, stroking his chin thoughtfully. Several stands of trees indicated that the meandering stream had flowed through the tract that was to be abandoned, and an interesting stone ledge lifted itself up from the plain in several places creating a wall twelve to twenty feet high.

At one point, the homesteader had dug in under the stone ledge and created what would have been a soddie dwelling, except it was more of a dugout, or cave, with a stone ceiling. Cut and trimmed cottonwood poles lay stacked about, obviously being dried.

Now, IF he was a few years younger, and IF he still had two feet, he would be interested... maybe. Pa had said to him, one time, that, "if IFs and BUTs were candy and nuts, we'd all get to go to a party." So, leaving aside the 'ifs', this is what he would do for the near future. Yes... here was a plan.

He would find a place among those trees by the stream... toss his oiled tarp over a limb... tie it down securely... clear a place for his plunder and make himself a bed in the cart. The covered space would be big enough for the "girls" to at least get their heads into the shade... or the dry, as the case may be. And their food grew all around them. He had provisions for himself for a while, the can of golden pebbles would last a longer while, maybe longer than he did, so....

Digging with the shovel was still difficult, but he managed to create a hole deep enough to hide the tobacco can. Just as he had at every overnight campsite since he left the mountain. With a grin, he had told himself, a thief might steal his plunder and his girls, and might do him in, but they wouldn't get the pebbles! Then he projected his thought farther to years ahead... to the time when an unsuspecting farmer would hook his plow point into the can, and realize he didn't need to plow anymore! The thought was worth a chuckle.

Great patience, Digby had perfected over the last 30 years. The answer would come to him. On his way to this land, he had noted with interest a shanty with a storefront proclaiming it to be Carlile's Corner. A sign nailed beside the door stated "Coffee and Cookie 5 cents. Conversation free." Someone with a sense of humor had scratched "maybe" above the word coffee. Did it mean that sometimes they did not even have coffee? Or that what they served was only distantly related to that popular brew? Didn't matter. It was something of interest to be looked into.

AT THE WILSON HOUSEHOLD

The dirt road leading south from Argyle was rock hard beneath the buggy wheels and it was fiercely rutted. The occupants of the buggy were slung wildly back and forth to the delight of any seven-year-old boy. Josie located the handhold straps attached to the buggy frame, and discovered that if she held tight, a few of the bumps and swings were made milder.

Jefferson turned his head to call back to her, "I'd apologize for this road, but it don't get no better. This here's the worst buggy, too. The one-seater ain't quite so bad, and the two-wheeled cart is even better. Don't seem like it would be, but it is. Wheels seem to fit in 'tween the deeper ruts."

As the morning passed, Josie's mind began to circle. *My only relatives in America. Will they like me? They didn't have a choice to say we couldn't come. Kind of like the snow that comes down when it comes, ready or not. Did I get everything I needed? Gun? Mr. Mac joked, but he sounded serious. Joshua's books. They should be already here. I've never taught anyone anything, but Uncle Blaine says I'll have to. What if I can't? Then I'd have to take Josh back to New York, then when would I ever see him? Cousin Darrell is his age and Josh'll not want to leave him. Which of the cousins is my age? What about other girls?*

"Jefferson? Are there any seventeen or eighteen year old girls close around?"

Jeff hesitated, then turned to face her, letting the team find their own way. "Yeah, well, maybe. They'd be a mile away or maybe two miles, and I think they're mostly married."

"Married?"

"Mostly. Cousin Josie, you gotta know one thing. There ain't too many girls out here, and quick as they get to courtin' age, the fellows descend on 'em like bees on a sunflower, wantin' to get married. They pretty much get their pick of the crop if they want to marry. They's some that won't look twice at a fellow, cause they see how hard their Ma has to work, and they ain't quite ready for that. Sorry to say that, but you asked."

"Hmmm, what's courting age?"

"For some, it's fourteen. Pa says that ain't gonna happen for Carmelita even if he has to use a gun. Maybe he was jokin', but I don't think so. Ma's teachin' Mellie things, but she ain't got much time."

"What things?"

"Lots, but right now she's been learnin' to darn."

"Darn... ?"

"Yeah. You don't know about that? It's when us fellows wear a hole in the heel or toe of a sock, it's gotta be fixed with thread so it ain't no hole again. Takes a fair amount'a time, and that's what Ma ain't got. Much of, anyway." He chuckled, "You gotta watch or she'll have you holdin' a darnin' egg and a needle!"

Egg? Josie hadn't the courage to ask what that was for fear it was more than she could handle today. Maybe tomorrow, but not today.

Jefferson again. "Josie? We got Carlile's Corner comin' up. We always stop as we go by to see if there's mail. You can come in if you want to, but you'll be there lots of times, anyway."

Josh leaped joyfully from the front seat of the buggy and sprinted toward the store-fronted building, Jeff's long-legged steps close behind. "Hold up, Sprout. Wait for your sister. That's no way to treat a lady."

"What lady?" Josh grinned, but obeyed.

Jeff held the screen door while Josie stepped up on the low porch and into the room. Smells. Warm peppermint and not quite fresh coffee. Cookies under a glass domed container. Pickle barrel with a checkerboard on the lid. Three stools gathered around the barrel but no one sat on the stools. Very few homesteaders had time for checkers of a morning that wasn't snowy or rainy.

Hand printed sign offered: "Soup 5 cents." "Sandwich till they're gone. 5 cents." Shelves along one wall were stocked with salt, baking soda, vanilla extract, envelopes and writing paper, a jar of number two pencils and a bottle of ink. Also, other items not identified at a quick glance.

More notable was the deep cushioned rocker and the wrinkled scrap of a person enthroned thereon. Skin, dark-aged. Eyes behind spectacles, bright. Apron, snowy white. Tiny hand extended toward Josie.

"Miz. Carlile? This here's my cousin Josie Wheeler that we was expectin'. I was the one got to go bring 'em in! Took me three days to do it. She'll be with us a few weeks or maybe a few years. I hope its years. That youngen is her little brother, Josh."

Josie lightly clasped the hand. Bones fragile as bird legs. Skin, smooth and papery. Smile, bright and wreathed in wrinkles.

"Glad to see you, Miss Wheeler. You'll be welcome like the flowers in May. Now, Jefferson, son, look under your mail hook for the package. Heavy, like. Thought maybe books, square shaped like it is."

Mail hooks were exactly that... hooks. Small strap was looped over the hook and equipped with clamp. Over each hook was a name and many of the clamps held letters within their pinching jaws. The wide shelf below the hooks held parcels and various items, apparently meant for the family whose name was above the hook.

The "WILSON" clamp held two addressed envelopes, and the shelf below held a wrapped package. Square. Likely books.

Back in the buggy, Josie had a question. "Jeff, what is 'Maybe Coffee'?"

After an amused chuckle, Jeff thrust the reins toward the boy. "Here, Sprout, you drive while I talk with your sister. That 'maybe coffee' is just what it says. If they have real coffee, that's what they brew, but if they run out like if they haven't had a chance to get over to Argyle, like what happens in the rain or snow, then they brew up what they have. There'll be tea, of course, but the 'coffee maybe' is made from toasted grain and something called chicory, and it's sweetened with molasses or maybe honey. Not bad, really. For a fact, they's some that like it better'n what they get from the east. So there'll always be a hot drink, and maybe it'll be coffee. Way I hear it, old Miz Carlile gets lonely and feels like she's worthless so she sells a hot drink and a cookie, and maybe someone'll stay and talk a bit, or there's fellows that'll meet here and play checkers when they get rained outta the field. She'll pack a lunch as long as the meat and biscuits last... the ones left over from her breakfast. Got her own little thing a'goin'."

Well, that answered that, and immediately there was another question. Beside the road, just across the fence, two girls carried a basket between them as they wandered over the grass. They each carried a stick, and seemed to be totally unafraid of the cattle grazing on each side of them. Cattle with horns as wide as the girls were high.

"What are those girls doing with that basket?"

"Oh, those are the McLaughlin sisters. They are collecting cow pats."

"Cow pats?"

"Well, a few years back they'd be buffalo pats, but the buffalos all got killed or chased off. Cow pats are... how do I say? What it is.... is poop. The girls have sticks to chase off snakes and to turn over the pats. If the pat turns over without breaking, they pick it up... but if it's still sticky, they leave it till it dries."

"But why do they want it?"

"Oh, of course. You wouldn't know it was to burn. That's what heats houses and cooks food. Mostly. It gets burned in the stoves. When it gets dry, it don't have no smell, and burns really hot. You notice we don't have many trees, and ones we have, we don't waste 'em in the stove when cow pats do better."

"You don't have coal?"

"Not that I know of. I'm thinkin' it'd cost too much to haul it out here from over the ridge, and I think we'd mostly rather have the cow pats. They're free."

Well, that made sense. As they moved along, Josie took long, deep breaths to calm her apprehension. They had to be almost there. And they were.

"Here, Sprout, I'll take over. You watch what I do to make the horses turn." And his voice called out, "Whoa! Haw up' there! Get on in there!" Obediently the team turned to the left and clomped up a long lane between two fences. Finally a shouted, "WHOA!"

Ahead was a neat house with white picketed yard. Clothes were pinned to a line and they moved in the breeze. People came out of the house, hesitated on the porch, and then came toward the buggy.

Tall man with dark red hair, trimmed with gray around the edges. Tall young men with red curls. Like Jeff's. Girl in dress and coverall apron. Woman...

Resting her eyes on the woman, she saw hair that was not molded into the current style, but twisted tightly and held with pins. But the eyes were her mother's. Round feminine face with her mother's smile. Dress, not made to fit but flowing loosely and covered with a roomy apron. Josie's eyes went back to the smile.

From the front seat of the buggy a small figure flew out and landed solidly on the ground. Like a flash, the legs carried him on, but he was caught in mid leap by the woman in the apron. Holding him securely, she peered into the face. "As I live and breathe, you are my little sister, Nora. I swear this little boy could'a been spit out by her, full made." She released her hold, and the child was gone, disappearing in a moment with the red haired boy about his size.

The woman in the apron turned her concerned attention to the other occupant of the buggy. Traveling outfit in sturdy wheat colored surge. Softly flared skirt. Fitted jacket trimmed modestly in brown and pink. Pink bonnet with wheat colored ribbon tie.

Brightly colored carpet bag over right shoulder. Right hand drawing aside the skirt as she lowered her foot to the buggy step. Left hand lightly resting on the arm of Nettie's own handsome son.

Stepping onto the ground, the shoulders straightened and the chin lifted. Measured steps... those expected of a lady. Somewhat broad of forehead, high bridge of nose. Sculptured cheek bones, well defined jaw line. More handsome than pretty. Arresting, actually. Deserving of a second look. Deep dimple softened the rounded chin. Straight brows and serious, gray-blue eyes.

And the girl looked toward the woman. Aunt Jeanette, called Nettie, who nodded in recognition. The woman continued, "And that one is Joseph Wheeler, dead to rights. I'd know him anywhere." The feminine version of her sister's husband moved toward her, eyes steady and expressionless.

Josie felt the moisture form in her eyes. She clenched her jaw in irritation. She would not cry. She would not... she would NOT! She was not a baby. The gray-blue eyes did not hear her and they filled anyway.

The woman in the apron, the one with her mother's eyes and smile, now opened her arms and waited while Josie's feet took her into them.

They closed around her, and a soft voice, almost her mother's voice, said into her ear, "Darling girl, you got here. I am so sad about our loss, but I am so glad you are here with me."

That was all it took. The squared shoulders under the wheat colored traveling suit shook with sobs, and bitter anguish gagged in her throat. Soft arms held firmly and knowing fingers patted with reassurance.

She felt a strong arm at her back, and knew that Uncle Matthew had his arm around them both, and a soft pat against her tear-drenched cheek were the fingers of twelve-year-old Carmelita.

Josie cried. Her tears flowed like summer honey from a bear tree. Tears held back for almost two months gushed free. She cried for the sudden loss of her parents. She cried for the suddenness of necessary decision making... for the frightening responsibility for herself and a young brother. She wept from the necessary words from Uncle Blaine as he was obliged to treat her as an adult, rather than the protected young lady she had always been.

There were tears for the loss of the city she knew, the plans that had been made for her and the culture she had understood. And there were tears of relief that someone knew how she felt, and had shared the tremendous loss. It was as though the horror of the last weeks had been melted into salty streams to be deposited upon the comforting shoulders of Aunt Nettie, whom she had not seen for more than six years.

Cousins stood around, arms at their sides... not knowing what to do. Finally, the heaving, gagging sobs dissolved into sniffles and hiccups. A free hand reached in her bag and drew out a handkerchief, stashed where a lady would always expect to find one.

Next came the embarrassment of having acted like such a baby before she had even greeted her aunt, but it didn't seem to have mattered. "Come, little one. You're here, now, with your family, and we're about to set on for dinner."

Food. The universal need that drew folks together, the salve to bridge a gapping wound, and it was now simmering fragrantly from the kitchen. Ten plates were spaced around the table and her aunt's apology for absent mindness. "Meant to have that extender leaf put in the table, and just didn't get to it. That'll give us spreadin' room."

Meat loaf with red gravy, steaming potatoes cooked with home canned green beans. Some kind of spring greens seared with bacon bits. Cornbread in a pan the size of a bed pillow. Eating left no need for conversation. The men finished off with sorghum syrup over more cornbread, and then they disappeared.

Nettie surveyed her new charge. "Now, Josie, honey, you're gonna stretch out on the bed for a bit..."

"Oh, no, I'm fine."

"No, you're not and I gotta say this. I'd be hopin' someone said the same for my Carmelita after she went through what you been through. You'll humor me by spendin' a little while in the bed, then you can get up feelin' fresher. I'll try to keep Esther out, so's you can get some rest."

The soft feather-stuffed mattress pressed warmly against her back and shoulders as the pillow cradled her head and drew the stiff pain of tension from her neck. The drawn curtains shut out the sunlight and when she again opened her eyes, hours had passed.

The evening moved by in an unreal dream, and the feather bed was once again her refuge. Twelve-year-old Mellie occupied one side and Josie the other. Small Esther claimed the middle, and Josie passed into sleep with tiny, soft fingers lovingly stroking her arm.

Hours later, flames again surrounded her. An unknown presence shared her bed, fright paralyzed her as she tried to scream. She knew she was not making a sound but that it was vitally important for her to scream loudly. Drawing in a deep breath, she forced her voice to make a sound. The strength of it pierced her own ears and raised fright bumps along her trembling arms. Moments later a lighted candle appeared, held in the steady hand of Aunt Nettie.

The terrified girl opened her eyes to Mellie hovering over her and Esther stretched across her chest, patting both cheeks with her tiny hands. Her whisper insisted, "It's all right. You're with us and nothin' can get you. Don't cry. It's all right!"

Aunt Nettie took over. "Mellie, go poke up the stove for tea. Essie, move back and let 'er breathe." Sitting on the bed beside her, the comforting words came, "Honey, don't feel bad. I was thinkin' this might happen. Sometimes lettin' down on pain hurts more'n holdin' in, and you've been holdin' in for weeks. I'm thinkin' you'll dream more times, but they'll finally go away. I want you to think on your nightmares as a good thing. We'll live through 'em, one by one, and then they'll gallop off and leave you with memories that don't pain so much. Mellie'll have that tea ready by the time we get settled so let's go on out to the table."

Esther trailed behind, holding to Josie's nightie and settled herself in a chair beside her. "See? I said to you that you was with us now. You got us to be with you when you cry. You can't cry with folks that don't know you and love you like we do." Such wisdom.

Josie looked down into the face... creamy skin and pink cheeks. Cupid's bow lips that could have been picked off a rose bush, so rosy pink and shapely they were. One arm spontaneously reached out to the four year old, who squeezed her small body up into her cousin's lap.

The steaming tea tasted of honey and smelled like peppermint candy. Cicada crickets and night birds sounded outside the open windows, through the breeze-ruffled curtains. No more words. They sat in silence and sipped. Such a relief! Sleep came immediately when the tea was gone and the lights were put out.

Digby's Camp

Digby, who had only known the Colorado mountains, was intrigued with the flat land and even more with it's people. Families. All members busy as a mound of beavers. Plowing. Animal tending. Making trips to the interesting place called Carlile Corners. Friendly when met on the road.

Leaving Hep at the campsite, he rode astride Worthless who willingly walked the rough and rutty roads, stopping as her rider surveyed this scene and that scene.

The place of his camp showed a lot of promise, though he had not yet made an effort to speak to the owners. The man seemed to have strange duties, mainly gathering things together, repairing equipment and tending animals. Two girls about eleven and twelve. Three younger boys, one of them coming onto the age of being of some use.

They were none of his business, of course, but it was time he was deciding what he could offer the family in return for permission to stay on the far corner of their land. The continuous rock ledge that stretched across the whole quarter section intrigued him. He had lived most of his life within dirt floors and stone walls and ceilings, and with this strip of stone he could easily make a snug place to spend the winter.

Josie Settles In

Behind the white picket fence, the New York girl coped with the clash of cultures. Nights often brought tears, but the terrified screams became fewer.

Days, however, were pulled forward by new experiences. Being one of a working family was completely foreign. Her brother was no long hers, only a moving shape, zipping here and there with his cousin. Small duties were assigned them, one of them being the need for cow pats. Wielding their sticks, swinging their basket between them, they scouted the pasture around the grazing animals. The boy seemed hardly to recognize his sister anymore.

Josie, however, met activities of another sort. Privies, for instance. She had known about the outdoor buildings sometimes called "necessary rooms", but they had been fast disappearing from New York City. So clever to have two of them here. There was the one a short walk behind the kitchen door, and another one far out behind the barn. Likely a good thing to have two, being that there were ten people. It also saved a lot of steps.

The huge iron cook stove was intriguing. In her mother's kitchen, a knob was turned, a match was struck and a flame was produced. Food was cooked over the flame. Not so in the territory.

First, cow pats must be brought in from the storage shed, called a wood shed, though there was precious little wood in it. The carrying of the light-weight chunks of burning material was a job for a four year old. Sometimes willing, sometimes not, but performed, never the less.

In preparation for the next meal (there was always another one to be started) the firebox must be prepared. The little metal knob sticking out the side of the stove must be moved back and forth so ashes would fall into the ash bin. But not jiggled too hard because there needed to be a few ashes left to start the next fire. Then the firebox had to be loaded.

A clever piece of bent wood was used to clasp the pats, to protect the clean hands of the cook. Really big pats had to be broken in two and the firebox could not be stacked over full. That would be a waste of fuel, and the fire would be hotter than needed.

If there were no left-over live coals, the flame quickly caught from a "go-fer" match, so named because the unequal mixing of combustible material left some of the slender sticks without enough heat to keep burning. So one was forced to "go fer" another one. At times they were called "lucifers" because of their propensity to burst into flame on their own when they accidentally came in contact with a solid surface... such as a penknife in overall pockets.

For a quick start, the flat "stove lids" could be removed so a skillet or pot could be set directly on the flame. Of course, that created black carbon that had to be cleaned off in the dishwater. However, if there was a LOT of carbon black, it was scraped off for its own use. It seemed to help prevent rust on the stove, itself, or, in an emergency, it made serviceable ink for letter writing or sign painting. Imagine that!

Then there was the hot water holder built in beside the firebox, called a reservoir. It was what created the means to wash dishes, floors or people. It, like the cow pat box, must be filled frequently so it could be emptied as needed. That was considered a suitable job for a seven year old boy, or maybe two of them.

There was the bread pan. It was a flat piece of metal with one-inch sides, and had been made as large as it could be and still fit in the oven. Actually, there needed to be two of them, for when there was to be company meals or when cookies were to be baked, one pan could be loaded as the other baked.

A special part of baking the bread was the turning. After 10 minutes or so, the huge pan was drawn out of the oven and turned, end for end. This created even browning.

The stove, with his uses and requirements, was a continuous fascination to the New York girl. Another important thing to remember was to keep an eye on the pipe that took the smoke out the roof. If it seemed too hot, or actually turned red, a knob on the side, called a damper, must be turned because that would shut down the air that came up the pipe and would quiet the flame in the firebox. But not too much, or the oven became too cool to brown the bread. The temperature was even more critical if there was a cake in the oven. Cakes "fell" if the temperature was not right... or if a small boy slammed the kitchen door. A lot to remember.

The adjustments created by the stove were a challenge to her mind, even more than the mathematical equations that had been demanded by her tutor at the insistence of her father.

The necessary kitchen animal called a stove, made even a further demand. Eventually, the ashbin was full. The lightweight flakes removed from the firebox had two uses. They were a valued addition to the soil in the petunia bed if they could be spared from the privy. Warm afternoons could produce a powerful smell in the necessary room, if left untended. Cow pat ash seemed to fill the bill and keep flies from hatching.

Another fact that intrigued her was that the cow pats themselves had conflicting uses. As badly as they were needed to replace the nonexistent trees, the alkaline soil of the flat land begged for the acid of the animal-produced residue. A grin escaped her lips as she considered that knowledge of the interworkings of cows, who, for a fact, might be more important in the territory than a book education.

On her second evening behind the white pickets, the family was called into the parlor for a conference. Uncle Matt began with unusual seriousness.

"Josie, it's necessary that we have a few family words, and I wanted everyone to be here when they happened. We received communication from your lawyer, and he mentioned that while he had the responsibility of the money your father left, it was your father's wish that your Aunt Nettie and I have the responsibility of you and your brother, at least for a while. All of that was as it should be, and we consider it a compliment and his faith in our ability to care for you... and that is much more important than any amount of money."

Josie nodded understanding, and offered, "Mr. Blaine gave me a little money and told me to leave it in the safe room in Argyle. He thought I might need some and it takes a while to get here and he said sometimes it doesn't make it at all if it's in the mail. I put my necklace and bracelet, that I got for my sweet sixteen party into the box. They were what my mother gave me." With a grin, she confided. "The man asked me if I was putting a gun in the box, 'cause if I didn't need it, he could sell it for me." She expected an amused smile from her uncle, but it did not come.

"Not bad idea, you having a gun. I think we need to tell the lawyer, in the next letter, that you need one suitable for killing snakes. As a matter of fact, we should ask for two. He'll have access to a better choice than we do, and it's time Mellie had a little target practice, as well as you. Those little rattlers are mean critters."

The request, when it was in the hands of Mr. Blaine, caused a surprised expression. "A gun? What would her father think of Josie needing a gun to protect her from snakes? What have we done to that girl?"

Whereupon his wife commented, "What if the gun saves her life? He trusted her uncle to take care of her, and her uncle HAS produced six children, and they're all still alive."

So the pair of guns, when they arrived, were tucked each into a glove made of serviceable material and lined with fleece. Gloves, the perfect size to fit the no nonsense-size of Josie's strong hands. Packed securely around the gloved weapons were an even dozen of soft, woolen stockings.

Cousin Mellie picked up a pair of the footwear, smoothing her fingers over the diamond pattern of the knit. "I never even saw stockings like these before." Josie picked up five more of the pairs and put them in Mellie's eager hands, saying, "And now you have six pairs."

Nettie picked up the note attached to one pair. The script was written in Mrs. Blaine's precise hand. "Josie, dear, I wouldn't want to think of you and your cousin having cold feet!" She instinctively knew if stockings like these had appeared in a store in Argyle, they would likely stay there for a long time. No one here had the money to squander on such a thing of luxury, but it wouldn't hurt for a little girl to have something fine and comfortable to wear, even if it had to be hidden within the high-top winter shoes and beneath the flannel winter petticoats.

But there was more to the family conference.

"As you know, Josie, and Joshua, too, it was your father's choice that you come here, at least for a while. All he really knows about me is that I have 6 healthy children, and he wanted the best for his two, so he asked me. Because of that, I plan to treat the both of you exactly as I would my own. If I didn't, I would be letting your father down, and I couldn't bear to do that.

"Because of your father's plans for Joshua's education, he could have been left in New York and put in the boarding school. That would mean we couldn't see him even during the summers until he was old enough to travel alone, likely 3 or 4 years from now." The little boy's huge, sky-blue eyes widened fearfully, and his arms clasped themselves protectively over his chest. His eyes, under the long, delicate lashes glanced at his new best friend, who looked equally alarmed.

Uncle Matt continued. "As it turned out, Joshua, your sister decided that you should come with her. A very good decision. There is another thing, however, and that is that you must still get the education your father wanted for you. Now, we don't really have a school here, and neither your Aunt Nettie or I have time to help you, even though he sent the books necessary for your first year. The lawyer is of the opinion that your sister is well qualified to teach the books, at least for a year or two." Josie's blue-gray eyes now widened in alarm. Yes, Uncle Blaine had mentioned something like that but... surely he didn't mean it.

Uncle Matt again. "Here's what we will do. There will be a set time each day for Josie to meet with Joshua in the parlor to learn the letters and numbers. He will work hard and do his best for an hour, during the summer. If he decides not to work hard, the lesson will be two hours long instead of one hour. Darrel will be there, too, and he will do exactly as Josie directs. Now, there's one other thing. Carmelita got a raw deal on our move out here, and she will have her turn. She will bring her sewing into the parlor during that hour, or two, and listen to the lesson. She may ask any question she likes, and if Josie can't help her, her mother or I will do our best. Does anyone see a problem?"

Josie took a deep breath. "Oh, I don't think I... well, I never have done anything like that. How could I be a teacher? I'm only barely seventeen."

"Well, Josie, perhaps you are too young. I thought Jefferson was too young to make the three-day trip to Oklahoma City to meet you, but I thought it was necessary for your safety that we meet you there, and the other boys were needed here. Jeff had never done anything like that before, but now he has, and he did well. Your father was very firm about education for his children. He educated you as well as if you had been a boy, needing to learn enough to get a job. The only other option would be to leave you both in New York, and he didn't want that. Now, Mr. Blaine stated that perhaps many girls your age could not do this, but he knew you and knew that you could. That was a compliment to you.

"Now what will it be? Do I send you back to New York with your brother, or will you do what you are well able to do? I'm sorry you have to make this decision. It isn't your fault, but it isn't mine, either. That's all I know to tell you."

All eyes were on Josie, two pairs of them pleading, pleading... Little Esther could stand the tension no longer, and eased herself into Josie's lap, pushing her small body back against Josie's chest while gathering Josie's arms against her own. Giving what comfort she could.

Aunt Nettie, cleared her throat. "Josie, honey, you've had to make a lot of decisions, but this may be your last hard one... at least for a while."

She finally realized there was no way out. She squared her chin and lifted her face. "My brother does not go anywhere without me. I'll do what you say. I mean I'll try."

Carmelita clasped her hands together before her face in an attitude of prayer, "Oh, thank you, Josie! You're going to stay here! I'm so excited!"

Travelers from Tennessee

Gaither Cullen was on the road again. He had directed his team, the roan and the bay, toward the west, and the iron capped wheels of the wagon rattled on the brick streets of Memphis, Tennessee.

It was six years ago that he first turned toward the west, but that was many problems ago. So, now, he felt a sense of relief but also depression... an excitement as well as a dread. Nevertheless, he must go on toward the pull of the invisible thread that drew him. A place had been found, and this was just the next milestone of his journey. It was a journey he knew he would take eventually, and the 'eventually' had now come.

The letter from Mac McConnell had settled the long-standing question, and he was now on his way to the Oklahoma Territory, just about six years too late. But nothing was easy... seemed like.

Behind him was beautiful fifteen-year-old Janine. Or did every father think his daughter was beautiful? Beside her slept the five-year-old boy.

A glance behind him revealed that the double seated buggy had now pulled onto the brick street. Tethered behind the buggy was the sleek young stallion, Bugger.

Gaither Cullen had known old Mac McConnell all his life. Their grandfathers fought together on the rugged hills of the old country. The Cullens and the McConnells fought with the Campbell clan against whatever enemy beset them, be it the king's army, the regiments from England, or even another highland clan. Tall, strong highlanders, they were, but they seemingly were forced to fight for every breath of freedom.

It was those two grandfathers who had decided there was nothing to be gained by raising sons only to be hacked apart in the many skirmishes. They had worked on the shipping docks until they had found a vessel willing to take them on as laborers in return for passage to the new country.

The shores of Virginia had welcomed them, and the hills of Kentucky seemed like their home in old Scotland. Mac and Gaither had struck out again, stopping for a while in Tennessee. Wives were found and families were started until, in the year of 1888, the rumors had begun.

New land. Free for the asking. All that was expected was what had always been expected... that a man should work and care for his family while he improved the land whereon he lived.

First it was on... then it was off. Did the government not know what to do with the little chunk of the Oklahoma Territory that was not yet assigned to any native tribe? But then, finally, the date was set.

Together the two families crossed the mountains of Tennessee, but then Gaither's problems began. His lovely English bride became ill.

Together he and Elizabeth had decided that, if they were ever to go west... to obey the tug the men had felt, then they must not let their growing children find mates in Tennessee. Gaither, himself, had Bradley, age fifteen, and Janine, barely ten. Both of them on the brink of marriageable age.

Then it happened, and in sight of the mighty Mississippi river, Elizabeth could go no farther. Mac and his family waved a sad goodbye and moved on. It was necessary to be in place by April 22, 1889. The race for the new land would wait for no man. Mac was successful and now had a small town settled on his quarter section. He named it Argyle after the stream that had flowed past his grandfather's land in the old country.

Gaither, himself, was faced with decisions. It was soon determined that Elizabeth expected a child, belatedly, and she was no longer young. Doctors were to be had in Memphis, so it would be foolish to take a sick woman over the journey that would be difficult for a healthy one. With a sigh he prepared to stay.

A place to live. An employment. Simple to find, as he had always been handy with horses, and where there were people, there would always be horses... else how could they move about? His son, Brad, now... that was a different story. While Gaither, himself could shape metal to a horse's hoof, he knew there was much more to be done with iron. He searched until he found what he sought.

The blacksmith shop in Memphis was large and well run. Customers waited their turn, and that spoke well for the skill of the owner. Taking the owner aside, Gaither offered the man the services of his strapping, strong son. He would expect no money to be paid to the boy until he was worth payment. When that happened, the successful owner would know what his son's services were worth. Gaither asked only that his son be exposed to every facet of blacksmithing that was known, and be allowed a chance to learn to create.

So it was that Brad learned to build the furnace to a white-hot blaze, how to hold the clamps to iron rods so the smithies could best shape them, and he learned to smooth and "round-up" iron bars to make many necessary items. He learned to sharpen rods for awls, and file the teeth of saws. He learned to put a fine edge on ax heads and hunting knives. Before the first year was out, Brad was paid in real money for his services, and the amount of the payment was increased every year.

A young man with a skill was very attractive to young women. It was then that Gaither remembered the need to move on before his son put down roots. Friend Mac agreed to look for a place somewhere in the territory.

It was with sadness that he remembered the pain of watching his beloved Elizabeth sink lower and lower, the pregnancy robbing every ounce of her strength. She had taken to her bed early on, and the care of the family had fallen onto the shoulders of the ten-year-old girl. Who else was there?

Gaither's days were spent caring for horses in a livery stable, and Brad was learning an important skill that every young man should have. Who else was there to care for Elizabeth? Janine, the happy, good-natured daughter then picked up duty after duty, finally carrying the whole lead. That was when her smiles and laughter became rare. Gaither did what he could, but what did he know of women's work?

The baby was born, seemingly healthy in spite of his ailing mother. The old woman who helped with the birth and filled out the papers necessary for a midwife and did with them whatever it was that had to be done. Name: Taylor. He had repeated it several times to the old woman. There was no way a mistake could be made.

Poor Elizabeth was hardly able to nurse the child, and the duty of bottle-feeding the infant became another duty to be performed by his daughter.

Nighttime rocking. Bottle cleaning. Gaither had insisted on helping, but after the time he went to sleep while feeding the baby, and had let him slide to the floor, he was banished from that duty. Janine would not hear to it when he promised to do better. She had put too much effort into that baby to risk his being damaged by another fall.

When the child was seven months old, his mother had used the last thread of her total strength, and had no ability to gain more. They had committed her frail body to the rich dirt of eastern Tennessee.

Years passed, and Gaither had no will to make changes. Food appeared on the table, horses needed care, Janine kept the floor swept, and Brad worked without complaint. Young Taylor grew.

More years flew by.

It was when he passed the blacksmith shop and saw an attractive young lady in bonnet and shawl speaking to Brad. She smiled and ducked her head, modestly. Brad seemed attentive. At that moment, Gaither Cullen awakened from his depression. What had he done! Was it already too late?

How could it have happened that on that very day, he received a letter from the territory? It must have been meant to be.

Was Gaither still interested in coming west? Mac had heard of a quarter section that was proved up and ready for sale. The young couple could not take the openness of the land and wished to locate in the city. If Gaither was interested, then he, Mac, would pay the earnest money and the young couple would wait for him to get there... if he started now.

Gaither answered immediately. Janine had somehow become a beautiful fifteen year old, and Brad was already his own man at age twenty. And there was that young lady at the smithy. Was it already too late?

Luck smiled, however, and the team now plodded on toward the wide Mississippi and the ferry platform that would convey them across the muddy water. It was already March, almost exactly six years later than he had planned... but what else could he have done? With a sad farewell to Elizabeth, he passed by the place where he had placed her body... relieved and reassured that she was now in a much better place.

He had been lucky. Brad was ready to go, on the condition that the tools of his trade be taken along. With his earnings he had acquired this and that, some of it frightfully heavy, but if that was the price of his agreement... ? Then, too, there was no assurance of smithing equipment being available in the territory.

The traveling wagons were pathetically small for trying to fit aboard all the things that Janine had said, emphatically, must go along. It turned out that Brad's belongings required their own small trailer with heavy springs to be drawn behind the wagon.

The town buggy was traded for a heavier one with two full seats. They would be days and days on the road, even with luck, and there must be a private place for Janine to sleep. Even now, Gaither could hear behind him the hooves of the buggy horses guided by the skillful hand of his son.

It was, however, not until he saw the frothy, brown water on either side and heard the shouts of the ferrymen that he felt that, finally, he was headed west into his dream. There was the wide Mississippi to be crossed and then he would be truly on his way.

He had urged the team off the ferryboat and onto the soil of the state of Arkansas and held back his tears of happiness as he watched the buggy horses climb onto the bank. The tears he knew he would shed must not be shed in the presence of his children. They must be private tears to be released only in the presence of God and himself.

Carlile Corners

The newness of the territory was now becoming commonplace to Josie Wheeler. Milk that had appeared in thick glass bottles upon her New York doorstep, now came in frothy buckets to be bottled and lowered into the well to keep cool. She had begun to help her aunt devise ways it could be used before it clabbered and was fed to the animals.

Leftover biscuits were not fed to the city birds, but were broken up into milk, eggs, honey and nutmeg and baked into a tasty and filling dessert. Leftover cornbread, if there was any, was dried, spiced and crumbled for a coating to fry fish, or for a thickening in the bean soup.

Challenges. They were everywhere. The row of persimmon trees beside the barn were put there so the dogs in the barn could keep the possums and raccoons from stealing the sweet fruit that was used in candy, pies and fruitcakes. The gathering of pecans and hazelnuts was no longer a lark for a pleasant afternoon, but a planned and serious accumulation of a necessary food source.

White flour was a delicacy that not everyone could often afford, and the finely woven sacks it came in were laundered carefully and put back for creating shirtwaists for ladies and to repair the collars of white Sunday shirts. Having white flour on hand continuously took more than money. It took planning. Several sacks would need to be ordered for delivery in Argyle, and then a trip in a cart to bring them home. Ten hungry people could consume a lot of flour.

And there were the lessons. Only an hour during the summer, to be expanded as necessary in the fall. It was Carmelita who proudly whispered to the older Canfield girl that her cousin from New York was a real, honest to goodness teacher, and that she, Carmelita, was allowed to listen in.

A teacher! Imagine! In their sparsely populated prairie, a teacher was as unexpected as snow in August! Women whispered over fences and men chatted about it at Carlile Corners. Could their own child, maybe, perhaps, just sit and listen and pick up what he could? What service could they provide the Wilson's in exchange for that prized gift of education for their child?

* * *

Fascinating games were played as Joshua, with his handful of stones, and Darrel with his, placed 6 stones, and 8 stones on the table and then counted them. The object of the game was to know later, without counting, that 6 and 8 would be fourteen... every time!

The first five letters of the alphabet were selected to learn sounds. Amazingly, most letters had two sounds. One sound said the name of the letter and the other one didn't. "A" was sometimes an "A" and sometimes an "Ah". "B" could be a "bee" or it might be a what? And the two little boys yelled, "bah"! Now, "C", on the other hand was a clown... a trickster! It pretended to be an "S" sometimes and other times it was a "K". Their teacher promised that, later on, it might even pretend to be other sounds.

The parlor room became crowded and very noisy, and the games were so fascinating that they extended far past the designated hour. At times the audience became so excited they could no longer watch quietly, but shouted out the answers themselves.

And that was not all. Interested mothers brought smaller ones, and stayed to visit with the lady of the house who had no time for daily visits, regardless of how well she liked their company. Something had to be done.

It was then that late night talk again spoke of the extra room, actually a yard cabin, to be used at night as a boys' bedroom, and during the day as a classroom, and the mothers must be informed, somehow, that the children must come alone... or not at all.

Maybe a room 12 by 12. Big enough for two full beds, a bureau of drawers and a potbelly stove for the worst winter days. But where would the students sit?

Maybe 14 by 14 would be better... or maybe 16 feet square. Of course, just for the boys, a section of the barn could be closed off and a stove put in. But that didn't allow for Josie's class.

Well, anyway, something had to be done. Summer was fine, but in the winter, with the house all closed up? And there'd need to be heat in the parlor. Also, how long would the expensive parlor furniture last... with a daily room-full of excited little boys?

Josie was aware of the problem, but she had her thoughts full with trying to remember her own first lessons, and adapting them to her strange class. Yes, it was becoming a problem, but not entirely her problem. Teaching had never been her idea... even though it was an interesting challenge, and her own tutor had been strong on challenges.

She even noticed that Carmelita and her friend, both of whom had a little schooling, had begun to help some of the younger children in the games... helping just so the same ones didn't win all the time. Maybe she could use that, because it was becoming time to copy words from the reader onto the four slates Uncle Blaine had thoughtfully included. The use of the slate and chalk would make it plainer for the students to see the differences of the "A" in "say" and the one in "saw", and to see how "L" with "C" in front turned it into a "K". Then why not use a "K"? Well, she'd wondered that, herself.

* * *

It was about this time that the dreaded news was passed around the community that Mrs. Sutter's time had come, but that she did not make it. It happened all too often. Mr. Sutter, in his sadness, anger and desperation, saw the only thing to do was to sell up and leave.

He would, of course, be leaving a lot of improvements and some livestock. He'd have to trade for horses for the wagon, as mules were too slow and plodding, and he must get back across the Mississippi before winter snow hit in the Ohio woodlands. He hoped he could find someone with a few gold pieces, maybe as much as $40.00 and that, added to the little he had, would see him through such emergencies as were sure to happen with 4 children under twelve on such a trip. And that included a baby.

Butcher a pig and cure what he could. The girls, 11 and 12, would can up what they could in the glass jars they had. There were potatoes left, and a lot of turnips—cleaned and packed in straw they would be useful. He'd have to leave the potbelly stove, but they'd have to find a place for the kitchen plunder, as it would be needed no matter what his final outcome for the family would be. He sighed. Just another set of problems.

He purchased a tablet and the girls printed several sheets with the pertinent information on it. It was a long shot, but it was possible one of the neighbors knew of someone... well, it was worth a try.

The first place he took a notice was to Carlile Corner. The next stop was the Wilson's. There always seemed to be a lot going on there, and Matt Wilson was a good hand at knowing answers. The sheet was discussed over a lot of dinner tables. Cryin' shame about the Sutters... them bein' such good neighbors, and all.

Uncle Matt and his sons discussed the situation. "Pa, we could likely make a trade for the stock. Him needin' three horses, we got 'em to spare, and we could use the mules. Seems like there was maybe four cows, and the other hog. Don't need 'em all that bad, but we could make use of 'em, and help a neighbor out."

"Could do that, son. That soddie where they lived, now that was an interesting place. More of a dugout, maybe. Heard 'im say how warm it was in the winter. He was fixin' it up to be the fruit cellar when he got a regular house put up."

"After we eat, we could run over and see what we could do to help."

Mellie spoke up. "Could I go, Pa? I'd like to tell Bessie goodbye."

"Hmmm, I don't know why not."

Mellie, again. "Josie, do you want to go, too? Their house is somethin' special to see."

At first, all the New York girl saw was a gaping hole in the side of a small hill, topped with a flat layer of stone stretching in both directions. A door opened out under the rock ledge, and several children were sorting potatoes by the door. Next, she was walking through the door behind Bessie.

The darkness was not as bad as she had supposed it would be, and what should have been a dirt floor was carefully laid with flat stones, chipped and shaped to fit like pieces of a puzzle. Bessie pointed it out with pride, saying it took her pa a 'heap'a time to do it', but that was what her ma had wanted. And she added that pa had said it would be a good fraidy-hole for when the cyclone storms came across the mountain.

Bessie also pointed out that the new heater stove had to stay, and also the iron bedstead her ma had insisted on bringing. Said her Gran and Grampa had given the bed to her ma when she was married to pa, over thirteen years ago.

Josie reached up to the ceiling, a flat layer of stone stretched just above her extended fingertips. The sidewalls were laid with stone, straight up and down like a regular house, but, Bessie pointed out, "them cracks sometimes lets in the spiders." And... "Most times in the winter, they's a cricket that comes a'chirpin'."

Amazed and fascinated, Josie circled and re-circled the large room. Talk about a challenge, her tutor would like to see this.

Cooking was apparently done in the small fireplace, as evidenced by the blackened hearth, but a smoke hole was inside the fireplace. How did the smoke get up through the stone ceiling? “Oh, pa, he dug through till he got past the stone, then he put in a pipe. Only thing is, one time a garden snake fell into the pipe and showed up in the fire.” She chuckled at the joke played on the reptile.

Near the door was a heap of the flat stones used for the floor, and a sizeable pile of cottonwood poles, trimmed and de-barked. Bessie was sober and sniffling, close to tears as she pointed out that was to be their new “regular” house, and it would have stone floors like the dugout.

Bessie pointed out, “Nuther thing ma liked was the water that come up out back and up the hill. Pa said it was part’a the stream over yonder that sunk down and come up again. Said he’d get it to come into a pipe, once he got the house up and ma’d have water in the kitchen. Ma was gonna like that.” Then she added, softly. “Guess ma don’t care no more. Likely got all the water she needs where she went.”

The deal was made, and three young horses would be traded for the remaining livestock. One pig was to be butchered, and one cow was to be taken along, tethered to the wagon. If it worked out, the little ones would have milk, and if it didn’t, it could be sold along the way. Traveling the way he would have to, Mr. Sutter was resigned to the fact that it would be a slow trip. The cow should have no trouble keeping up.

All the way home and through the day, Josie thought of the Sutter’s loss. What a lot of work to let go for $40.00. How much was “$40.00” worth, anyway? Her old tutor would have made up a problem, somehow, using the value of the work, the scarcity of hard cash and the time constraints with winter coming on. It would have been interesting to hear what he came up with. He liked to do problems like that.

It was on that night in April that she again saw the flames. They danced and leaped around her, casting shadows and flashes of light, just as before, except this time the flames had voices. Like hellish demons they "yipped" and "squealed" threatening to consume her. She turned this way and that to avoid them, and the bed shook... waking cousin Mellie before the screams had a chance to start.

"Josie! Wake up, Josie. You got that dream again."

Gratefully, Josie forced her eyes open, but her shaky, terrified voice whispered, "I still hear the demons!"

Mellie chuckled. "I've known 'em to be called demons, all right, but they're really just little fuzzy pups, learnin' to hunt. Them's coyote pups, born this year and just now out of the den."

Josie smiled in relief. She'd often heard the wailing whine of the adult dogs, "song dogs" the natives had called them. The moonlight streamed into the window and across the colorfully pieced quilt. Long after her cousins were back to sleep, she stared out the window into the brightness. So many new things. New thoughts. Not the least of them was the guns. Small and shiny, they seemed no bigger than a case for face powder, or maybe an unusually shaped casket for rings and broaches. Actually, they were a far different thing.

She and Mellie had spent hours with the pair of shiny weapons. The first target was a plate-sized circle drawn in the dirt. Then they graduated to a thick rope looped over the clothesline. These small guns had one purpose, and that was to protect herself and her cousin from snakes. Most were harmless, but they were not to take chances. When they became proficient, the guns would fit in a bag, or in an apron pocket when the girls must be out and about. Their safety would be assured.

When the request for the guns had reached Uncle Elias Blaine, he had gasped with horror, but now, after a bit of consideration, he had thought of sending a weapon with a bit more power. Surely there were horrors worse than snakes and requiring a more powerful punch. He'd check and see if that would be appropriate. He already had a request for the lesson books for the next level, and was smugly pleased with himself for his faith in Josie's ability. His valued friend and partner could have sired no less than this strong, intelligent girl who was also a lady. It would be interesting to follow her activities.

Lawyer Blaine, however, was totally unprepared for the next request he received.

Josie slept no more after the fire "demons" had awakened her. It was close to morning, and it was just before the rooster sounded the alarm, that it hit her, as one might say, right between the eyes. Full blown and formed, the idea spread itself in her head with all its possibilities, and it would solve more than one problem.

She would buy the Sutter place. She would go through the motions of asking permission from her guardian, but she would buy it. Practically at arm's length, she had $40.00. He had said that he trusted her to make well thought out decisions, but there was no time to think about this one. It was a good deal, and someone would snap it up. She knew, for a fact, that she would never return to New York, except maybe for a visit. And that would be long time from now.

After that, there was absolutely no sleep to be had, and she was in a fever to get up and let her decision be known. One thing though, it would mean a trip to Argyle. Though she had the coins with her, she was not to let anyone know about them. She had to pretend she must visit the box in the strong room. Too bad, but it was Uncle Blaine's way of protecting her, and she saw the wisdom of it. Who knew what would be said without thinking if it was known that she had money in her trunk beside her bed? He had been clever and he had trusted her to do what he said.

While the men were doing the morning chores, she ran the words through her mind. Her family would think she had surely lost her mind, but to her it was as clear as a bell. Her "students" were about to ruin Aunt Nettie's nice parlor, and they messed it up each day by tracking dirt and grass seeds into the carpet and crushing the satin pillows. It would be only a matter of time before one of the cut-glass lamps was knocked over in their enthusiasm. Her aunt had never mentioned it, though she had spoken about the visiting neighbors setting her behind in her work.

Josie could picture the children on the flagstone floor, each one furnishing a cushion if they expected to use one. The potbelly stove would be left, and a kettle of soup would simmer nicely on it. She was getting good at making soup. If the eleven and twelve year old Sutter girls could do a family's cooking in the fireplace, so could she. Or on the potbelly.

She would manage for a stack of shelves against the flat stonewall to take care of the books that would be coming. She had requested that storybooks for older children be sent along. Maybe eight or ten books would be nice. And, oh yes, she had asked for a map and had been puzzled as to where she could hang it. See there? Her mind had known all along what was going to happen!

It was not her fault, really. She did not intend to be a teacher, but when forced by circumstances, it was clear she would have to have a place to do it. Isn't that plain to see? By anyone?

It wasn't.

"Oh, Josie, honey. You can't want to buy a quarter section of land. You have no way to take care of it, and things have to be done to prove it up. There has to be a well, cross fencing and at least forty acres under cultivation or in cattle production. The Sutter's haven't nearly..." And more was said.

Josie sadly poured syrup on her buttered biscuit and proceeded to cut it with a knife and fork. The sweetness of the honey was bitter on her tongue, and she forced herself to swallow. Of course! Why did she ever think she could do what seemed to be exactly what she needed to do? She was only a seventeen year old girl... what did she know?

Another bite, and a sip of the delicious coffee that suddenly had no taste. Now what? She had been contented until she saw the wonderful underground room. She just couldn't go back to not knowing it was there. But now her dreams had scattered like a broken feather pillow tossed up in a windstorm. Scattered. Irretrievable.

The family ate in silence. Then, cousin Douglas. "Pa, a body's gotta be 21 to sign for one of them land transfers that ain't been proved up, don't they? To make it legal, like? Well, Josie ain't 21 but Junior is."

"What're you sayin', son?"

Junior Wilson lay down his fork and forgot the gravy-covered biscuit in his plate. He had been with his brother for nigh onto twenty years and could read his thoughts very well. "Pa, listen to this. Doug and me, and Jeff if he's a mind to, we been wantin' to set up with the Angus cows on a place'a our own. Didn't say nothin', knowin' there wasn't nothin' you could do about it. Been no time to think it through, but if I was to sign for Josie, makin' it legal like... ? The fencin' and cultivatin' that'd have to be done, that was what we'd have to do, anyway. We'd need a barn, and we'd put it up with them poles down there..."

He paused, and Douglas took up the planning. "And diggin' that water well, it'd be no trick before the provin' time was up, almost a year away, and anyway, it's got water comin' and goin', the way them little streams meander."

Jeff was fit to burst with words. "You bet fer sure I want in on it. Place that'd raise cows'd raise horses. Maybe mules, too. There's gonna be a big need for 'em, the way this place is a'fillin' up."

Josie glanced at her aunt. Nettie was silent, as a proper lady might expect to be while the men plan and figure, but her eyes were alive with interest, as they had been when Josie first outlined her plan. This plan would get the lively little boys out of her parlor, and if the mothers attended with their children, it would be Josie's problem, not hers. And, as she was getting to know her niece, she felt Josie could take care of the problem perhaps better than she, herself, could. All this was written plainly on her aunt's face, and as Josie watched, her aunt caught her eye and they exchanged the tiniest of smiles. And a miniature wink.

"Well, boys..."

Josie could stand the tension no longer. "Then someone's gotta tell Mr. Sutter so he don't let it go before the boys can get there. Same time, I've got to have a trip to Argyle to get the money."

Then her uncle. "But, Josie, we gotta get word to New York to get permission. All that'll take time."

Josie's head shook violently back and forth, swinging her honey colored hair into a wavy fan. "Please! No time. Like I said, I'm going to buy it. I know he'll give permission. He trusts me. He said so, and he let me make other decisions. If you can't spare someone to take me to Argyle, I'll go down to Carlile Corners and try to hire someone. I have enough money with me to do that. I know what I want, and I want that dugout."

Silence. This was a new Josie, and there was thinking to do. "Well, likely you're right. I can assure the lawyer that the land will sell for more every year, and he'll surely trust my boys to do right by you."

Jeff was breathless. "I'll take her, Pa. We'll go in the cart and it'll be easier ridin' and faster'n the big buggy. We'll be there and back by noon."

Then Junior. "I'll saddle up and get on over there to Sutter's place. No use in him a'wastin' time handin' out more'a them flyers."

Doug was next. "Junior, remember to pick up that one he left at the Corners. No one has time to waste, checkin' on what's already been took."

Uncle Matt cast his eyes toward his wife in time to note her wide smile. "I'm thinkin' this is all right with you?"

A bigger smile and a nod. Aunt Nettie was clever. Some things just simply took care of themselves if you let them. The trick was to know your people and have patience. Another thing she had thought of in the last few minutes... her sons were almost grown, and Junior was past 21. Any day or any moment one or more of them would be gone, intent on setting up something for themselves. Somewhere. This project would keep them around for a while longer, and give them a start with their own animals.

Finishing the meal was forgotten. Jefferson had the cart with the single seat hitched up to frisky paint filly as Josie was handed the pocket gun. She was to slip it into her carpet bag (having been filled already with the necessary coins, their jingle dulled by inserting them into stockings) and advised to keep it handy on the return trip. Seeing robbers or anyone who would cause trouble was highly remote, but it was better to be safe.

She was instructed, if trouble became seemingly, to take the weapon from the bag and fire at the ground outside the cart, while bracing herself for any fright activity that might happen with the filly. The gun was to be her responsibility, not Jeff's, so the mischief maker would know that the lady was armed and would not be an easy victim. If trouble did not go away, the next shot was to be in his direction, and the filly would be required to put on speed.

Josie nodded. The shape of the small weapon was now familiar to her hand after the hours of practice with the circle on the ground, and then the rope over the clothesline. Mellie, being of fine bone and years younger, was still working on holding a steady hand, but Josie had "graduated" to a moving rope across the ground, and was proving to be surprisingly adept.

Jeff chattered excitedly all the way to Argyle about all the things that could be done at the Sutter place. Josie searched her mind for what she needed beside more chalk, and did they carry slates?

She was locked in the safe room and left with her strong box, still securely chained to the wall. She took the coins from their protective stocking and counted them before slipping them back into the knotted stocking bag.

No, the store did not carry chalk as there had never been a call for it. Did she want some ordered? If she did, she would have to pay half now and the other half when it was picked up. When would that be? With a shake of his head, the clerk said it would be just as soon as they could get it. Josie thanked him and said she would think it over. It might be slower to order from New York, but it was certain to get here.

Three days later, Matthew Wilson, Junior, signed responsibility for the tract of land, and was given a receipt for the $40.00. The Sutter family was still gathering their needed plunder, but planned to be gone before the week was out.

The Cullen's Journey

Far to the east, the wagon pulling the trailer and the heavy-duty buggy rolled away from the ferryboat yard at the Mississippi River. There was still daylight, and Gaither Cullen wished to make a few miles before camping for the night. He had assigned Janine and the boy over to the buggy "to see how it rode" because he wanted to be alone.

He knew there would be tears as soon as he permitted them, and now was a good time. His three children would never understand them, but the tears were necessary. Loneliness and pent-up longing... discouragement and anticipation... excitement and weariness... All of the emotions that had taken their toll... they must be dealt with. Here was a good time and now was a good place.

Tears streamed down his face when he thought of Elizabeth, being long ago in the churchyard. He wept with gratefulness for Janine, though he knew he had expected too much from a child. He wept for pride in the way Brad had taken his advice at the smithy, and he wept with relief over the letter from Mac in the territory. It took time and a lot of tears to attend to every disappointment in his life, but when they found a camp at sundown, he knew that the worst of the tears had past.

He pulled the wagon aside near a stream and a pasture that was pale green with new grass shoots. Dotted among the rotted logs at the stream were puffy balls of white that brought a smile to Janine's face. A rare and welcome smile. She was so, so beautiful when she smiled that it made Gaither's heart ache. Oh, Elizabeth, you should see our daughter!

Mushrooms. The dinky little stove powered with smelly kerosene was fired up. Maybe wood would be better, but the oil stove was quicker. Janine did what she did best, and assigned mushroom picking to her brothers while she mixed the cornbread.

Mushrooms. Browned and swimming in gravy. Cornbread. Crusty and buttered. Water in the jug and milk for the child. How could heaven be better, though Janine commented that the cornbread should have been lighter, and she hoped there would soon be a place to get more eggs.

Darkness settled in, and the girl crawled into the back seat of the buggy, fastening down the storm flaps against night-flying insects. It had not been a bad day. If the fellows were happy to be on this trip, she'd be fine. She could do only what she could do, but tomorrow she would arrange to walk part of the way to get exercise for herself and the little brother. The fellows would just have to go slow enough for them to keep up.

Digby Decides

It was a new world for Digby. For a man whose days were centered around the dirt inside a Colorado mountain, and one who knew, to intensity, the way to survive... and now the activity on the flatland was intriguing and full of endless avenues of opportunity, there was much to see.

Under his tent on the far corner of what soon would be Josie's quarter section, he did not escape notice, but was seemingly not important enough to cause concern community concern. At least, not at first.

Rumors abounded, and arose in the air like the pollen from spring flowers. Stories seemed to move with a communal knowledge and without being put into words. What was known by the O'Days was almost instantly known by the Canfields though they be two miles away. Back fences, shouted greetings to passers by, maybe coffee at the Corners and the reports brought back by children who were everywhere.

The passage of news had accelerated, as Josie's lessons became known. The hope for a school, somehow, and discussions of how to get one was a binding thread in many conversations. The usual method was to advertise for a spinster lady of some bit of training to come to the community and educate the children. Involved families expected to "put up" the teacher for their divided share of the time, based often on the number of children in the family to be taught... which often put the teacher boarding the most time in the largest families.

Two great problems existed, and the community around Carlile Corners added another of their own. They had no community center for gatherings or, more importantly, a place of learning.

The next two problems vied for first place. There was the scarcity of hard money, and gross lack of actual space in their homes for the teacher, assuming one could be found and be persuaded to come. Add these together, and toss in the fact that anyone who called herself a teacher could find sudden employment in the bigger cities... with more comforts. Small, rural communities were at the bottom of the desirability pile.

Therefore, when the news circulated that Matt Wilson's New York niece was a "bonified teacher", nothing could convince them otherwise. She was from New York, certainly a seat of learning. She carried herself as one with education, dressed the part, and did not merely "entertain" the children but actually taught them. What more was to be expected?

When 5 and 6 year-olds displayed their ability to count a handful of rocks, and to recite the alphabet, it drew attention. No matter that they had no idea of what it meant that "C" was a clown, and pretended to be other than what it was.

The O'Days and the McLaughlins furnished the most children, therefore felt free to start the ball rolling. It was clear that if there was a teacher among them, then they'd better do what they could to keep her before she went on to Argyle, or even Oklahoma City.

The ink was hardly dry on the agreement before the eight square mile area knew that, somehow, the niece and the sons of Matt Wilson were going to take over the Sutter place. Just what the agreement was seemed unimportant when stacked up beside the possibility of a teacher having somehow fallen into their midst and had not yet put down roots.

The continued insistence by the Wilson family and Miss Wheeler, herself, that she was not a teacher was patently disregarded. Logic told them that if you could plant, you were a farmer. If you raised cattle, you were a cattleman. Consequently, if you could teach, you were a teacher, no matter what you said.

So...what could they do to keep her? Well, that was the subject of many parlor gatherings, and one was held currently in the parlor of the O'Day family. One huge difficulty was cast aside when they knew Josie would be at the Sutter place. That meant no one would have to "put her up" in their turn. It was not that they wouldn't like her, or that she would be a trouble to them... it was more the fact that no one actually had the room, considering their own expanding families.

So, if they were not putting her up, the value of board for the teacher must be made in other ways. How much money would be required to hire her for all the children, not just the two seven year-olds of her family and their closest buddies? The fact that they sincerely desired a teacher did not increase their cash flow, which was mostly zero at the moment.

"The Sutter's had 'em a good garden plot. Does a New York lady know about growin' food?" Hmmmm, an idea for thought.

"Them clothes she wears... they must take a heap'a sudsin' and pressin'." Definitely another idea.

Silence. A circle of thoughtful faces. "Well," began Mr. O'Day, after clearing his throat in a meaningful way. "Me bein' right here like you might say, across the road from the Sutter place, I say I can furnish the lady with milk and butter. If she likes cheese, my wife makes the best. Could that get the ball t'rollin'?"

Nods. More thought. Mrs. Canfield was next. "Reckon I could take on her washin' and ironin'. With the washin' I got, what's a few more things? 'Sides, if she'll take on my two oldest girls, they'll be more'n glad to do their part."

More thought. Frowns furrowed the foreheads as the more obvious offerings were volunteered. What could they do... that a young New York lady needed done?

Mr. McLaughlin drew in a breath. “Well... way I’m a’seein’ it, that lady is gonna need a way to get around. I’m sayin’, bein’ close here like I am, that I could furnish my little buggy and a horse for whatever and whenever she needed it. I’d have it ready and not use it for anything else, less’n I knew for sure she’d not need it. I’m allowin’ there’ll be trips over to Argyle and who knows where else, that she’ll need to make.”

Then leaning back on the uncomfortable settee, he continued. “I’m sayin’, ‘course that won’t be all I’d expect to offer. There’ll be this and that she’ll need, things what we won’t know about for a while. I’ve got three youngens a’needin’ learnin’ and I’d shore want to do my part.”

“I keep thinkin’ about that garden,” put in Mr. Hastings. “There’s them three cousins’a hers, any one of ‘em could take care’a the growin’, but, way I hear it, they all three got plans a’their own. I’m a’thinkin’ that fenced off place they got staked out is gonna be so full’a animals you couldn’t stir ‘em with a stick, meanin’ them cousins’ll not have time. I’d like to take on the spadin’, plantin’ and weedin’, and the pickin’ if she didn’t want to do it.”

Mr. O’Grady, whose quarter section was almost two miles away, rapped his knuckles on the arm of the chair for a chance to speak. “I seen that potbelly that Sutter moved in there, and it’s gotta be a cow pat gobbler. Likely need that much heat, though, with all them fancy stonewalls. I’ll have to send my two girls up there on horseback, and it’ll not hurt ‘em to take along a bag’a fuel. If that don’t be enough, I’ll load up a wagon. With all the cows I got, it’ll be no trick, a’tall.” And then, not to be outdone by McLaughlin, he added, “...And I stand ready to do my part on other problems that might come up.”

Mr. Owen had been impatiently trying to hear what was going on, with his wife insistently whispering in his ear. “Folks, my wife here, she’s a’talkin’ me blue in the face. She’s about the best in the country with a needle, to hear her tell it. She’s sayin’ she’d like the duty’a patchin’ and sewin’ up what needed it, and the makin’a aprons and what all. She's sayin' she's got another idea. Says we could ask that girl what she likes to eat that comes in cannin' jars, and each decide on what we got that we could send her."

Mrs. O'Day held up a hand for a chance to speak. "Is that girl a'gonna stay over there? I was thinkin' she was gonna stay bedded down at her aunt's and use the Sutter place for the school."

Julie Canfield took her turn. "Likely that's what they're sayin' but come November rain and February snow, that girl'll be glad enough to fire up that Sutter stove with O'Grady cow pats and huddle up by the fire. I'm a'sayin' Betty O'Day's got the right idea. I could can up some beef in them little pint jars that'd be just right for her to heat up."

"Yes," put in Mrs. McLaughlin. "I'm a'thinkin' cured ham and bacon'd be somethin' she'd fix easy. Maud Sutter cooked on that dinky little fireplace, but I'm thinkin' a New York girl might not know about how to keep that thing a'goin' and stop the smoke. The top side'a that potbelly'd be the place for her to do her cookin'. At least for a time."

Dwight Haasfield stroked his whiskery chin. "What'll them youngens sit on whilst they're learnin'?"

The answer from Harriet Hastings. "Word I hear is that she said that everyone that didn't want to sit on the stone floor could bring a cushion or whatever they wanted."

A chuckle floated around the crowded parlor. A loud clearing of the McLaughlin throat, and he announced. "Looks like us men folks gonna be makin' some tables. Reckon how she'd like them picnic type tables with a bench hooked on? We could maybe make three, and one of 'em could be made to fit the little fellers."

Nods and smiles of agreement. "Well, we'd have to ask her. After all, it is her house..." Chuckles of amusements. Here they were planning her life and from the looks of her, that New York lady already knew what she would do with her life!

While the discussion was being held in the crowded O'Day parlor, the subject of the discussion, herself, was enthroned upon the uncomfortable horsehair stuffed sofa in the Wilson house. Shutting the door to keep out cousins, Josephine Wheeler propped her tablet on her knee and leaned toward the kerosene lamp, the better to make her list. If she was going to do a job, she had to have something to do it with. Uncle Blaine had said she would have money for whatever she wanted, not just what she needed, and she sincerely wanted books to put in the strange house she had also sincerely wanted.

When she had asked permission to buy it, she had already paid the money, but her local guardian pretended that she had not. The lawyer had said that it seemed like a good investment, particularly since Uncle Matt had sent along a note that even at this moment it could be sold for more than she had paid... it was just that the Sutter's could not wait for the better price.

The excited children had come with pillows, that is the girls had. The boys thought they were tough, and could sit on the bare stones. We'd see how that went! Now she needed books and a blackboard. Maybe two blackboards.

There would be the New McGuffey Readers. They had been barely available when she was studying, but her tutor said they were the very best, and they had made his job a lot easier. They had seven graded steps of learning, primer through the sixth level. She would be very brave and order 6 complete sets, while she was at it. Aunt Sharon Blaine would have a lot of fun picking them out.

She would need the numbers books, level three to six. She would teach grade one and two from the blackboard. That's what her tutor had done, and little ones might learn quicker that way. History for level 4, 5, and 6. Aunt Sharon would do a good job there, and also the storybooks. She wanted a lot of them because reading was so important for understanding. How many...?

How about 25 books in levels three through six. And while she was at it, maybe a few that would interest the teacher. Teacher! How strange it sounded, but there was no convincing the parents that she was not a teacher... and that she hadn't even taken the test for a certificate. What did she want with a certificate? All she was doing was making sure her brother and cousin were ready for... ? What? Oh, well. She was just doing what she was told to do.

Uncle Matt had a way of making people see their duty. He faced Josh and Darrell at the breakfast table, his favorite place to give orders because no one wanted to leave the food!

He had said, "Now you two boys are seven. You have learned how many are seven and seven. That's fourteen... yes? All right, together you two boys make a boy of fourteen, and that's old enough to harness the pony to the cart and see that your sister and cousins get down to the schoolhouse. Then, you'll see that it gets tied securely. Understood?"

Two nods. Then Josh wondered, "We don't have to take off the harness?"

"Good question. No, not during the summer for one hour, but in the fall when you stay all day, you will take off the harness and put the pony in the pen. That's what a fourteen-year-old boy would do. I'll help you tomorrow and one more day, and then the job is yours."

Josie grinned at the memory. He had a way of making the job seem important and almost a gift, and that they would be foolish to argue.

What else? Oh, the slates and a crate of chalk. How many... let's see. There are sixteen counting the bigger girls. So, maybe 25 to start with. I can always order more. And I need one book with the penmanship letters.

Finishing her letter, she blew out the lamp and crawled in bed with her cousins. Esther turned over in her sleep, her tiny hand resting warmly and possessively on Josie's arm. The bed was just a little crowded. It didn't seem so much when the weather was cooler, but July was about half past and the days were hot. She'd thought of maybe moving to the floor, but Aunt Nettie would feel bad about it.

* * *

It was a week later that the children had gone home, and Josie stood alone in the center of her flag-stoned floor looking around her. The stones of the floor blended seamlessly into the layers of stone on the walls. Potbelly stove. Solid, firm and business-like. Reassuring.

Bed. It had cost the Sutter girls a pang of anguish to leave the bed because their mother had loved it so much. Mrs. Sutter's wedding bed. Heavy iron trimmed with curls and flowers of shaped iron, made to retain its beauty for the ages. Rods circled the top to hold the canopy and side curtains. Could be she'd need the top cover and curtains in the winter. How cold did it get between stonewalls? Well, it was hers, and she'd get to see.

Wall shelves. They'd work until she could get a bureau with drawers. Stools. Well, that was a decision for another day.

She took another turn around. Hers. From the depth of her being was shouted the word "MINE!" Demon flames could never devour this house. The sturdy stones from the territory would break out the fiery teeth of the demons and tame them down into a servant that would fill the potbelly with warmth, and maybe later, the fireplace.

Hers! So there! Got that, old fire demons?

Her tutor had thoroughly drilled her in problems and solutions. When she had completed the requirements for young men of wealthy parents, she was fourteen, the correct age be to be apprenticed. No further study was available unless she was preparing to read the law. Her father had forbad that, saying that no matter how good she was at that, no female would ever be trusted to become a solicitor. Too dangerous. Still, he wanted her active mind expanded.

For that reason, he told the tutor to concentrate on problem solving in the best manner than he could, and the young man accepted the challenge. He devised situations and circumstances that would present a problem, and allowed her to suggest solutions. Then, together, they would discuss her findings.

That must have been how she came to be standing among these rocks. Her mind had seen how she continuously fought against the flames, and had now provided for herself something that would not burn so she could ease her mind. Is that possible?

She had chosen to walk home, so the pony cart had gone on. At the Corner, she stepped inside to check the mail hook. Nothing today, but rolling and tumbling at her feet were the three small furry pups, competing for her attention. Small rounded bodies, pointed tails, ears that aimed skyward. Sparkling eyes and laughing mouths. Toy pups. Not pups that would grow into valuable farm dogs.

She stooped to pet the closest animal, and it was nudged aside by a wriggling creature that pushed his head under her hand. Turning to grab her fingers in his mouth, then to stoop on his front legs to push himself into a leap, whirling in the air and landing again on his feet.

Startled, Josie turned to old Mrs. Carlile who smilingly told her, “That’en, he’s the onliest one that does that. Couldn’t’a been taught, cause he ain’t been alive long enough to learn nothing. I’m thinkin’ that animal should ought’a be yours.”

“Mine?”

The old woman pointed to a penciled sign, FREE PUPPIES. She nodded, “You can see them ain’t gonna be stock dogs, and there ain’t too much call for dogs that don’t work for their keep. Folks tell me you got the Sutter house. You need a dog.”

Mine. The house made of stone... mine. This puppy that thinks I might take him, and then he would be mine. MINE!

She walked out with the small dog in her arms, but soon put him down on the road. Circling, dashing ahead, yipping and occasionally flipping in the air, he led her all the way to the Wilson house.

Carmelita was first to see him. "Oh, a puppy! What are you... ? I mean, whose is he... ?"

"He's mine and his name is Flip."

"Hmmm, well, mom... she don't... Well, she mostly thinks dogs gotta stay in the barn. You reckon he'll stay there?"

Oops! Problem. Quick thought. "I'm thinking on making him a box, and not letting him run around."

Carmelita looked doubtful. "Well, I don't know... I guess...?"

She left him in the yard playing with an interesting stick, and at night put him in the box beside her bed. The weary puppy seemed to take to the soft bed, until his need for nature came on him. Like any well-bred pup, he left the box and searched for an absorbent place to deposit the liquid. What he found was even better than he had hoped for, and did his duty between the red petunia's and the woven daisies on Nettie's parlor carpet. Then he obediently came back to bed.

Esther, whose turn it was to wipe the accumulated dust from the parlor furniture, was first to find the evidence. Still faintly damp and slightly tan. "Mama? Someone tried to water the flowers on the carpet!"

"What?" It must be said that Aunt Nettie took the damage better than her family expected, patiently showing Josie how to softly brush the thick suds onto the carpet, not going against the grain. It wouldn't remove any odor, but maybe such a little bit... ?

Without actual words coming her direction, Josie knew the puppy must sleep somewhere else. She put the box on the porch, but the yips and puppy howls kept the family awake until Josie joined the small animal on the porch. She leaned against the wall, and the pup curled up in her lap without another sound.

No sleep. A doze and a jerk, and she was awake again. Another problem. This puppy could not go to the barn. He would be no fun to play with if he was not with her, and the farm did NOT need such a tiny animal.

The sun was rosy in the east when the solution to the problem became apparent. When it settled into her mind, Josie knew that it would have eventually come to this, and the pup had just brought it about quicker than expected. It was discussed at the breakfast table.

"But Uncle Matt, I was going to move into my house eventually, anyway. I need to be there, learning to do things and taking care of myself."

"No, Josie. I can't allow that. It isn't safe for a girl of your age to..." And he paused for a good reason, so Josie spoke up.

"But Uncle Matt, how old would I have to be to be safe? If I was 25 would I be safer? You taught me to shoot, so would a bullet know it was being shot by me, and not a fellow?"

Cousin Douglas came to the rescue. "Pa, I'll stay over. There's room already in our pole barn, and we expected to take turns anyway on account'a the livestock... an' poachin' thieves. It's just that I'll start my turn right now. I'll rake in some hay and it'll be just like home."

Matt Wilson took a deep breath. It was strange to see control slipping from his fingers into his niece's and his son's hands, but it was somehow reassuring. "Well, you'd be close enough to hear if she was to let off a shot. And there's the O'Day's pretty near just across the road... At least, till we think of something better..."

Josie packed her few belongings into the big trunks to be brought later, but a small feather mattress and other bedding rode on the cart behind the fourteen-year-old boy who came in two bodies. Second load would be food and this and that to get her started, as well as a loaned skillet and kettle.

Josie hugged the puppy and he strained his warm tongue to reach her cheek. As the cart pulled away for the second trip, she put Flip on the floor and watched as he snooped the corners.

Mine. My house and my dog... they're mine. Someday my life will be mine. Now, what made her say that? Hmmm, this was going to take some thought.

Bacon and hams came, and were attached to the ceiling where the Sutter's had prepared hooks for hanging meat. Small jars of this and that... green beans and peas... tomatoes and pickles. A small basket of potatoes and box of turnips. (What does one do with a turnip?) A pint jar with what looked like golden gravy. She lifted the lid and was amazed to realize the jar was filled with strained honey. She had been in the territory long enough to imagine the value of this sweet! This gift would have been from the O'Grady's, who had wild bees on their land.

A pair of embroidered pillowcases and an apron with two pockets. Chunks of... ? A snip and a sniff told her that it was lye soap! And cow pats! There had to be cow pats!

She stood in the center of the room and looked around. *Mine*, she thought, *and now I have to make it work. I CAN make it work.*

The children came. Bright, excited eyes cast about the stone floored room. "You live here, now?" "Is that puppy yours, truly?" "Can I play with him?"

She eventually had them seated on the floor, and sincerely wished for more teaching material. She passed out the books, assigning cousin Mellie to read out of the first reader to the 5 and 6 year-olds. The girl could use the practice to be ready for what had been ordered for her and the Canfield girls.

Back to the mathematical rocks again. Josh put his 11 rocks on the floor. Darrell was told to put two rocks beside them. Now, how many rocks would Darrell need to have the same number as Josh? Pairs of eyes studied the problem.

Nine-year-old Kristie McLaughlin shot out a quick fist and grabbed up two of Josh's rocks, pointed to the rest, then exclaimed, "That many!" The group turned to her with all eyes wide, demanding, "Count 'em!"

Josie stood back and watched as Raymond Canfield shouted, "One, two, three..." as he pointed to each rock, and the rest of the group shouted with him until they reached nine.

Josie nodded, "So how many would Darrell need?" The answer came back in a united shout, "NINE!"

"Let's see," continued their teacher. "Raymond, pick up nine rocks from the bowl and give them to Darrell, and Kristie will see if it works."

For the entire hour they added and subtracted small hard chunks of the Oklahoma territory. Books and slates will be nice when they come, but until then, another solution must be found. That's what her tutor would have said, showing her that there were often several solutions, though some were more efficient than others.

She had to shoo them away when the hour was over, but she wanted, with a desire that was almost a living thing, to be alone for a few minutes. Moving the box of rocks to the wall, she sat on the floor and furry, tail-wagging Flip crawled into her lap. Josie bent over him and wrapped him into her arms. *Mine...* she said as her eyes filled with moisture.

She pulled her sleeve across her eyes, sopping away the tears as Flip jumped with his paws on her chest, swabbing her face with his tongue. She was alone in her home, and it was all right to cry if she wanted to. So she did. Finishing with a few sniffles, she stepped out the door with the pup crowding between her feet.

The afternoon sun was lowering behind the hill above her rock ceiling. Far down the road, an old man rode on the back of a donkey, heading toward her. He stopped and examined something beside the road.

On a whim, now that her life was totally her own, she stepped into the house and shouldered her carpet bag. A cup of maybe coffee and a cookie, and a change of scene. Her actions were her own. *Mine*, she repeated.

Flip was excited to see his sibling, the one that was left at the Corners. Immediately a growling, rolling tussle developed. Josie sat on a stool and sipped the warm liquid, actually coffee this time, and nibbled the cookie.

People. Her neighbors. They came... then went, and everyone of them had a thing to say. In a few short words, old Mrs. Carlile brought them up to date on what had been said that day, and added their words to her accumulation of community gossip.

Rested and satisfied, Josie called to her dog and waved goodbye. The July sun was past the tops of the western cottonwood trees. They cast long shadows across the front of her home. Hers.

The man on the animal had reached the Corners, and he had dismounted. Josie looked aside and would have passed him, but he said, in a low voice, "Miss? Could I have a word?"

Josie cast a sharp, appraising glance. The whiskered man leaned on a crutch. He wore a clean, thoroughly wrinkled shirt under his almost new overalls. The warning against strangers flashed through her mind, but in the territory, everyone was a stranger to her so... what to do?

"Miss, don't be a'feared. I'm just wantin a few words with you. I wouldn't stop at the house down the road, wantin' to wait to be closer to folks so's you'd not run off."

"But, mister..." as she hesitated, her hand worked its way into her carpet bag and felt the comfort of the shiny little weapon.

The man continued, "Miss, there ain't no need to reach for that toy gun, I ain't no threat. I got no weapon, and if you was to yell, there'd be help come from all over the land in a minute. I'm just needin' to talk and maybe conduct a little business with you."

Josie relaxed, "Well, that'd be my Uncle..."

"I'm thinkin' it'd be you. I been here listenin', wantin' to see how the ownership'a that little stone house settled out. I'm thinking it's you, with your cousins helpin' out. Now, I got me a plan, and if it works out, it might be good for the both of us, but if it don't work out with you, I gotta get on outta here and make my plans for the winter somewhere else."

Josie hesitated, her hand still on the gun. "What business?"

"Well now, me, my name is Digby. If I need two names, Jones'll work out. Could be Jones as well as any other. Names don't matter just now, till we see how our mind's fit together.

"Now you got yourself a nice place there. I been watchin' and I saw poles piled like there was to be a built-on room. Them poles was the wrong thing, and I was glad to see 'em go fer a barn. They're a sight better for the barn than a room for you."

Now Josie was intrigued, and wild horses couldn't... well, maybe they could drag her away, but she clearly wanted to hear what he had in mind.

"I can say to you, I lived the most'a my life in stone walls in a mountain, so I know what you got there. I hear you like them walls. I ain't seen 'em, but I know what they'd look like inside. It's what I had up in the Colorado hills where I lived. Now, if you was to want a new room put on, I'm the one as could do it. You got the best rocks that ever was formed, right out on your land. Like as not, you ain't been to the end'a it, but that stone ledge, it runs on south and then west. It's like when the earth laid down that ledge, they grew grass in 'tween the parts, like butter in a biscuit, and them rocks come up in layers, all ready to lay. You got rocks enough to build whatever you want."

"I have rocks... ?"

"You betcha. The very best rocks, and they'd be a heap sight better'n them poles. Now if there's a thing I know, it's rocks and how to fit 'em together so's they'd keep out the wind. I can do it with clay you got right here, or with plaster that can be bought. I could do it and I could start in three weeks. That'd get me nigh up the walls afore winter. Now, I ain't able to put on the roof, but they's them as can, and they can be bought a dime a dozen.

"When I got them walls up, there'd be something you'd be proud of and it'd last longer than any grand-youngens you might have. That new room could have a flat, stone floor like the one I hear you already got. The thing is, I'm needin' a answer so's I can make my own plans 'afore cold sets in." He paused, expectantly. "Now, iffn I need to talk with your Uncle, I can do that. I was thinkin' you might be in position to decide, and I'd give you the chance. I been watchin', and I see the kind'a lady you are."

"The kind of lady I am...?"

"Yes, ma'am. I look around and see, and they's young ladies with eyes full'a pretty things, flowers and butterflies, and that ain't no bad thing. The world needs pretty things. The truth of it is, though, that ain't you. I see your eyes, and they're eyes like the prairie hawk... or maybe the eagle. Level and far-seein'. They look out straight and true, right over the tops of the trees, and even the mountains, a'lookin' for what's out there and what can be made of it. Lookin' for answers to the problems that might be comin' at you."

Silence. This strange man had pretty much looked inside her and explained what she had only begun to suspect. He was treating her as though she was a grown-up so she might as well ask a grown-up question. "Mister... er... Digby...? If I was to agree with you, how much money would you need to build those walls?"

"Law, sakes, Miss, I'd not want any money now nor later. I got what I earned in the mountain and it'll keep me all my days. What I want is somethin' my money don't buy. I want a spot'a ground, maybe 15 feet square to put up a place for me to spend my days. I'd need space to put a bed, a stove, a table and chair and a shelf. I'd be puttin' it up on the exact spot wherever you say. I could put it on the backside where it'd not be seen, or I could put it closer where I'd be there to help out if you was to need somethin'.

"I'm a good hand at animals, and I'm thinkin' them cousins'a yours gonna be busy as a pup with five youngens to follow, and they'll not have time to take you where you need to go. Now, there's a thing your uncle'll agree with, and that'd be that a young lady like you don't need to be goin' about by herself no matter how good'a shot she is. You needin' a trip to Argyle, I'd be there. You wantin' a prairie hen to roast on the coals, you'd need to let me know. Most important, if you was to be bothered by a varmint, be he two legged or four, I can shoot the eyelash off a gnat. Think on that and see what it's worth."

Yes, she had already noticed it was a sacrifice to take Jeff away from his duties. She was already trying to formulate words to explain to Uncle Matt why she should take up this man's offer.

"Miss, I see you cogitatin' on my words, and I can leave you to think on it. I wouldn't think you'd be one to say, right off, what you could do. You'd need to do the lookin' this way and that to see all sides. Now, I'm not wantin' to come to your house till we decide we can trust one another, so I'll say I leave now and be here again tomorrow at this time. You havin' good news, I'll be waitin' to hear it. You thinkin' it's not what you want, you say nothin' and I'll cart up my plunder and look for another place. I can say right now there'll not be another fellow to put up stone walls better'n I can. They's those to put on a roof a dime a dozen, like I said, but workin' with rocks, that's like a puzzle, and I'm the best."

"Mr... uh?"

"Just Digby, Miss Josie. Don't need no other name till we write up a paper. I'm think your uncle'll want to see writin' and to tell the truth, that's what I want. Then I'd be able to show it to those a'thinkin' I was bein' a bum and expectin' something for nothin' at the expense of a lady." He paused.

"Digby, I'm just thinking out loud. If you build your cabin about a hundred feet to the south, could a stone wall be put up to enclose both places?"

"Law, sakes, Miss Josie, if you ain't lookin' out over them treetops agin! That'd be no trick, a'tall! Now, when I see you tomorrow, I'll be ready to meet with your uncle and the cousins, too, if you want. I'm thinkin' they'll see the sense of a bargain." Tipping his cap in her direction, he hoisted his crippled foot over the back of Worthless, turned her around, and rode away without looking back.

Josie watched until he disappeared in the distance, then she turned back toward the Corners store. Faces were glued to the windows so word of the prolonged meeting would be spread before the sun went all the way down. No conversation could have been overheard, so who knows what the words will say?

A slight sigh escaped her lungs. More decisions. Each one seemed sure to be the last one for a while, and then another one was there, demanding her attention. Best she head out right now and talk with Uncle Matt. One thing about Digby, he was convincing, and everything he offered was something she'd like and all he asked for was something that cost her nothing to give.

The mile to the Wilson house was more than the puppy could manage, and Josie had not changed into more serviceable shoes, but the trip had to be done. Her uncle listened soberly but agreed to a meeting.So far, so good. She spent a sleepless night, however, dozing a while after the sun was already on its way up.

Breakfast. Reality set in. No steaming biscuits from the oven or breakfast table chatter. Josie nodded to herself. Just like her tutor had explained, decisions always had consequences. One just had access the value and to be ready to pay the price.

Breakfast. She remembered seeing a pint jar of peaches on her shelf. That would make a suitable breakfast, and she'd have to make better plans.

A tap at the door and a small voice shouting, "Hello?"

Students already? She'd just have to send the owner of the voice back home for a few hours. She opened the door and looked into the smiling face of Kristie McLaughlin, with her sister, Gwinnie, behind her. Kristie held a pan of biscuits, the heat of the pan absorbed in a thick towel. Gwinnie had the butter and a small bowl of fruit preserve on a platter with a slice of ham, pink, juicy and steaming hot.

"Ma says for us not to come in. We was to hand this to you and tell you goodbye. So, goodbye!" With that, the two girls dashed away giggling at their joke.

Well, that takes care of breakfast, Josie told herself. How hard is it to cook in a fireplace? I wonder if Digby knows how.... Oh, well, there was time later for that.

The mountaineer was very explicit in his conversation with Matt Wilson. Man to man, he was bargaining with an equal, and with the confidence of one knowing he had a skill of value.

"If we was to come onto an agreement, sir, I'd have my own place up inside'a three weeks, bein' ready to start in on Miss Josie's. Now what I'd need from her'd be a rod called a prybar for liftin' them rock layers, and a sledge hammer for dressin' 'em into a shape to fit together. One other little thing, I got a cart that'll pull those rocks from the ledge up to the building site, the thing is, it's slow work and it's an old cart.

"If Miss Josie was to work it out with that young cousin to load the rocks onto your sled, that'd make the work go quicker. 'Course, that's none'a my concern. It don't have no bearin' on this deal." He paused, allowing the uncle to voice a question. When none came about, he went on.

"I'm thinkin' you'll need to sleep on this, but I hopin' for the answer soon on... lettin' me get with the work, or get myself on the road."

Matt Wilson nodded. Yes, an answer was needed, and there had been no doubt on which way it would go. "Well, Mr. Jones, seems like you're bendin' over backward to be fair, and there don't seem no way my niece could be hurt. I'm thinkin' I could spare my third son one day a week to sled the stones. I'm thinkin' that'd be enough to keep up ahead'a you. Fact is, if you're plannin' to hang around and be a help to her on other things, could be you'd want to drive her on over to Argyle and pick out what you'd need in the way's tools.

"I got a buggy she can use, but I can't spare a driver. Don't hardly want to see her on the road without a bodyguard, so to speak."

Nettie Wilson knew the meeting went well, but she also knew she would not get the details of it until lights were out at the end of the day. Family discussions happened at breakfast but private ones happened in the bedroom after dark.

"Figure I'm still a fairly good judge'a character... ain't been wrong too many times. That fellow talks a good game, and we'll see how it pans out 'afore too long. Says he's a good hand at laying stone. Soon find out. That couldn't hardly be somethin' a fellow could lie about. Sutter had them poles for putting on an addition, and the boys took 'em for the barn. This'll take care of the house.

"All he's askin' is a place to spend his later years around people and a few more comforts than he's had on the road. Been campin' over there since April, waitin' to see how the ownership went. Says he'll put his cabin anywhere Josie says, and he thought she already had a place picked out.

"It's a sight how I get pulled into that girl's plans after she's already made a decision, but at least I can let that lawyer know that the most of the risk is on Mr. Jones. The paper the fellow wants is just for the neighbors, to show he ain't a tramp, squattin' where he ain't wanted. Nothin' legal about it, and if Josie changed her mind, he'd have to hit the road.

"He brought up something I'd thought of. Them boys'a ours, they're young and got plans, and they'd help Josie any way they could, but they'd likely not think of offerin' or maybe bein' there when they was needed. The old man will be. He'll be wantin' most of all to please her so he can stay, after all that work on a place for himself, and he'll know that if he let somethin' happen to her, he'd be on the road again, or dealin' with someone else and not havin' the house buildin' work to offer to 'em".

Nettie nodded to herself. It seemed to work out well... not how she expected it to go, but then her sister, Nora, did not always do what was expected, either. The full moon shone in the window, and the outside was full of chirping crickets. She was just about to doze off when her bedmate had one more thing to add.

"Still say it's a sight how the decisions crowd around that girl, but likely this'n'll hold 'er for a while."

Nettie Wilson was awake just enough to say to herself, "No, there's one more for her to make, and it'll affect her brother. Please, Lord, let it go the right way!"

NOTES FROM THE EAST

Jefferson Wilson sang and whistled as he went about his duties. The thing he dreamed of, but thought couldn't happen, just maybe could come to pass. From the time he heard about those solid gray-white Irish horses, Conamara's they were called, he wanted a start of them so badly that it had become almost a physical pain. Strong built, they were, and trimmed with charcoal around the ears, nose and hooves. He even knew where the animals could be gotten, though it would take a trip all the way to Oklahoma City.

A place over there on the far side of the Santa Fe tracks had a fellow specializing in different kinds of horses. High dollar, they were. Thing was, if he, Jeff, was to take young animals that were just weaned, he could get four fillies and one colt for about the same price as an adult breeding pair. Reason reminded him that he had more time than money, even with what Josie would trade out. It was clever of Pa to help him to swap labor to Josie for the cash money for his animals.

'Course, there was still the problem of getting them home, but he'd take one thing at a time. Reckon how many rocks could he sled out over that ridge in a day? Who would'a thought about that ridge back there? But then, no one knew the old man was back there, either, or if they did, they didn't think it strange.

Josie had biscuits with ham, topping off with jelly. A thought nagged her that she would, eventually, have to think of a way to have food around, but that was a problem for later. Too many problems jumbled up together could give a body a headache. Right now, she'd like to think up some "thought" problems in the form of puzzles. That is how her tutor taught, so it must be the right way. Actually, it was the only way she knew. She sighed with resignation as she handed Flip a jelly coated biscuit crust.

She sat on the cool floor rocks and leaned back against her bed pillow, her tablet across her knees. She thought through the times her tutor had taken her to this place or that one, to create a puzzle problem for her.

Triangles! Yes! They may have been a favorite of his, because he talked of them so many times. The world's only totally solid shape. There was the time he took her in his buggy to a tall building in the city. Very tall! It must have had at least five rows of windows. He told her that the top of the bottom row of windows was 18 feet from the ground.

The problem for her was, if each of the next rows of windows was the same distance from window top to window top, how tall could it be? That one was easy, but the next one wasn't so much.

He took a board about as tall as he was, and stood it up at the edge of the shade of the building, leaning the board toward the building until the shadow fell right down the center of the board. With her measuring instrument, she must measure the angle of the board. Then she must measure the distance from the building to the edge of the shade.

"Now, Miss Wheeler!" he has said. "You will tell me the exact amount of shade that is made by that building, not just the amount on the ground." While he watched, silently, she had tried just about every way she knew. There had to be a way... there always was. He would never trick her with a puzzle that had no answer.

Eventually, she stepped back and stared at the problem. Now if she had an invisible line from the edge of the shadow all the way straight up as high as the building, and extending horizontally to the top of the building, she would have a square... or rather a rectangle. Hmmm, well, she knew how to find the area of a rectangle and the shade of this building exactly cut it in two. The two triangles of the same shape made a rectangle.

Hey, easy! Divide the invisible shade by two and she would have the actual shade. Two minutes of scribbling and she had the answer. It was such fun to be successful and he nodded and smiled at her scribbled page. He was not big on neatness, but he insisted on accuracy.

Now, if she could only think up problems like that for beginners. It was a challenge, but she was used to challenges, wasn't she?

Another favorite time was when he took her to the play park and put her on the seesaw after explaining about the fulcrum that held up the board. He got on the other end, and she went up in the air. What was wrong, he asked? Why was the seesaw board not level?

She had shouted, "You're too heavy!" But he had countered, "Or you're too light. But I can fix it easily."

Then he had scooted closer to the fulcrum and the board became level. How did that happen, he asked. "Because you moved," she had answered, and he told her she was wrong. "I'll show you," and he scooted back to the end. "See, I moved and the board is no longer level." Then he pointed out that their weight and the weight of the board remained the same, no matter where he sat, so the answer could not be that he was too heavy.

Hmmm, that was a hard one. Think triangles because that's what he likes. Where is a triangle? The fulcrum goes up, the board goes crossways and the invisible line is from the end of the board to the ground below the fulcrum. Triangle!

The problem was, that the triangle made from the end, where she was sitting was not the same shape as the one where he was sitting. So it has to have something to do with the size or shape on the triangles... or maybe the length of the legs of the triangle. The only thing that was different was the distance from the fulcrum to where they were sitting. Answer? Sometimes length of the triangle arms created weight, and that action was called 'leverage'. A new word that explained it all.

He told her of the scientist who proclaimed that he could move the whole earth by himself, alone, if he just had a fulcrum in space and a pole long enough.

Digby had to have a prybar so he would have leverage. He could not use a bar only a foot long because it would not have enough force. It must be at least six feet long if he was to separate the layers of stone he needed to build her school room. Leg length.

Now, problems like that were what she needed, only for much younger children. Those problems had been for her when she was fifteen, but there had to be some that fitted ages 6, 7, and 8. The small rocks were fun, but the students were getting too good at adding and subtracting and needed a new challenge.

It began to appear that the challenge of creating new problems was a bit more difficult than working out the sizes of triangles! But it didn't really matter. A challenge was a challenge, just another thing to overcome!

* * *

The Wilson mail hook in Carlile's Corner contained a note and a letter to Miss Josephine Wheeler. The note told her that she had boxes at Argyle that could not be delivered by the mail buggy, and would she please see to picking them up. Marvelous! The books! But were they that big? Oh, it must be the blackboards.

The letter might explain. It was written in Sharon Blaine's precise copperplate script. "... such fun we had shopping for you. The wholesaler at the book factory was very interested in your project... as we are. He pointed out that if you needed two of the blackboard panels, you likely needed six and if you bought a package of six, you got a better single price. So you'll get six. When I read of your lovely bed, I just couldn't resist selecting a canopy and curtain. It was hard to choose, but I really like the one I finally picked, and I hope you do too. We thought you might like being able to close the bed off with the side curtains if the weather gets really cold in the territory. We were glad you got a puppy, they are good for hearing noises in the night.

"We also had fun choosing the 25 story books you asked for, trying to pick the most interesting ones by different companies. That's when the owner told us he had several books whose titles were not selling well, and would you like them? We said, let's send them on and ask her... so there will be more than 25 books in the crate, but the extras will not cost you anything. Two of the crates contain something you did not order. They are our gift to you because we are so proud of you, just as we knew we would be. Thinking of you, Elias and Sharon Blaine."

Oh, the books and the slates! There had to be a quick way to get to Argyle. Jefferson was busy with the sled freighting out the heap of rocks Digby had shaped. Douglas was plowing on the forty acres that must be put under cultivation to qualify for the homestead. Also to provide rich hay for the animals. Junior was swinging the sharpened scythe in the tall native prairie grass to store the hay in the barn for their animals. Cutting it in August often encouraged the land to produce the second crop that they so greatly needed. That was what she was told. Only Digby was available to make the trip.

Josie climbed aboard the Wilson's double buggy, and the whiskered man clicked the team onto the road toward Argyle. He had delivered a lengthy speech and she ran his words through her mind.

"...now we got us a business deal. Like I said to your uncle, I go as your bodyguard. You must sit back in the seat and rest because this is my job and I do it good. You got things to think on, and I got a buggy to drive."

The girl took him at his word and settled back on the supporting pillow. She had time, now, to think on her problems.

She had learned, from the puzzle of the building and the shadow, that there were times that it was best to move backward to get a different view of the puzzle. This was a good chance to step backward and think of the ten, eleven, and twelve year-old girls who had refused to miss a day of "school" even if attention was centered on Joshua and Darrell.

Only five and six years ago, she had been their ages. She had nothing to do but attend her class of one, learning things she would not have thought of alone. These girls had spent the last few years caring for siblings, eating what was handy, sleeping where it was possible, moving across the miles and unsure of what would happen to them. Most of them had learned to count, and could determine the shape of the numbers. They knew the names of the alphabet letters, and some words they had just learned the shape of. They had no idea of the different sounds the letters represented, sounds that were called phonics. How could they learn to read, if they had to memorize the shape of every word? Likely it was possible, but it would be so much quicker if they knew the sounds. Even just a few would help.

They could not, of course, work out shadows and triangles. Not yet. But there were surely interesting puzzles that they could work out... that would be interesting to them. It was Josie's job to think them up.

Extending her feet out before her, she studied the shiny toes of her traveling shoes. Her mother had been firm about shoes. Never go out without solid, comfortable shoes because you might have to walk a long way. Things happened to carriages, horses, wheels, rough roads and temperamental drivers. One must be prepared to take care of oneself, if there was no one there to help. Shiny toes on the shoes. Stout ties held the shoes in place.

Shoestrings... what could be done with them? All the girls had shoestrings. There was a row of "Xs" where the strings crossed. If the leg of every "X" was an inch and the crossover at the bottom was an inch... and if it took 7 inches for a tie, how long would the shoestring have to be? Smiling to herself, she pictured the girls working on the problem, and guessing what they would say when they realized they had to know how many "Xs" were involved, because some shoes had higher sides than others. Good, that would be problem number one.

What if candy was five pieces for one cent, and she had seven pennies? How many pieces of candy in all? If there were six children to get the same number of pieces, how many pieces would each get... and what would the girls say about the remainder? Problem number two.

If a carrot was 12 inches long, how many ½ inch pieces would it make to add to the soup? If there were 6 carrots, how many pieces? Problem number three.

Oops! For that one she needed rulers. She would also need protractors to figure angles. A string and a pencil made a good compass. Problem number four. Buy rulers.

What good would these puzzle problems be to girls on the prairie? Well, it would let them know there were many things to learn. And something to think on... also, it would make them feel special, instead of just looking over someone else's lessons. There was another thing, too. It was a family sacrifice to allow a girl of that age to be away from home on a regular basis... there was just too much to do. Would their parents be pleased with their accomplishments? She wondered, for a fact, how they would feel? Maybe a girl didn't need to learn those things?

Josie sighed deeply and leaned back on the back of the buggy seat as it bounced and swayed along the road. So much she didn't know, but one thing was sure, and it would not change. She was not hired to accomplish even one thing. Anything she could offer these children was only a gift... no strings attached. Not even shoe strings!

She had made that clear when the parents began to offer gifts and services. I appreciate everything, she had told them, but I want you to know. I am not a teacher. I have not taken the test to be a teacher, and I am not being hired by anyone. I can accept what you want to give, but I have not asked for anything. I love your children and I will do what pleases me, and what I think will be useful to them. I don't want any student who doesn't want to come, and if any child does not obey me, he will not be permitted to come. She was sure there had been a lot of conversation about that, but be it as it may be. This was going to be her home, and these were her neighbors, so they might as well understand each other.

Since that time, no one had taken back gift offers, and the gift of the small buggy with a pony was still available. As soon as a shed and paddock was built, she would take the pony, but the small conveyance would not have held the cargo she expected today. Digby was just one person, and the rockwork came first. Not animal care. The pony and buggy were well taken care of during that time.

Aunt Nettie had been surprisingly pleased with the offer of the buggy, also with Digby as a "bodyguard". Digby had insisted that caring for a pony was only a pleasure, and he'd have the "little fellow" in the dry by cold weather. We'd see.

Puzzles. Challenges. This was a good time to think up a few more. There would be slates for the girls to work individually. Paper to take a puzzle home... and here was another one just entering in her head!

Biscuits. Breakfast biscuits. All the girls were well acquainted with the necessity of daily biscuits. Scribbling rapidly, she wrote:

"For breakfast at the Wilsons there would be a pan of biscuits. Mr. Wilson would eat 4 biscuits, Junior and Douglas would eat five each. Jefferson would eat 2 for breakfast, and take 2 with him for later. Mellie (and her cousin would grin happily at being part of the puzzle) would take 3 biscuits, but she would give one to Esther after it was buttered and jellied. Darrell and Josh would take 3 each, eating 2 at the table, and putting the other one in their pockets. They would forget the biscuits were in their pockets, and would sit down and squash them so flat that they had to give them to the dogs. Josie didn't get any!

"How many biscuits would Mrs. Wilson have to put in the pan?"

She would copy four sheets and let the four oldest girls work on it. It would be such fun to see what they did, and which of them thought to ask whether Mrs. Wilson got any or not? The thought of it made her smile... puzzles were such fun!

Argyle was just ahead. She set aside her tablet in anticipation of the awaited packages. The usual crowd of wagons and buggies surrounded the station. Other buggies and strolling people were here and there, going in and out the other buildings. Signs hung on the fronts of buildings... HATS, SHOES, HARNESS & TACK, HARDWEAR...

Oops! She was planning to figure what she needed at the hardware store. Instead, she had thought up puzzles. A skillet and a pan, for certain, so she could give Aunt Nettie's back to her. A few plates and cups. Knife, forks and spoons... a long handled spoon and an egg turner. She'd just step down there and pick out a few things while Digby saw to the loading... he had insisted that that was part of the duty of a bodyguard.

A wagon with a covered canopy and pulling a small trailer behind, had just stopped by the station. Following it was a double buggy, much like the Wilson's, and Josie paused to let it get settled. Horses did not need people walking out in front of them.

The buggy settled, and an older man twisted the reins onto the hook and prepared to step down, but right in front of Josie a small body came sailing out of the front seat, landing solidly on the packed dirt. Like a dart of an arrow, he shot past her, bumping against her carpet bag, and swishing against her skirt.

Josie turned quickly and saw the girl in the rear seat, a girl maybe a bit younger than she was. Tired. Very weary. The set of her shoulders indicated she had been riding a lot longer than she had wished, and now sincerely wished for the end of it. As the small boy had sailed out of the buggy seat, she had raised her arm against her eyes as though shutting out the sight. As Josie paused, the arm came down, and the girl's eyes caught Josie's.

"Little brother...?" Josie offered.

The girl nodded wearily. "Don't know where he gets that energy. Seems like we've been ridin' all my life."

She did not seem to mind talking, so Josie asked, "Do you live around here?"

"Not yet, but we're going to. We came from Tennessee and it's a long way. I've sat so long I got a cramp in by backside. I'm going to lay down while we're stopped and I got the chance. It was nice to speak with you."

"Yes, it was. Have a good nap." Poor girl. It had been hard enough to ride on the train, but if she had been in that buggy since Tennessee... no wonder she wanted to get a little rest while it was stopped.

Jugs. She needed jugs to bring water from the spring back up over the hill behind her home. Extra jugs, because the children got thirsty and drank it up. That would be a good boy's job, bringing in extra water. Also, little tin cups with curled handles. She bought 25 of them. She gathered her purchases and put them by the door. Digby would have to bring the buggy down to the hardware store to get them.

Walking back, she saw a large box being stuffed into the front seat beside the driver, and another on the back bench where she had sat. Hmmm, what was wrong with the back of the buggy where Jeff had put her trunks? Coming closer, she saw the answer. The luggage rack was packed full. Two massive, crated boxes and a great number of smaller ones. What was going on? Were books that bulky?

Digby had a grin behind his whiskers. "Got 'em on! Thought for a while there, we'd have to make two trips! No tellin' what all you got in there!"

But Josie, puzzled as she was about the contents, noticed first the boards making up the crate. About four feet long and as wide as a book! BOOK! When those boxes were empty, she was certain Digby could put the boards together to make a bookcase! She had thought the books would have to be stacked on the floor until she had more time.

Books! Lovely, lovely books! Colorful covers! Pages of words! Such magic on the pages! Such trips of fantasy the readers would have! Or was she just dreaming about how she would feel?

It would be a long trip home before she could see the books... to see what titles Sharon had picked out and what the book manager had given her. Oh, what a wealth! Her big girls would get to read and see how different writers put their words together! Would they enjoy it as much as she had? Somehow, they must! She'd have to see to it!

The sun was passing through the western treetops as Digby crammed the last of her purchases into nooks and crannies of the buggy and headed the horses toward Carlile Corners. As the vehicle turned, she saw the girl from Tennessee walking toward the station, holding firmly to the shirt collar of the small boy. Maybe they would be staying the night, and she would get to sleep on the canvas folding bed. It really was quite comfortable, especially if one was very, very tired.

Either way, she wouldn't have to be concerned with the brother... boys were not allowed in the woman's room!

Retrieving her tablet from beneath the back cushion, she set herself to inventing more math puzzles. While she had them going through her mind, she'd better write down what she could. There would be plenty of other things to do when she got home with this buggy full of boxes!

When the boxes were finally spread over the stones of her house, Josie surveyed her floor virtually covered with boxes and crates.

Decisions! Boxes of square cardboard enclosed in layers of tape! Secrets contained within! Surprises! She could tear into them now, or savor them later. Decisions! Decision!

Turning her back on the lovely boxes, she watched as Digby used the new tools to pry apart the crates, the contents of which she had not requested.

First to appear was created from beautifully finished wood wrapped protectively in a colorful... ? Bedspread? Yes, a lovely cream color with tan and brown designs. Lifted away from the wooden object, she saw the desk. Not just a desk... this was clearly a teacher's desk. Drawers down each side and a kneehole in the center. Top... smooth and shiny, glistening with newness.

Digby set the desk upright, and Josie stood back to more clearly admire it, savoring the moment. Of course, she was not a teacher, but there stood the desk in all its shining glory. She MUST be a teacher to deserve all of this. Oh... that would be so handy. No more working with her tablet on her knees.

But there was more. The squeak of nails being pulled apart from the crating boards. More surprises. A lift of the final board that captured the surprise, revealed the chair to match the beautiful desk. A chair! One that could be raised and lowered to fit the sitter! And there, poked between the chair legs, was the folded canopy for the bed the Sutter girls were reluctant to leave behind. Thickly woven tapestry with a pattern of baskets woven in browns and tans, with colorful vines and flowers in clumps and sprays. The draw curtains matched the ruffled canopy.

Josie smiled as she imagined the picky Sharon Blaine trying to choose what would look best when she had no idea of the stone walls, floor and ceiling. Admittedly, she had done a good job!

Back to the lovely desk. Drawers moved smoothly in their metal guides. Something was packed inside the drawers. Hmmmm. Loose fitting leather boots with thick fur lining. Note attached. Sharon's script advised that she thought stone floors might be cold and winter was coming. Her feet might appreciate cozy fur. Another smile, as Josie wondered if her stone floor would be any colder than Sharon's expensive tile, and had she failed to mention that the Sutter girls had made a point of the thick braided rugs that had been made by their mother? Nevertheless, the boots would be well used as winter house slippers.

Folded tightly and stuffed into the next drawer was the fleecy robe. Pale blue as the territory sky. Fluffy as the afternoon clouds drifting over the midday horizon.

The bottom drawer contained a bag... satchel...? Bulky handbag? Was this what was popular in New York? Made of leather, tooled in patterns of checks and swirls. Wide shoulder strap with adjustable buckles. A very serious looking satchel. Lifting it from the drawer, she puzzled over the weight. Very heavy.

Opening the safety catch, she noted the interior pocket with a protective flap. Inside was shiny metal... very purposeful metal. Gripping tightly, she withdrew the gun, as long as her arm from her elbow to the end of her thumb. Note attached:

> *We thought that if you needed a small gun for legless varmints, you might also need a bigger weapon for the bigger varmints that have legs. Two, four, or however many.*

She hefted the weapon. The weight of it was a definite pull against her wrist. Cousin Mellie with her delicate bones and tiny wrist could never use this gun... but then, Mellie would never have to. On the other hand, she, Josie, was very likely to see the time... well, anyway, it wouldn't hurt to learn how it worked.

The squeaking and tearing of nails from boards had stopped. A pile of separated crating boards lay against the wall, and Digby stood staring at Josie as she examined the gun. Approval. Pleased nods. She handed the weapon to him, and he raised it to his eyes, sighting down the barrel. Aiming it toward the floor, he squeezed the trigger. Click!

With a deeper nod he handed it back and watched as she returned to the bag and placed it in the drawer. Wordlessly, the bodyguard/handyman/driver set about freeing the square boxes from their layers of tape.

The top drawer on the other side of the desk revealed a box with inlaid wood of different colored patterns. Lifting the lid, she found handkerchiefs... several trimmed in lace, but many more in a larger, more substantial size. Each of the snowy squares was marked with a "J" in blue thread. How many? At least a dozen... maybe two dozen.

Note attached:

Josie, darling, the contents in the drawer of this box are at the suggestion of your Aunt Nettie. She thought the marking would make sure the handkerchiefs get back to you after being washed, and she felt you would have uses for the larger ones.

Also, the contents of the next drawer are for her. She indicated that Joshua would likely spend the winter with her, and would prefer to be dressed like his cousin. She thought she should order his clothes from the catalog, as she did Darrell's. It would only be right that you pay for them. Now, honey, I hope we were not taking on decisions that should have been yours. We are both so proud of you, but we see that you have your hands full... at least right now. Forgive us if we guessed wrong.

There was another thing she said. She was not sure you would think to ask, but you could likely use what she called a "clothes press". We decided it must be what is called a wardrobe, and you remember how important they are. She also said that the family doing your laundry could deliver only once a week, so you might need more dresses and underclothes. If that is true, you might need two wardrobes, and two would ship as easily as one. As for the dresses, I still have your size measurements, and if what we picked out for you is still suitable, I would be delighted to shop for additional items.

Another smile! Shopping was what Sharon did best.

I'll wait to hear from you, about that. I'm sure you know what you like best.

Be careful, Josie, darling, and do your best as you always do.

Thinking of you,

Elias and Sharon Blaine.

Clasping the tiny handle of the drawer, she pulled carefully. There, packed in layers, were shining coins. Nodding in approval, Josie remembered that she had forgotten how fast little boys grow. Josh had to be outgrowing and wearing out his clothes. She had never had to think about his clothes, but she'd need to start. With the new addition to the house, she'd have room to bring him home.

The next drawer contained fluffy bath towels. Did she ever need those! The bottom drawer was packed full of wash clothes wrapped around perfumed face soap. Another smile as she pictured Sharon's expression if she knew that Josie was washing her face with homemade lye soap, and thinking how lucky she was that it was given to her. It was especially good for washing hair... making it smooth and shiny, and aiding the soft wave and curl at the end.

Last drawer of the desk. At first sight, it seemed to be packed with washcloths, but she soon learned they were packed carefully around a cut glass lamp made for burning kerosene. Good light! So much better than a candle, and likely safer, too. Also packed in the drawer were the shiny glass globes... two of them. How thoughtful, because the thin glass of the globes was so easy to break. The lamp would be in a special place on the wall, just as soon as she figured out where. But that was tomorrow's problem.

Sweet thoughtful Sharon, and sure enough, she had begun to realize she would need a few more items of clothing. It just hadn't seemed as important and pressing a need as devising puzzle-problems that would intrigue her students the way her own tutor's had intrigued her. She needed some "boy" problems now. Ages seven and eight.

Tennessee Travelers Arrive

The weary girl at the station in Argyle moved tiredly into the women's room and sank into a bed. One that was long enough for her to stretch out her feet. Pure heaven! One that was solid and did not jiggle on its springs when she turned over. One that did not let the nighttime dewy mist settle stickily in her hair. It was not, however, one that she did not dream on.

Her eyes had no more closed than she crossed the Mississippi, and no more had she reached the bank when she was again chugging over the water. She crossed and re-crossed the muddy Arkansas river. On the first part of the trip across Arkansas to the Oklahoma Territory, she had looked forward to the end, and later she knew, for an absolute fact that she would NEVER reach the end of her life's journey. She would be jiggling along for the next century or so.

Janine Cullen had just decided that this journey was only an extension of the series of duties that had become hers. No choice. They had just descended onto her like a sudden spring shower.

She was now, however juggled awake to get up and help start the day... to pull up another tomorrow... to face another sunrise and sunset. She finally opened her eyes to a strange room with empty beds. What was going on? Had she really slept all night?

But beside her was a girl of about her age with a tray containing hot tea and a bowl of steaming cereal, liberally swimming in golden streams of butter. A fragrant biscuit and a small pot of red jelly. And a smile.

"Miss Janine? Your fellows said to wake you up to eat so you wouldn't starve to death in bed. Then when you ate, you were to lay back down and rest as long as you wanted to. Maybe all day." Then she grinned with mischief, "Don't worry about the little fellow. He's found him some friends to play with."

Janine smiled, and looked about with unbelief. Had she died? This couldn't be heaven, but somehow it felt like it.

She ate and slept again. It was mid afternoon when she became restless and dressed in her least wrinkled clean clothes and went for a walk.

Argyle. Interesting name for a town. Nice little town, too. Most necessary goods and services were available. Hardwear, blacksmith, hat shop... a feed store proclaiming that they also carried white flour. And was that a café...? It surely looked like it!

Hmmm, a catalog store. She stepped inside and saw a counter with stools and a couple of ladies turning the pages and chatting. This was a really good thing to know. If she found herself without something that she totally had to have, it would for certain be available in the Montgomery Ward Catalog.

The evening meal was served in the house of Pa's friend, the one whose granddad fought with the Campbells in the old country, the way her own relative had. Well, she knew what that was like. She had her own battle to fight. No Campbells there to help, either.

When they drove on to their own place in the morning, she would pick up her duties as she had in Memphis, only there would likely be fewer comforts. Pa made the best decisions he could and he never complained or found fault with what she did. She was lucky about that, and the little fellow was a lot less trouble now... just harder to keep up with. She'd manage, she always had.

* * *

Jefferson Wilson doffed his hat and mopped the perspiration from his head. The dampness had plastered his red curls against his ears and forehead. At least he knew what he was doing when he loaded the flat stones on the sled. Smaller ones he lifted, but the larger ones required the pry bar. The old man had said he needed mostly bigger ones at first... and he was the boss.

What Jeff didn't know was how he was going to get the five young animals from the other side of Oklahoma City out here to the Corner. Tying them together seemed the only way, and maybe bringing a couple of grown horses on a tether would be possible, how else could five of them be managed?

He really needed a wagon to hitch them behind. That was one way to keep them together, and the pace of the team pulling the wagon was about what would be needed for them. He couldn't ask his brothers for help as they already had more than they could do before cold weather set in. And he certainly had no money to spare to hire help.

Hat back on, and return for another load. After this one, he'd need to change mules. A loaded sled was a hard pull and it was a handy thing to have the two Sutter mules. Mules just naturally pulled stronger than horses, even if they were thicker in the skull. But even a mule could pull only so long, and then he stopped. Wherever he happened to be standing, he would stop and go no farther.

Next load. The exhausted mule lowered his head, and let his ears sag. Jeff snapped him from the harness and led him to the paddock. Returning with the fresher one, he saw he was being watched by the old man.

"Young fella, how you think you a'gonna get them fancy horses home?"

"Still thinkin' on it. Ain't got too much luck yet. The thing is, the older they get, the more they cost, and they cost enough already."

Digby nodded his understanding. Then continued to stretch the string that would insure the walls of the 15-foot square building would be straight. Corner stones were first, set carefully 6 inches below the soil, squared at the corners and chipped smooth on the inside.

By dark, three courses had been laid, bringing the walls halfway to his knees. The first two had been the hardest. Though the cabin would have a stone floor, still the outside wall had to be set just right to keep out moisture. The building would face the stone ledge, insuring that its single door would be protected from the wind. The back of the building would face the road.

That night he stretched his bedroll within the enclosure. It was a symbol. His first night within the walls of his new home. Among his few possessions was the document received back from the New York lawyers. Wheeler and Blaine, it said, and in clear printing were the items of the agreement. What he would do for Josie and what he expected in return. It was clearly signed by her uncle and her older cousin, giving their consent to the agreement.

There had been more.

He had wanted to say more and hoped for a chance. It came earlier in the day. "Now, Miss Josie, so there don't be no misunderstanding, I got a few words to say, and you tell me how you feel.

"Me, I got no wife nor child, but that was never a problem in my mind. There was a time, though, that I thought a daughter would be a good thing in a man's later years. Never had one. If I had one, I'd be pleased in every way if she was like you. Now, I know it can't be, but there's a thing I want to do and that'd be to have the privilege of doin' for you like I would have liked to do for a daughter, and take care of her and not let anything hurt her. Never thought I'd have the chance.

"I'm sorry you ain't got no pa, and that ain't your fault but it leaves open the things a pa could do for you. That good uncle of yours... he ain't got time for nothin'. I'm hopin' for a chance to do some'a them things. Makin' you happy, that'd go a long way toward makin' me happy. So, right now at the start, you tell me if I do somethin' that makes you unhappy or makes a trial'a myself. You can do that, can't you? They's things I'd like to do to make things easier around your property. I'll be askin' and you'll be tellin' what you want, and whether I do what I got no business doin'?"

The question hung in the air while Josie thought, then nodded. "Right now I'm thinking there isn't anything you could do that wouldn't improve things, but I'll do what you say. If I don't say not to, you just go on ahead and do what you see to do. Is that a good answer?"

As he settled into his bedroll with old Tangle pushed up against him, like a dog should be, he looked up at the expanse of starry August sky and thought the answer couldn't have been worded in a better way.

Tomorrow would see his walls up to window level and he must decide if he wanted a window in every direction. Likely he would. There was a good chance Argyle had window glass and framing boards. He'd make the roof sloping so he could use cottonwood poles for roof beams. That would be quicker, and he was purely eager to get at Josie's addition. He could picture her walking around with her smile of contentment. Seemed like where she stayed didn't ever to get to her and fret her mind anywhere near like the schooling she gave those youngens.

* * *

Janine Cullen had spent weeks jogging along on rough and rutty roads, heading to a place she could only imagine. She had absolutely no eagerness to see what she was going toward. Now, though, she was a bit rested, and there would be no more camping along the road. One good thing!

Farms. Horses. Workmen in the field. Fences being repaired. A wagon in the distance. A small store... ? A STORE! She sat up straight and stared. Carlile Corners. It had a name, so it must be a store. Hmmmm, well...

It had been Brad's turn to drive the buggy and the youngen was with Papa. "Sis, I know you're just about all in, and you ain't had too much to be happy about, but I picked up a little good news back there in Argyle."

"I could use a little good news."

"Well, what they tell me for the truth is that there'll be a school out our way."

"School? When?"

"I hear it'll start this year."

"They got a real teacher... and not just a neighbor that can read?"

"Real teacher. Trained in New York."

"I don't believe it. Ain't no way the territory'd have the money to get a teacher outta New York, and if they did, she'd be in a town."

"I don't know, Sis. This one seems different. She's not bein' paid, except what the parents want to give her. Someone gave her the use of a pony and trap, and someone else is doin' up her clothes."

A few yards of bumpy ground crawled under the dusty wagon wheels. She spoke the first thought in her mind. "What you think you got that'll be worth her teachin' our little brother?"

A few more yards, and a lot of fence posts went by. He responded, "Well, that's what I ain't really thought out... yet... Got it in my mind to be workin' on it, though. There's bound to be somethin'."

Janine tried to take comfort from his words. It was certainly a concern and had been one for a couple of years. She could feed him, but how could she teach him when she, herself, had hardly been taught?

She knew numbers and letters, and a few words. Her period of education had been three sketchy years taught by a neighbor, and then they had moved across Tennessee. From then on, she had taken care of her mother and the baby, and then just the baby. When had there been time? And now it had seemed that the little fellow was going to get the same raw deal.

But... miracles could happen... couldn't they?

She knew that her new home had been acquired "lock, stock and barrel" the name used for taking over everything, and the former owner just practically walking out. That meant a house, at least some furniture, a decent place to cook, windows to keep out the biting insects and the promise of shelter when winter came. At this point, she took relief in the sound of it.

The wagon ahead of the buggy stopped, and her brother walked ahead. Together the fellows consulted the hand-drawn map. Janine leaned back and waited. The fellows had started this, and they could just figure out together whatever problem they had. The news about the school, however puzzling, was the one bright spot on the horizon of her mind. If it could only be true...

Brad was back. "We're there, Sis. That drive up ahead is it!"

Janine Cullen spent that night in a regular bed, and the fellows bunked out on the parlor floor. She had a PARLOR! At daybreak, the very pregnant wife showed Janine the oddities of the cook stove, and Janine could have shown her the oddities of the metal box she had used for cooking during the past weeks... but she didn't.

By mid morning the papers were signed and the former owners were on their way, waving joyfully at leaving, and Janine was waving just as joyfully for getting to stay. Four big rooms, and there was a lean-to 'mud room' off the kitchen. A place for the fellows to wash up. And (joy of joys!) a small summer kitchen was right there in the back yard!

Now she could cook a meal during the summer and bring the food back to a cooler kitchen to eat. She could can tomatoes all day, and leave the stove heat out there. She could...! Oh, it would be wonderful! She had heard of summer kitchens, but never expected to actually have one! That news ranked right up there with the school... almost!

* * *

Josie sat on her cool stone floor with the tablet on her knee. There had to be some organization... a planned direction, actually... or she might loose track of her goal. Her tutor had been firm on that. Before an important project was begun, a goal must be set. It must not be absolute, as there were always circumstances that affected an outcome, but there had to be a baseline... a starting post...and a direction. It must be set with the hope and intention of moving it farther as time went on. So. . .

GOAL FOR THE MONTH OF SEPTEMBER

Level one:	Level two:
Esther.........5	Josh........7
David.........5	Darrell.....7
Isaac...........6	Luke.......7
Bettina.........6	Bridgit....7

Level three:	Level four:
Raymond.......8	Carmelita ...12
Henry...........8	Rosalie...... 11
Gwinnie.........8	Francine.... 10
Kristie...........9	Carlotta......10
Patricia..........9	

She nodded with satisfaction at her divisions. Part of setting a goal was to create measurable and attainable parts within the goal. She was sure she would get a complaint from Kristie and Patricia who would want to be in the higher level, but Kristie was barely 9, and Josie had set very high achievement requirements for the four older girls. Girls so often got the short end of education, and that had been true for all four of these.

ACHIEVEMENT GOALS

Level Four will: Create their own puzzle problems, five puzzles each for each day. This will provide the opportunity to add, subtract, multiply and divide. (Later lessons will cover efficiency in multiplication and division.) To enforce reading ability, they will create lists of words with long and short vowel sounds. (These can be used later in other classes) They will assist Level One with slate and chalk drawings, and will help them to recite numbers 1-25 and all 26 letters of the alphabet from flash cards. For reading practice they will read stories from the Third Level McGuffey Reader to Level One group.

Level Three will: Create add and subtract examples, ten of each for each day. Will practice reading from Level Two McGuffey and will study word lists from Level One and Primer McGuffey. Will make lists of words with long and short vowel sounds.

Level Two will: Work with chalk and slate, writing numbers 1-35 and alphabet in perfect order and letter shape. Will practice reading from Primer McGuffey, will receive help as needed working with phonic sounds. Will practice adding and subtracting single digits from practice cards, orally.

Level One will: Will practice sight recognition of numbers 1-25 and all alphabet letters, from practice cards held by Level Four students. Will practice free hand drawing to familiarize with slate and chalk. Will listen to stories from Level Three McGuffey, as read by Level Four students. Hearing these stories will help familiarize them with correct sentence structure.

* * *

A spell of weather had come through last week, resulting in a day of downpour and two days of mud. There were certainly plenty of things a homesteader can do in a day of rain, but the eight fathers had scrounged scarce scraps of lumber and constructed small tables with a bench attached on either side. Paint had not been available, but could be applied later. These tables were obviously needed now, though the teacher (who was not a teacher) had not requested them.

It was the students who had commented on their stone-floor seats. Measuring the dimensions of Kristie, they determined the size for the tables. Changes could be made later, if necessary.

It was as Josie sat on the cool floor (the better to stare at the shiny new desk and chair and the better to admire their beauty) that the first table arrived carried by fathers McLaughlin and O'Day. The other two tables proceeded closely behind.

"Figured not to bother you about these till we got 'em done. Likely this'll save you bendin' over to check what the youngens are up to." A hearty, depreciating laugh followed, as the six men stood back to see how their efforts affected her.

Speechless. Awestruck. Staring from one to the other and nodding. Tables! Real tables, and so cleverly made that they required no chairs.

"We wisht these didn't take up all the space in your house. Couldn't hardly make 'em no littler."

Josie waved aside their apologies. "Perfect! Just perfect. Would you line them up with one end toward my desk, here, and the other end toward the door. Perfect! That way no one has their back toward me." She paused, staring soberly at the men. "I'd thank you better if I knew how. Who shall I pay, and what did they cost?"

The surprised men stared at her and at each other. "Law, sakes! There ain't no money due. These was scrap boards and we was rained outta the fields, anyway." Josie knew better than that. There was no such thing as scrap lumber in this treeless land, and a rainy day was never a waste.

* * *

Digby had put his makeshift roof on his stone house just the day before the rain came in. Nodding to himself, he proclaimed it a success, and when he was able to get a real door in the door frame, it would work even better.

The stakes and string that would outline the foundation of Josie's addition had been in place, and examined at length by every passerby. The students stepped carefully over the stretched string, all except for 6 and 7 year old boys, who gleefully leaped from one side to the other.

* * *

The Wilson mail hook held a pair of notations for Josie. One said that she now had her own mail hook. A Wheeler hook was attached and marked beside Wilson. The other notation said there were two large freight shipments in the Santa Fe depot in Oklahoma City, and they would hold them without charge for 30 days, but request they be picked up as soon as possible.

Two freight shipments? What...? Oh, they must be the wardrobe closets sent on by Sharon Blaine. Wasn't she going to wait until they were requested before they were purchased? Apparently not.

What now? No one had time to go all the way to Oklahoma City on her errand. Staring toward her house, she saw the busy figure of Digby, stroking his chin and planning his next move.

Digby! Could she ask him? Well, if she had a pa close by, that's where she'd go first, and... well, she'd see.

He listened and the chin stroking continued. "Well, Miss Josie. Could be that two problems done collided themselves, smashin' each other down to size. That red haired cousin'a yours, he's been stewin' over them animals getting' brought out here 'afore they got grown. Same direction.

"Talk to your uncle for the loan'a his heavy wagon and a couple'a horses. That cousin and me, we'll take off over to the city, load on your packages, tie them prize pieces'a horse flesh onto the wagon and head back. Three days, tops."

Hmmmm, well..? Seems like two problems really did collide, and practically erased themselves.

Jeff hurried off a message to the horse farm. Could they get his five animals over to the Oklahoma City Santa Fe depot five days from now? If they could, he'd pay what the transport for the 22 miles would be. Surely it couldn't be much and the day of time saved would be worth it.

So the stonework stopped. Little boys continued to jump over Digby's stretched string.

Daylight was hours away when Jeff and Digby set out, armed with money for the animals and a letter from Josie permitting her "handyman" to sign for the two freight shipments.

Ohs and Ahs greeted the newly installed work tables. Level Two students were enthroned on one of the tables, and Level Three class on another. Level Four girls would share their table with Level One class, as they would be working together a lot of the time, anyway, and this would enable almost one–on-one help if difficulties arose.

* * *

Gaither Cullen had wandered up the road to the Corner, and Brad had taken the boy and headed out... somewhere. Janine slipped out the back door and walked toward the remains of a summer kitchen garden.

Fenced. Large, actually, for a kitchen garden. Dried husk-wrapped cornstalks still standing. Need to be pulled out. A few late tomatoes on the ragged plants. She'd slice some for dinner.

Turnips! Lots of them still in the ground. Leave them there, always fresh for variety during winter. Onions. Tops bent over to let them make big bulbs. A lot of blank rows where the remains of summer had been cleared away.

A sigh of satisfaction escaped her lips. Maybe not excitement... but the garden promised a bit of freedom from frustration. New raw land. She was tired of starting from scratch, and this one had been well tended. Maybe even fertilized.

With arms folded across the top panel of the garden gate, she allowed her mind to rest. Well, anyway, the fellows were finally where they were going, and there would be no more moving on. What she saw before her now, she could reasonably well count on continuing. All in all, it seemed good. The September air with a hint of crispness held her spellbound... fascinated... an unexplainable sense of newness and expectation.

Expectation of what...? With a shrug of the shoulders, she dismissed the feeling, but still she stood... enjoying a sense of newness she had never felt before.

Brad Cullen strolled with long steps down the dry, rutted road. The lively child ran ahead, dropped behind and circled him, chattering like a magpie. Brad tolerated the activity as he would a slightly bothersome horsefly. He had some talking to do, and a lot depended on his success today.

Several times before, he had stopped and chatted with the whiskered man with the lame leg. Right clever with those stones, he was, and he said he found them out on the back of the quarter section. He had just finished a free-standing stone cabin that still needed windows and a door, but he now measured and dug a footing in front of what seemed to be a cave under a massive stone ledge.

Little cabin had a shed roof. The fellow said that was all he could make without help, but allowed it'd serve till he could do better. Allowed he'd have to put the same kind on Miss Josie's new addition. Not too strong on looks, a shed roof was, but it turned the rain. Yes, he'd agreed, the 20 foot span across the narrow side of the new addition would stretch the ability of the available cottonwood logs, and, yes, it was going to be a tussle to get them felled and prepared, his lame foot being what it was. And too, there'd likely have to be a pillar or two on the inside of the rooms. Takin' up space.

"The thing of it was," the man confided sadly, "the teacher in there is a'bustin' at the seams, needin' more space. Time is the master right now, ya' see?"

Brad had asked, "How many students does she have?"

The man mopped his sweat-soaked brow and readjusted his hat. "Don't rightly know, bein' I never stopped to count 'em. Could be a hunnerd for all the racket they make." With that he returned to his work, essentially dismissing the young man with the questions.

So, today was the day. He had thought and thought, throughout all the morning and till now, in mid-afternoon, and the best words had still not come, so he'd just plunge on ahead. The troupe of children had just flowed out and spread in various directions, so the teacher was likely as free and alone as she would ever be.

Clutching the circling child by the collar, he tapped at the door, then called, "Hello?"

The door opened. The woman... girl?... stood before him. She was taller than she had seemed at a distance. Her head was clearly even with his chin, and he, himself, extended somewhat above most men. His pa had said that it was necessary to 'grow 'em tall' in the old country so they could see the enemy coming from over the Scottish hills. Here on the plains, that wouldn't be necessary, Brad thought with a wry smile. One could actually see forever, seemed like.

Josie stood, unsmiling, a question in her eyes. What was he there for, and how soon would he leave to let her get on with her duties? Brad opened his mouth and bravely began.

"Miss... Wheeler? I come about the school. I have a youngen here needin' to be taught, and there's talk that you can do it. I've been askin' around, and I think I know how... well, I was told that if you take on a youngen, you don't take money, but you would accept a gift... maybe... I been thinkin' on something big enough to let you put up with this live wire, here. If you got room."

Josie stared at the small boy. Something about him seemed familiar. "Come in," she invited. "However, I don't really work that way. I'm not a teacher, but I can show the students how to do some things. There is no expectation of a gift, as you call it. There are some parents, though, who want to do special things for me so I will have more time to devote to their child."

The man nodded. "Yes, ma'am... Miss Wheeler. That's what I understood, but I put it wrong. That's what I'm in a hurry to do, and I'm thinkin' on how to tell you what. It's that my pa and me, we have plans to stay here at Carlile Corners and set up shop. Me, I'm a blacksmith by trade, and my pa hankers to have a livery stable, maybe someday, since he's a good hand at carin' for horses. It takes a while to get things like that started, so we was thinkin', after talkin' with the workman, outside....." Hesitated. Thinking.

So far, so good. The teacher was still listening, so he continued, "The fellow was sayin' it'd be slow work to get poles for your roof, and pa and me, we heard tell of a sawmill down south a ways. If we was to head on down there with a wagon, we could have sawed boards hauled up here, and put up a roof that'd look good and last a lifetime. Didn't say nothin' to the fellow, thinking it was your decision. We're just millin' around, doin' nothin' right now, and we could have that lumber here, measured and cut by the time the fellow gets his rock work up and ready."

The steady blue-gray eyes were expressionless, and suddenly Brad had no more words. He didn't need them.

"This sawmill, you know for sure they have what you'd need, and have you checked on the price?"

"Not yet, Miss. We thought that'd seem too pushy, without talkin' to you first. The thing is, I could jump on a pony in the morning, and have news back by night. I'd need to do some measurin' to figure on how much you'd need."

Josie turned her attention to the boy, now climbing onto the bench of Level Four table. Fists pounded on the boards as feet kicked the underside of the table.

"How old is your little boy?" Couldn't be six, maybe five...?

"Oh, ma'am, he'd not my boy. He's my little brother."

"Brother...?"

"Fer a fact. He came on along, unexpected like, with his ma not being able to hang onto life long enough to raise him. Gone on ahead, she has. Fact is, he's sorta like my boy... mine and my sister's. He's five years old... well, he will be five before Christmas. Big for his age. Took after me."

Why did he look familiar? "What is your name, and his, of course?"

"Oh, where at is my manners? I'm Brad Cullen, and the kid's name is Trailer."

"Tra... ? Repeat the name, please."

With his one-sided smile, Brad explained. "It's Trailer, just like it sounds. The midwife wasn't too handy with a pencil, and ma was too sick to talk plain. Aimed to call him Taylor, what was her maiden name, but when we found out that didn't happen, it was already registered. Ma said to leave it like it was, 'cause that's just about how he got started, and her bein' past the time for... Well, he was a surprise, you might say."

At that point, the boy took a flying leap off the bench and landed, with a whoop of explosive joy, onto the stone floor. With arms extended like bird wings, he sailed around the room.

"Mr. Cullen...? Brad, is it? Were you in Argyle a week or so ago? I seem to..." As she hesitated, Brad picked up the question.

"Fer a fact, I was. My pa has friends there, and my sister was so done in, we stayed over for a couple's nights to get her some rest. You were there...?"

With a nod of satisfaction, Josie explained, "I saw him jump from the buggy, and I saw a girl... maybe your sister?"

Ah, things were going well. He had thought she might say she should wait until Tray acquired some manners, but she hadn't yet so perhaps the deal was not off... yet.

"Yes, ma'am, that'd be Janine. And it's about her that we got another gift, if you'd take it. Our Janine, she's barely fifteen, but the deal she got outta her life is about as rough as it gets. She was moved away after three years of what was not really school, just a good meanin' neighbor, and after that, our ma took down sick with everything that came along, havin' to have constant help from Janine, her bein' only ten years old at the time." He paused, thoughtfully, and the teacher waited.

"After that, she was left alone with a baby to care for, hardly knowin' what to do next, and there weren't much to be done about it, her bein' the one to do the job best, and the job havin' to be done. Now, Janine, she ain't lazy and there ain't much she can't tackle, but she got the raw end'a life, there for a while.

"What we was thinkin' me and pa, that with all these youngens, and just one'a you, there'd be times you'd have need of a body taller'n three feet. Youngens just naturally have things happen, get sick, that sort of thing. That's when Janine'd be her best... takin' over when it was necessary. There'd be more, though. We was hopin' she'd be someone to help you, but just bein' here and hearin' the lessons, that'd be a help to her. She hardly got to learn to read, and you'd be teachin' that..." Once more running out of words, Brad paused, looking helplessly around the room. Then he began again.

"Fer a fact, we was thinkin' you'd be a few years older... maybe... and could...? Well, we didn't know, and she'd be able to make Tray sit still a minute, like I can't hardly. Anyway, we was thinkin', me and our pa, that our help with the roof, that'd be one gift we'd give, even if you don't want to take on the boy. The best gift we have to give, though, is Janine. We know what a gift she is, and it'll be a trial for us to get on without her at home, but we decided to take it on... me and pa. That is, if you could see the value in it."

There. He had said it, for good or bad. If that didn't clear the path for both Tray and Janine, it was beyond his ability to do so.

After a painful silence, Josie decided, "Let me think. You could see me again tomorrow, and you'd have the price of the boards...?"

The eyes lit up and the smile broadened. The tension in Brad's shoulder's relaxed and he stood to go, being surprised again at the height of the teacher, the lift of her chin and the set of her shoulders. She might... yes, she just might be the one to manage Tray.

At least, her and Janine together. Now, what he had to do was go home and convince Janine that she was going back to school.

* * *

His sister sat in her NEW living room in her NEW (passed down) sofa that was hardly worn. Her mending was in her lap but it was utterly disregarded. Brad shook his head and blinked in amazement, yet once more, at the beauty of his sister. She had inherited the milk white skin from the Scottish highlands along with the black, black hair. Glossy as a blackbird's wing and darker than an hour past midnight. Cheeks and lips tinted with the shade of rosy pink of the Seven Sisters rose bush outside their Kentucky home... a lifetime ago.

After a deep breath, he began. "Lot goin' on up at the school teacher's house. Addin' on, it seems. Seems they'll take on the youngen, maybe."

"What do you mean... maybe?"

"Well, he should'a been born a year earlier. But there's another thing. There's gonna be a passel of youngens over there, and that teacher... she's a sight younger'n I would'a thought. Pa and me, we talked and it might work out if you was to go with Tray, helpin' maybe... at least for a while?"

"Huh?"

"Pa and me, we sort'a offered... maybe... well, we said to her that you'd be there to help. That many youngens, there'll be times, well, maybe he can go, but there'll be conditions to be met. I said to her that you'd be willing to..."

"YOU TOLD HER WHAT?"

"Hold on. I wasn't finished. We're facin' a situation here, Pa at loose ends tryin' to find hisself, and me... well, I gotta be gone all day tomorrow, with what may turn into business for me. I'm havin' to start from the bottom to let folks know I can blacksmith. Havin' to decide on where and..."

"Whoa, stop and tell me why I gotta do another job when I got plenty of 'em already? Right here!"

"All right. He can't go with me, and that leaves Pa. We know how that goes. Pa wasn't too sharp on takin' care'a me, and I wasn't half'a what the boy is. I'm thinkin' pa'd get a talk started, and wander off to see someone's sick animal, and Tray'd be in... maybe Argyle or farther. You know better'n anyone how fast he is, and how you're the only that..."

"Well, I'll take care'a him here. At least I'll know what to do. If it's another year, it's just..."

"I know, sis. It was a big change to come here, and it was mostly for you that we came. Havin' a nice house and meetin' more people, it's somethin' you deserve. Pa and me, we was hopin' it'd be now. We was thinkin' that teacher was older, and she don't appear to be more'n 3 or 4 years older'n you. 'Course she ain't as pretty, but that ain't her fault."

At last he got a grin, so he plunged ahead, emptying the last bullet in his persuasion gun. "Was hopin' to get myself back up there for a little job. Guess it'll have to wait."

After a pause, "That teacher got boards layin' loose, and I'm thinkin' they need to be part of a bookcase. Got herself boxes and boxes of books, settin' all over the floor, needin' to be put up so the youngens can see 'em. They're gonna be lucky..."

"Boxes of books? What kind?"

"Oh, I'd think there'd be lots of kinds. You know... a teacher, she'd want all kinds..." Did the last shot make its mark? "Guess I have to wait on that. One thing about them books stayin' in the box, they'll stay fresh and new."

Janine rolled her mending together and tucked it away. Mending could be kept forever, if one tucked it low enough. She walked away from her older brother to give attention to the younger one.

Brad leaned back in the leather-covered chair and waited. He'd given it his best. The sounds coming from her kitchen were encouraging. There was the scrape and jingle of metal that indicated she had something on her mind, and it was not entirely pleasant. A drawer slammed shut.

"Come on, Tray. We're gonna get potatoes for supper." Then the solid bang of the back door. She was definitely thinking. Maybe...

Janine's mind was a whirl, thoughts whizzing around... creating their own fog. The screech of the garden gate sang, "Boxes of books!" The chickens scratching in the next pen clucked and twittered, "Boxes of.. boxes of.. boxes of books!" She plunged the spade-fork into the fine soil, fairly flipping the tan-jacketed spuds into the air. Laughing, the boy grabbed them and tossed them in the basket.

A "V" shaped flock of geese came over, heading south. "BoxES, boxes, boxes! BOoks, BOoks, Boxes of 'em."

She allowed the fork to sink too close to the vine and lifted a potato onto the tine of the digging tool. She held the pierced vegetable out to the boy, who giggled and grabbed it. "Do it again!"

"No." she answered him, crossly. "We got enough. Let's go in."

A neighbor went down the road, and someone's dog sounded an alarm... "BOOKS! BOOKS! BOOKS!"

As she walked past the still buried onions, she yanked up three of them. Potatoes fried with onions were always a favorite, and she was in no mood to deal with any words from anyone. Crisp bacon, fried green tomatoes and cornbread. Good enough for anyone.

Brad steered the conversation toward their pa's activities, warding off any stray questions. He told his pa that he was headed to the south... likely be gone most of the day... and he'd look around for opportunities. This thinly populated territory was a far cry from the city, job wise. Money wouldn't last forever. Pa was bent over the table forking in the potatoes (with onions) and agreeing. Money. It was needed.

Tray poked his mouth full, and thought of something to say. "Big

Papa, I saw books in boxes. We got things in boxes."

Janine started up in surprise. "Tray, don't talk with food in your mouth. Look, you're dripping grease on your shirt. Come quick, and we'll clean it off."

Fortunately, Big Papa was engrossed in his own business, as was usual.

Brad continued, "Been thinkin' I'd unpack them carpentry tools and do some sharpenin'. Could be, we'll be usin' them more'n we wanted to while we get some other business worked up. Good thing we know how." Big Papa nodded in agreement while buttering a chunk of cornbread.

Janine cleared the kitchen and swabbed the mess from her small brother's face. Poking him into the bed (which was still in her room, but that was going to change) and slipped into her own nightie. The creek just outside her window held bullfrogs. Brad would soon be after them for their legs. Loved fried froglegs. Right now, though, they croaked, "BOOKS! Books! BOXES OF books." A night bird on a limb replied in a high-pitched voice, "BooOOKS? BooOOKS? BooOOKS?"

She sat up, pounded the pillow and flopped back down slamming her head into the feathers. She flipped over to her stomach and buried her face, "SHUT UP!" she told the feathers. Bouncing onto her back again, she set the bedsprings to creaking and complaining.

* * *

Less than a mile away, Josie was also tossing and turning. What did I do, she asked herself, and there was no answer. I don't need anyone, she pronounced, while refusing to listen to the disagreement in her mind.

I didn't agree to take a four-year-old. I don't even know how to teach, much less take care of someone's four-year-old. Of course, her mind argued back, the boy's sister seemed to be able to.... There'll be fives and sixes, and I don't know how to take care of them, either.

What, in the name of good sense, do I think I'm doing? Well, if she comes, we can try it a week, or maybe a couple of days. I know I've seen that boy before.

Her fancy iron bedstead had been pushed back into the cave as far as it would go, to make room for the two wardrobe closets. They were going to be a big help, but things sure were crowded now. Books all over the floor.

She needed to get some organizing done, but there seemed to be no time. Every evening she felt she needed to go over her lesson plans. How was she to know what happened in a schoolroom? She had never been there!

The thought of the wardrobe closets reminded her of the great pleasure Jeff took with his new baby horses. He was too excited to talk of anything else... solid white, trimmed with speckled gray feet and face. Long legged little fellows with pretty faces. Charcoal trim around eyes and on hooves. Were horses supposed to have pretty faces? They'd likely change and look just like other horses when they grew up.

Good thing for Digby to be along so they could spell each other on night watch for the two nights they were away. Jeff had been smart to think of that, because the animals were so valuable, they would surely attract thieves. He was out there in the barn now, making sure they were all right. Good thing. They had cost a LOT of money, but it was worth it to get the rocks sledded for Digby.

The new space was going to be wonderful. The narrow room at the north end of the addition would be her bedroom. BEDROOM! Sharon Blaine had sent along a beautiful foldable screen, obviously meant for bedroom privacy. Such a thoughtful person... however, it was the truth that no one was living here but herself, so what was the need? Anyway, she would have her bedroom by spring, for certain.

The screen, then, would find a new use... as a divider in the classroom, when needed. She would order more maps, possibly geography books, and remove the page-sized outlines of the continents, oceans and meridian lines. Pasted on the folds of the screen, they would a handy teaching aid.

By her sketches and measurements, the narrow room would contain her beautiful bed, the small nightstand that had come with the wardrobe closets, and also both of the closets. That would make such a nice space in the back of the room.

Book shelves. The books needed to be unpacked, but with no place to display them, they would be in danger of being damaged. Oh, well, eventually...

And there was the girl... Brad's sister. Would she be brave enough to come? And if she did, what could be done with her? Hardly even a third level achievement... Hey, maybe she could listen as Level Three read, marking the places they stumbled, or didn't know a word. That would be a big help, because Josie really needed to push Level Four on their numbers computations. They were bringing puzzle problems that were much too easy.

Level Two should be moving up to inches, feet and yards. She couldn't remember when she was introduced to measurements, but it seemed to be a good lead-in to multiplication and division.

And then, there was... still... With that incomplete thought, Josie Wheeler dropped into a weary sleep.

* * *

Brad woke up with apprehension. Breakfast at the Cullen house went much the same. Janine wore her usual apron, but it was over one of her better summer dresses. Hair was still tousled from sleep. Hard to tell what she had in mind.

He couldn't wait around to see, however, because he had work to do at the sawmill. Likely it would be for the best that he be gone. His sister was very good at reading intentions, and he certainly wanted to avoid any confrontation.

He needed to check the wheels and springs on the wagon. There would be at least two trips, probably three, to get the dimension lumber hauled in from the mill. Likely he could get some help in the unloading. With those three red haired fellows working around in the back pasture, it was impossible to tell which one belonged to the teacher, but whichever he was, he'd obviously have an interest in the addition. After all it was his house... even though it seemed that she made the decisions and controlled the money.

The stonemason took on a strange look and hesitated when Brad had asked if the teacher was part of his family. His eventual answer was simply, "After a manner'a speakin'." Now, what kind of an answer was that? She either was... or she wasn't.

* * *

Janine's Pa, Gaither Cullen, left the house to tend to whatever he had in mind, and her older brother saddled a mare and headed south. Janine called her remaining area of concern to her, issuing a much used command.

"Tray, don't be getting dirty, we're goin' out, directly. Right now, we gotta change this bed."

"What will we change it for?" He'd been sleeping on it quite comfortably, but now it seemed to be going away.

"We're going to take it apart and put it in Big Papa's room. Your brother needs to have a bed, and stop havin' to sleep on the floor. You're gonna sleep in the big bed with Big Papa."

"Big bed?"

"Yep! Tonight!" True, it was going to be a big surprise to her father. Janine had found, however, that it was better to explain an action after it happened than to ask permission.The boy needed to be out of her bedroom. It was past time, actually. Brad, whose job it was to pretty much keep the family going and make decisions, needed a more comfortable bed, and the single bed would fit nicely in the room with pa's double bed.

The bed came apart easily. The worse thing was finding where the hammer had been hidden. She'd be glad when she had time to get organized so she could know where everything was. And here she was, intending to leave the house for the day, doing whatever .....? Where was her head, anyway?

"Here, Tray. You take the side rails, and I'll bring the headboard. Then you and me, we'll team up on the springs and mattress."

Tray straddled one rail like a horse and galloped off, narrowly missing the doorframe. The other rail trailed along in his left hand like he was leading a spare mount. His sister watched, a small smile on her face. Strong! Didn't complain! Was tractable as long as he was not allowed to get ahead. She hadn't done a bad job with him... actually. Especially considering that most girls don't start with their first newborn at age ten. As she had.

Bed in place and bedding spread, Janine set Tray about getting dressed while she took off her apron and brushed her hair. Twisting it into coils on top of her head, she adjusted her bonnet to shade the sun (it was a fright how little sun it took to burn her skin) and located her parasol.

Grasping firmly to Tray's hand, she left the lovely new house that badly needed care and organization. Setting her chin into a square of determination, she headed up the road. The school (?) was very close. Less than a mile, and that seemed about like being next door in this land of space and distance.

* * *

Josie had gathered her teaching aids together, and stepped out for a moment in the sunshine. The yard was already alive with small milling bodies, stepping over and crawling through Digby's string creation. He was extremely patient.

Down the road toward the south, someone was coming. A woman (girl?) who was holding to the hand of a small child. The hand was jerked away from the girl, but, quicker than lightening; the girl's hand grabbed a shirt collar. The small person was jerked back into step, and the walking continued with never a hesitation. Remembering the boy's activity of yesterday, she smiled, thinking that now someone was in charge and the boy obviously knew it. Somehow, that seemed to be a plus, and she was feeling much better about this person. Obviously no pushover.

"So glad to see you, Janine. Your brother indicated you might come by. I'm hoping you'll stay a while. I almost feel like I know you, just a little. I think I met you in Argyle a couple of weeks ago."

"Uh, well..."

With a grin, Josie continued, "Well, you wouldn't remember, I think. Mostly, I remember Tray."

"Yes, I remember... almost. I was feelin' like a horse that'd been rode hard and put away wet, as they say. Arkansas is a long state to come through with all its ups and downs, and the territory is even longer. I think it might be worth it, though. Reason I'm here, my older brother thought maybe you could use a little... I mean, there might be something..."

Josie butted in, "There certainly is. I really need someone to help with Level Three. Those students have hardly gotten through Level Three McGuffy Readers, and I'm wanting them through book Four by Christmas. I really need someone to follow along as they read and mark in my book any word they don't know, or have to hesitate on."

"Well, if I can...." Her voice hesitated.

"You can. I don't want you to tell them the word if they can't figure it out. That way, we'll practice together using the letter sounds. I want each girl to read four pages while the others keep up with her in their own book. If the reader doesn't know the word and one of the others does, they can tell her, but I still want it marked. I want them to get used to saying words they don't know."

Janine felt herself being wide-eyed and trembly. What did she know about sounding words? But maybe...? It wasn't like she was going to have to tell them the word. She watched as Josie distributed slates and chalk to the 5 and 6 year-olds.

Then Josie continued, "You can sit here with them, and Tray can sit by you for now. Level One, his class, has been sitting with the older girls, anyway." She indicated one of the larger tables.

"Now, Level Three, Miss Janine is going to listen as you each read four pages each. You may begin on page 27, starting at the top. Do you girls understand?"

Heads nodded, and turned their eyes to Janine. Tiny half-smiles greeted her and several pairs of eyes took in her shiny hair and bright eyes, and the fact that she was older... so it must be all right to admire her appearance. Janine drew in a deep breath and bravely picked up a sharpened pencil, as Kristie began to read.

Now, Janine had years of practice at seeing more than what she was looking at, and she clearly saw that her little brother was easing down from his bench seat into the area under the table, while sneaking a peek at his sister to see if he was getting away with it.

Janine did not miss a word from the reading as she stood, book in hand, and crooked a finger at Tray and pointed to the bench. Wordlessly, he drew himself back where he belonged and hunched his shoulders together.

As Patricia began her turn to read, Janine's pencil took a quick tap on the black hair on Tray's head, and he quickly picked up his chalk and slate and began to draw pictures as he had been told to do.

None of this was lost on the rest of Level One. Isaac, Bettina, David and Esther had seen the escape attempt, the capture and the punishment, all done without a word from this teacher. The picture was clear. If she would do that to her own brother, there was no figuring what she might do to them if they misbehaved, so the four of them quickly joined Tray in the drawings.

Next, Level Four worked math from the Level Four McGuffey

numbers book. The wonderful slates were two sided, and on one side, the girls numbered one to twenty for the twenty subtraction examples. Turning the slate over, they did their figuring on the back of the slate, then posted their answer by its number. This way, they did not need to use the paper tablets. Paper could be expensive.

Josie stepped over to her. “Janine, will you write the numbers 1 to 5 at the top of the slates for Level One. Then help them copy the shape under each number? Thanks...”

Level Two, the 7 year olds, were adding single digit numbers, using fingers and chalk marks, then counting. Not good. Josie picked up a slate and wrote 1+2 and demanded, “How much?” Wide eyes stared, but no words came. “Quick! Think!”

With a grin, Bridgit whispered, “Three,” and shyly ducked her head.

“Good job!” Josie yelled loud enough for every class to hear. “Very good job!”Next came 5+1. A pause, a look around at each other, and two voices shouted, “Six!”

Josie favored them with a wide smile. “See, you don’t need to count. You have the answer right there in your head.” Nodding with satisfaction, she decided, yes, it was time for numbered cards so she could flash the examples faster. They had to learn to say answers without counting. Fast.

Level Three, the 8 and 9 year-olds were supposed to be reading in the First Grade McGuffey book. Raymond and Henry, the two boys of the group had decided to scribble chalk on their slates to make dust, then blow it off at the girls. After a pair of irritated squeals from the girls, Josie demanded. “Boys? Noses in the books!” Whereupon the boys opened their books on the desk and poked their noses flat against the pages.

Janine, put down her chalk and tapped Raymond on his tousled head, crooking her finger. He hesitated, then started to stand, and Janine motioned him to bring his book. Leading him to a blank wall, she positioned the book against the rocks of the wall just above his eye level.Then she opened it, placed his hands on either side, and pointed to the words.

The four remaining pairs of eyes in Level Three were trained on the actions and followed Janine as she returned to the table and crooked her finger for Henry. He didn't have to be told, but picked up his book and followed her. Spaced farther down the wall, she placed him before his book, holding each side in one hand. It wouldn't be long before there would be a pair of tired arms for each boy, but that was the price of disobedience.

Gwinnie, Kristie and Patricia were taking no chances. Their eyes followed the words of their book as it was placed on their table before them. Standing against the wall would be just too embarrassing for words, and they followed their place on the page with a pointing finger.

Janine went back to the 5 and 6 year-olds who were struggling with the numbers, whispering to themselves, "One, two, three, four, five," to correspond with their shaky attempts. The beautiful Janine made a correction or two, and favored them with pleased smiles.

It was nearly twenty minutes later that the two boys were shrugging their aching shoulders and stretching their necks, cramped and stiff from looking up at the book. Janine tapped shoulders lightly and crooked her finger, pointing to their worktable. The two boys gratefully accepted their reprieve and returned to their seats.

Lunch time. Containers had been piled on Josie's small eating table to keep them from tempting Flip, the pup. Janine realized what she had forgotten.

"Miss... Wheeler?"

With a shake of the head, Josie corrected, "Call me Josie. We're neighbors."

"Thank you. I'm afraid we'll have to run home for lunch. I was intent on moving furniture this morning, and plum forgot."

"No, no! You're not getting away! I get breakfast sent to me and there's always too many biscuits. I have sliced beef and mustard for sandwiches. Maybe Tray could have his with the others."

"Right! I love mustard, but it's hard to keep at my house."

"So pull a stool up to the table. How did you... uh, like... ?

Small hesitation, then, "A lot to think on. I never went to a real school."

"Me, either. My pa had someone come to my house to teach me, so we're alike, there."

Biscuits were sliced open and meat was inserted. "Here, Tray, you take your sandwich and go eat with the others. Be sure to stay over the table so you won't spread crumbs."

Duty done, Janine opened another biscuit. "Nice big biscuits. I like them big."

"Me, too, but I usually get too many. Of course, Flip likes to help out. Is it all right to ask how you liked the day... or did I make you work too hard?"

"Oh, no, no, no! I didn't work at all. I'm really glad I came. Uh... Josie, I didn't mean to take over when those boys decided not to mind you. I just did it without thinkin', but I'll be more careful if I... well, if I'm here again."

Amazed, Josie put her food on the table and stared at the black haired girl. "Oh, my! You HAVE to be here again, and you did the very right thing. I'm not used to correcting bigger boys, and I'm really not a teacher and I don't know that I'm doing, really. I just started because of my little brother and my cousin, and it sort of grew. Now I'm particularly interested in Level Four. Those girls were like you, the way things kept them from what they wanted to do. I really want them to learn fast." Nervous words poured forth. She must not let Janine go!

She paused, and bravely asked, "Could I have you do something, maybe not today, but when you can? I have a lot of books in boxes and they were selected by someone else. I'm not sure what's in them, and I've been so concerned with lesson plans that I can't think of anything else. Could you maybe look through them, if you get a chance, and see what is there that would interest your little brother?I'm thinking it would be good for them to hear stories read, just for fun, and would help them learn to read. The McGuffey primer is a bit dull for listening to, because they're trying to teach certain words and..."

Janine now put her food on the table, and her hands against her cheeks. "Oh, if I could! I would just love to and I could set the others out for you, if you had... We really need a place... a bookcase, really! Or did you want to keep them in boxes? They might stay cleaner that way. It seems dusty here in the territory."

"Bookcases would be perfect. My friend, Mr. Digby, could make them, but he'll not be through with the stone until spring... maybe. But I'd really like you to sort out some that you could read, and to let the big girls take home, if they wanted to. That way, you might help them... a little, maybe?"

"I could do that. Today, I left a note that I'd be right home, but I could stay later tomorrow, after the youngens have gone.Would that be good?"

From one thing to another, the afternoon passed. Janine felt her feet as light as dandelion fuzz as she walked home, holding to Tray's collar. Then she let go. "Run if you want to, Tray. You know the way home."

A deep breath and a pleasant sigh. Tomorrow, she would sort through the boxes of books. She loved neatness and order, and decided she would examine each book and put the easy ones together, because they would be the ones mostly used. At first, anyway. She could then thumb through the others and think about when she could read them herself. She was bound to learn a lot, just listening to what was being done.

Brad was home from wherever he went, and was sorting through some of his tools. Maybe he got a job!

Time to think about supper. Let's see... Her big crock was setting on the table full of water. Hmmmm, looks like he got a couple of squirrels and a rabbit on the way home. All cleaned and cut up. Perfect. They looked young enough to fry, so potatoes and gravy would make the meal. An easy meal. And an onion. Humming a nameless tune, she set about her evening.

Immediately after the early supper, Brad set out and was almost dark getting back. She had made up his new bed and put Tray in with Big Papa, much to his excitement. Settling into her own bed, she sighed with a pleasure she could scarcely remember having. Or even imagine.

She was sitting on a swing. It was a swing in a big woodland, and the rope was tied to a long, flowing limb. There were birds singing overhead. A breeze blew across her face, and she was wearing a favorite blue-checked dress.

She stretched her feet toward the ground but couldn't quite touch it. Extending her legs out in front of her, she saw her black stockings, those she must wear when she played, but she had on her shiny Mary Jane shoes... not the high topped, lace up shoes for play. Hmmm.

Big brother Brad was not with her, and she didn't know where he was. He must be far away because he didn't come when she called. He usually didn't mind getting the swing started for her, but where was he?

Then the swing started moving gently. Swinging forward and back. Oh, he must have heard her and come to help. She looked around to see him, and it was not Brad. It was another girl, not much bigger than she was, but she was big enough to push the swing really well.

Higher and higher, and small Janine extended her legs and pulled back, sending herself even higher. She called to the girl behind her, "I can do it now! I just needed a push to get started!"

The girl pushed a few more times, and let her go, but suddenly she was on a swing beside Janine... one tied to the same limb as her swing. Both girls swung merrily back and forth, giggling and laughing as the breeze fanned their faces and fluffed the ruffles on their aprons.

Janine did not ask the girl what her name was. She knew they had played together a lot, and, of course, she knew her name. Why would she ask? But when she suddenly woke up, she knew she had never had a friend with hair the color of dry prairie grass, hair that flowed around her shoulders, waving at the ends. And she never had a friend with gray eyes the color of a shiny new nickel. Turning over in the bed, she sleepily told herself, names didn't matter. It was only a dream.

The morning meal went rapidly. Clearing away the table quickly... not with her usual care, she swabbed down her brother, dressed him and herself and headed north toward the school

Tightly clutching his small hand, she suddenly looked down at her almost five-year-old brother. There was no one within miles who might be interested in stealing him. After all, he was no longer a dimpled baby that everyone wanted to admire. Also, there was no place for him to go if he should want to run away.

"Tray... I'm going to make a bargain with you. If you can walk beside me and promise not to get dirty until we get there, I'll let you walk without holding my hand. Is that a bargain?"

The small face brightened, the rosy cheeks dimpled and the cupid's bow mouth squealed a shriek of joy as he clutched his sister around the thighs. She looked into the perfect little face and had the urge to go back on her word and clutch the adorable child tightly once more... but she resisted.

The small boy strained to keep his feet steady and not stir up dust, and refused to pick up an attractive pebble to throw. Until he walked into Josie's fenced yard, he was able to keep his bargain. But there on the ground, he saw a pile of yellow wooden curls created by the smoothing plane.

Squealing with delight and recognition, he ran to the pile and tossed the wood shavings into the air. "Brad!" he exclaimed as he tossed a handful at his sister.

Nodding, Janine agreed, Brad had surely been here, and that would explain his lateness for supper. Then, stepping through the opening in the stone wall, and entering Josie's open door, she saw the result of the smoothing plane and her brother's skill. There against the stone wall stood four small bookcases made from the new wood making up the packing crates.

"Bookcases!" she exclaimed, and Josie looked up from her tablet with a grin at Janine's obvious surprise. "Oh, I can unpack the boxes and put the books up! I mean, is it all right? I know the shelves haven't been oiled, but I just can't wait to see how they look."

Nodding, Josie told her. "Yes, why not? You could put the books all in the bookcases, and don't bother to sort them until later. I'm tired of looking at all those boxes, and besides, I want them cut into squares to teach numbers."

"Oh, I can do that! If I know the size of the squares, I can do that! I can stay later if I need to because there's so many boxes."

Carefully slitting the gummed paper strips that held the boxes together, the excited girl gently lifted out the precious contents. "Oh, here's a Bible Story Book! Could I... I mean, if I was very careful, could I take this book home for one night? I'd be really careful, that is if it would be all right." She ducked her head with concern that she might have overstepped her duties.

Josie looked up again and tapped her pencil against her teeth as her thoughts progressed. "Janine, why don't you set that one aside and take it with you. You could look at the stories at home and see one you can read to the children each day before they start studying. I think that would be a way to get them settled down, and the stories seem rather short. Could you do that?"

Janine clasped the book in both hands. "Oh, yes. I think I could do that. Maybe. I might need some help with some words. You know I told you... that...?I didn't really get to...?" Her words faded away as her eyes became down cast.

Josie thought. "I have an idea. Why don't you pick a story as soon as you put up the books, and look through it? If there are words you aren't sure of, you could write them down and we'll look at them before you go home. That way you'd be sure. Why not pick the first story in the book to start with?"

Nodding, Janine put the book on top of the case, marveling that her problems seemed to disappear as fast as they appeared. She turned to look at Josie who was again attending to her tablet, and she noted the wheat-colored hair with the waves at the end. It sheeted over her shoulder like a fan. Janine remembered the gray-blue eyes as they had watched her.

A catch of her breath. A tremble. A small shudder of a chill passed up her arms and across her neck. She heard herself in the dream... "I can do it now! I just needed a push to get started." A connection? She shook her head and lifted more books from the boxes. She'd think about it later. The thought was much too big to consider right now.

* * *

Digby had been riding Worthless to the back of the tract of land. He would be needing more stone, and it was necessary to break some loose for Jeff to sled to the building site. It was the first of November, and where had the summer gone?

According to the Farmer's Almanac that he had looked at over at the Corner, the fair weather would hold during the first week of November. How did they know that... way back when the book was printed? It didn't matter. Tomorrow would be a perfect day to spend breaking loose the thick sheets of building stone from the layers created by the formation of the earth. Good stone. Easier to work with than that of the mountains of Colorado.

Today, however, it was time to look at the grove of persimmon trees. While lying in bed in his snug little room, he had been thinking. His Josie was obviously planning to spend a lot of years here, and the natural sugar from that sweet native fruit had so many uses. For candy, to sweeten oatmeal, for fruitcakes and pumpkin and sweet potato pies.

He could shovel up a dozen or so of the saplings and carry them over the ridge and set them so they would be handy for her when they began to bear fruit. Oh, yes, and fattening pigs. There was nothing better than persimmons for that! It would actually be worth the loss of a day on the room to get a start on her fruit orchard.

Next, he'd start some seedlings from apple, peach and plum trees. Also, pears. Wasn't much better for a hot buttered biscuit than a dollop of pear honey. It had a taste of the wind-swept prairie in the fall sunshine! And grapes... would they grow here? Certainly the tiny 'possum' grapes climbed every upright stalk they could find. Why not the bigger, cultivated ones?

What a land this was! As he had stretched out on his shelf bed last night, glancing through the window at the starry covering of the prairie sky, he had cast his mind back to the years of his life. Surely, he could not be that person who met each day with the pick and mucking shovel, with only the expectation of exposing a few crumbly, yellow stones.He had thought himself contented, and for years had put off making a move from what he had always known.

A smile shone through his gray-sprinkled whiskers as he thought, with unexpected kindness, of the rattler that had cost him half of his foot. If not for that reptile, he would likely still be living inside the mountain, and he would have never known about his Josie. A fate not to be considered!

A movement caught his eye, and raising his weapon silently, he stopped a rabbit... full grown with summer flesh and marbled with fat. A rare catch. Only the autumn could give marbled flesh to the animals and make them so perfect for roasting. Or stewing with dumplings. Squinting his eyes against the sun, he panned the prairie for the mate of the rabbit.

Bang! Got it! Now, his Josie had likely never roasted a rabbit because he had never been with her to teach her. It would be like that dinky little fireplace of hers. How did the Sutter family ever make do with it? When the roof was on her new room... well, it wouldn't be long with the help of that young neighbor and his pa who promised to give him a couple of days work. Then things would change.

The rabbit. Of course, his Josie had mentioned a stove like her aunt had... one that she had said she could operate with cow pats. Maybe he could find some scraps of wood to cook these rabbits... the smoke from cow pats just didn't work right for roasting. Not hot enough, he presumed.

Anyway, that brought him to another plan he had. Lying on his shelf bed at night was a wonderful way to think and plan. He knew about permanent woodlots. His pa had started one in the mountain and it had lasted for at least 30 years and was still going strong.

So easy. Worked so well. Just chop down the tree and leave a good stump. When sprouts popped out in the spring, break out all but the strongest and let it grow. The huge root, accustomed to supporting an entire tree, now had only a sprout to feed, and the new tree grew in a third of the time the original tree had grown.

Black Jack oaks were best. Many were growing down here on the prairie, and come winter, he'd have time to pick out forty or fifty good sprouts to start. Maybe more next year, and he'd line them up along the little creek that meandered around on his Josie's land. Wood always burns better and longer than cow pats. His Josie should have the best.

Digby tossed the heavy fall rabbits over the saddle, and poked a few pieces of dead wood into his saddlebags. Maybe it would be enough to roast the rabbits.

His small house was a continuous comfort, and he could happily stay there until the end of his days. No more wandering. His Josie had made a deal with him, and he knew she would keep it. He had no idea of how it felt to have a granddaughter, but already he could hardly imagine being without her. She let him do things for her and did not object to his advice on small things. Were all young ladies this agreeable?

Like the windows. High and smaller, he had advised. Less glass to get cold in the winter and set high to remove summer heat from the ceiling in the hotter parts of the year. And the butchered pig. He had suggested she send most of it to her uncle with the family. Keep just the bacon and hams, the cured feet for bean soup and dried jerky from the loin.

And the calf. After the little bull calf was born, the milk from the cow was more than either she or he could use. The greedy little calf was happy to use the rest of it. When it came time to wean it, he would check around for another pig. She seemed glad that he made these decisions for her. Likely her uncle or cousins would help, but they were so busy... the way men always were on the territory.

The neighbor who wanted to give her the loan of a pony and trap, had insisted it be brought to her house, now that she had Digby, himself, to take care of it for her. The small buggy just held two people comfortably and had a small place for the luggage. They had twice taken it to Argyle. School supplies.

Sweet riding little contraption it was, and they had ridden along in quiet enjoyment. She never chattered, as some women seemed to feel they must, and she seemed to be comfortable just looking about while he fingered the reins. The little pony was no good for heavy work or plowing, being much too lightly built. Digby could think ahead, though, at times she may want to drive herself as she visited locally with friends. He had heard that ladies liked to do that. This pony would be perfect. He would teach her.

And friends. Was there something happening with the young lady from a quarter of a mile south? Sister of the young man who was to help on the roof? Well, she needs friends. She should not allow herself to be always alone... the way he, himself, had been. Just now it seemed she could never get far from that tablet and pencil and the decisions about her classes. Maybe that girl would be the friend his Josie needed. And maybe help her. Interesting how that girl's older brother had insisted of making the shelves for her books.

Digby had intended to do that, but knew it had to wait till the stonework was done. When he looked at the finished cases, he knew the young man had done a much better job then he could have... smoothed and with squared corners. Skill and experience were a wonderful thing. Also good tools.

Stone. Two more tiers for the walls to be completed, and he hoped to find good stones for the tops of the windows. So much better if they could be long enough to span the entire length of the window, or he would have to try to locate a bar of iron for a bridge. Such good stone! Next would be the floor, and he would work on it while the neighbors put on the roof. He was glad of the help. It wouldn't be safe for him to be on the rafters with his foot like it was.

Floor stones. Referred to as flagstones, they were, because they were big and flat. First, though, he wanted to treat the dirt beneath the stones. Thinned tar poured over the leveled dirt to discourage insects, then the oiled tarp over the tar. No moisture could come through that like it did in her cave room. He'd learned that little trick in his own cave home.

Then the flag stones. They would be chipped and fitted together like a child's toy puzzle. A plaster powder mixed with glue would be carefully trained into the hair-line cracks between the stones. It would be beautiful. A lot of work and time, but worth it, and he could see it in his mind. Only the best for his Josie. It would be easy to clean, and a school room with children was bound to get dirty.

Two more pieces of dead wood. Letting himself off the back of the jenny, he stuffed the dead limbs into the saddlebag. Plenty of wood now. He could imagine the dressed rabbits on a green stick spit, oozing fat and juices into the flames, spitting and sputtering and making fragrant smoke! He would be able to tell how well his Josie liked them, and if they seemed as good to her as the prairie chickens had been... well, there were a lot of rabbits.

Such a pleasure he had never known existed! Another person who was important to him! Imagine the magic of it all, and it could have been missed, had not the rattler... Well, surely it was meant to be, and there would be days and days more, and marvelous wonders yet to occur... to a man who had finally acquired what so many would think was a natural happening. Daughter! Granddaughter! Both in one marvelous package!

Not natural for Digby... for him it was magic.

* * *

November. Her first November in the territory. In New York, November had barreled in with wet wind and snow flutters, a dire warning of what was to come. Ice skating children. Closed carriage rides and the smell of pecan logs and cedar branches. The tinkle of sleigh bells. Sleighs? She had not even seen one anywhere in the territory. What would it be like? With no sleigh?

She could feel the chill of the stone walls, though she had made a fire in the potbelly stove. It was dying out now. Digby had said that was the trouble with cow pats. He'd said that wood was the thing for long heat and he would take care of it for her as soon as he had time.

The last row of stones had been lifted to the top of the walls, with the help of Janine's brother. Brad had put out a shingle sign stating that he did horseshoeing and all forms of blacksmithing but there had not been much activity. Folks didn't know about him, yet, but they soon would. Just wait until a stallion throws a shoe, or a wagon axel bends.

Now, however, he was climbing about over the stone walls, nailing beams into place. Drilling into the top stone with the masonry drill to insert braces. Hard work. Looked good, though. Her new addition seemed like a creature that just grew, and took care of itself. Digby seemed to know how to do everything, and he was busy now with the floor.

* * *

Josie opened the doors of one of her wardrobe closets and searched among the long gowns. The fleece of the gown of Sharon's choice felt cozy and warm to the touch. Drawing it out, she removed it from its hanger and lowered it over her head... feeling the warmth of it even before she thrust her arms into the sleeves. Like a friendly hug. Bless Sharon and her friendly pushiness. Trying to fill the place of her friend, Josie's mother, by caring for the friend's daughter. Hoping to ease the pain of loss for them both.

House boots. Fur lined. Cozy even down to the toes, and with warm wool socks? The coolness of the stone floor would never penetrate through to her feet.

Her hand reached out and picked up her tablet and pencil... her mind never being far from the next lesson to be planned. A small smile flitted across her face as she thought of her New York tutor. Would he ever be surprised at what she was doing now!

Darkness came so early in November. She paused to light the wick of her kerosene lamp (that Sharon had sent without her asking) and a soft, yellow glow filled the cave room. So much better than a candle, or even two candles. No flicker of the flame in draft, and no smell of burning paraffin.

Seating herself at her desk, she began. Janine had unpacked the books and put them in the cases, and the cardboard boxes had been flattened and set aside. They were much too valuable to be allowed to ruin, and they would be perfect made into practice cards for learning numbers.

A bit of thought had produced a way for the same cards to work for addition, subtraction and multiplication. If she made the examples with the smaller number always on the bottom, and made with no activity sign, they would work. Like, for instance, 6 on top and 3 on bottom, the answer on the back could be: 6 plus 3 equals 9, 6 minus 3 equals 3, and even 6 times 3 equals 18. Maybe even division... no, that would be too awkward. She'd just have to wait for more cardboard boxes!

Janine would like making the cards. All Josie would have to do was make a list of what she wanted, and Janine would take care of the rest. What a lucky break to get Janine! It was amazing how different their lives had been, but now they were nearly like sisters. It was almost as though the flat, level prairie could level people as well, and make them see each other, eye to eye. Maybe it had something to do with need. She had never felt a need in New York, because everything had been planned and thought out for her, and then handed to her at the exact right time of requirement.

She had desperately needed her aunt and uncle. She had needed Digby, though she hadn't realized how much until lately. Apparently, Digby needed to be needed, and surely that counted! Janine had needed help in the one area that Josie was best able to give it, and Josie had needed Janine in so many ways.

Janine's big brother was so eager to have Janine helped, that it seemed he was continually striving to pay her back for what she had given to the family. Who would know that the burden of a house, a child, and the care of adult family members would fall on the shoulders of an eleven year old girl who hardly had time to grieve for her mother?

Need, yes... It popped up in the most unexpected places. When Digby pointed out that, with the help of the neighbor, the new roof shape would provide a space that could be used for a lot of things... that it was often used as the bedroom for younger children. Immediately, she had thought of Joshua. It bore on her mind that she had left her little brother with her aunt, who had never a moment to herself, and she had hardly asked permission. But it would be different, now.

She could provide a space for him in the attic, and he could stay with her... but then the surprise came. When she mentioned it at Sunday dinner, her aunt's eyes had become round with surprise and... alarm? Then, while washing up the dishes, her aunt had said, hesitantly, "Josie, honey, I know he's your brother and all the family you have, and I know you want him with you. I am trying to be grateful for the time I've had him here, but I will miss him so much."

"Miss him?" Surprise sharpened Josie's voice.

Her aunt actually sniffed politely, her soapy hands wrapped in her apron. Nodding, she explained, "I know you wouldn't know it, but that Darrel of mine is so much like me, and Joshua is the spit and image of my lost sister, I can see them together, and it reminds me of the good times we had when we were growing up, she and I. It's almost been like she was making one last present for me, letting me watch after her son, but I know it isn't a present from her... it's a gift from you. You have every right to take him with you, because it's so likely he'll be leaving to go back to New York in two or three years."

In stunned silence Josie had stared at her aunt, holding the platter she was drying in one hand, and the drying towel in the other.

Her aunt continued, "I wasn't meaning anything except that they needn't hurry up with your attic on my account. It'll be a month or two, won't it, before its ready... the attic, that is?"

Josie's hands and arms had moved on their own, and had put down the platter. Stepping toward the older woman, she spread her arms, and found herself locked in a damp embrace. "Oh, Aunt Nettie! How could I have been so blind and selfish! The 'present' was from you to me when I could barely care for myself, and I didn't even think to thank you. Even now, I have hardly a minute that isn't used to plan what I'm doing, and I do see Joshua every day! I would like nothing more than to let him stay here with you. I know he would like it much better than with me, and he would hate being away from Darrell, being almost like twins that they are."

Within her arms, she felt a relieved sob from the older woman. "Oh, darling Josie! We needed to talk about this, didn't we? I was dreading it so! If you could do that, I would be so grateful. Of course, you know you could be here with him any time you could spare." After a hesitation, she continued, "You are so much like your father, staying within yourself and doing what needs to be done... doing it so well. I can see now that, of course, you have not had time to hardly miss him... seeing him every day. I can't imagine how you can just pick up on what needs to be done, and do it. It would my intense pleasure to keep Joshua until the day you decide he must leave."

Later, Josie thought. So much like her father. Chin propped in hand and elbow on the desk, Josie nodded to herself. Yes, it was likely a fault of hers that she could not speak more, and explain how she felt. She must actually be like her father. But every minute, there seemed to be a new class decision to make. Like now. She had sat there, dreaming, for at least a half an hour.

Level Four was moving so fast; it was hard to know which direction to turn them. They were sailing through the fifth grade McGuffey reader, the Fourth Grade numbers and spelling was coming along... not good, but it would improve.

Level Three had begun to write out their own problems in numbers class. It was interesting to see the direction they came from in making up the puzzle problems... subjects that were interesting to them... and what fun trying to figure those problems made by each other. Their reading was now almost as good as the older class.

It was clearly time for the seven-year-olds to read. Maybe two or three more weeks on phonics, on long and short vowels and the hard and soft consonant sounds. But definitely soon.

Her eyes drooped, tiredly, and her head nodded. Jerking up, she tried to focus on the tablet before her. No use. Laying down her pencil and blowing out the oil lamp, she left the desk and crawled under the soft quilts. No more thoughts until morning.

Before daylight, the neighbor's rooster crowed her awake. Digby had said that maybe she should wait on having chickens of her own. He would need to help with them, and he had no time just yet. Sensible thinking. Besides, she got more eggs brought to her than she could possibly use and Digby was very regular on bringing in prairie chickens for the roasting spit.

One thing led to another, and she again had a house full of children. Janine was busy cutting 3-inch by 6-inch chunks from the cardboard boxes, and printing numbers on them. Josie sat on the end of the seven-year-old's bench explaining long and short sounds... once more.

"Sometimes an 'A' sounds like an 'ay' and sometimes it sounds like an 'aw'. Sometimes like 'say' and sometimes like 'saw'. Now, we're going to think up some words with long 'A' that sound like 'say'."

Examples were offered. "Day." "May." "Hay." "Tray."

From behind her came a voice calling out "Play!" Turning quickly, she saw Janine's finger over her lips. "Not yet, Tray! Not playtime, yet. You mustn't shout out that way."

The small boy's eyes became fierce with indignation. "No! Not outside! I meant 'play'. I was just helpin' with the long A."

Janine cast an apologetic look toward Josie, but Josie turned to the child. "Did you mean that 'play' had a long A"?

"Yes! And I have a long 'A'. Like Tray!" He beamed, triumphantly at his sister and at his teacher.

"Tray, you are exactly right. I want you to come over here and help out with these sounds. All of you come on if you want to." She paused as the entire Level One class crowded onto the benches with

Level Two, giggling and wriggling, excitedly.

Janine shrugged, continuing to cut rectangles from the packing boxes, and Josie smiled to herself as she learned another thing. Never underestimate a child. From then on, in most instances, she combined the two classes. Some liked to participate, and those who didn't seemed to learn just from listening.

Numbers. It was hard for the youngest ones to print the numbers on their slates, but they had no trouble shouting their names, holding up the right number of fingers.

As the laughing, shouting children skipped through the door of the crowded room, dashing this way and that in their freedom. Then finally sorting themselves out to go in the direction of their homes, while Josie sighed a long, audible sigh and sunk onto the bench of the nearest table.

Janine caressed the shiny cover of a book and carefully put it on the shelf. Glancing toward Josie she sympathized, "Tired?"

With a grin, Josie admitted, "I don't really know. I haven't done anything but talk and walk around these tables. I shouldn't be tired, really."

"I know. One time, the tiredest I ever was came when I sprained my ankle and couldn't walk much. I sat and saw everything that needed to be done, and it flat wore me out. Could be you're thinkin' a lot about too many things and it's your head that's tired."

"You may be right. Anyway, tomorrow is Saturday. That may help me. Do you need help with the rest of those books?"

"Oh, no! Please, I want to do them... unless you really want to, I mean. I never saw so many books in my life, not even in a store. I saw some of these with what looked like grown up stories and I hope I get smart enough to read them."

Josie watched as Janine selected a book here, and two over there and put them together in another shelf.

She explained, "I'm kinda sortin' 'em now with all the littlest stories together. I can do better sortin' later after they're all unpacked. I'm bein' slow 'cause I've never had so much fun in all my life and I'm makin' it last. Does that seem funny?"

"Not funny at all. I feel the same way about them. You know what? I think we should list all the books in a notebook... that is, after you have them sorted. We'll want to let the children take books home sometimes so we'll have to keep track of them."

"Do you reckon they'll be careful and not let them get messed up?"

"Hmmm, we'll have to think of some way so that doesn't happen. Maybe we'll have an idea." Josie smiled a small smile to herself at the use of "we". It was so easy to think of Janine and herself as a pair, instead of herself alone. She watched as the dark haired girl nodded, thoughtfully.

Then Janine stood, stretching her cramped legs, and pushed the last two boxes against the wall. "I'd like to save the last two so I can have fun Monday. If that's all right. I'm thinkin' I'll have hungry fellows at home before too long. Fellows are hungry most all the time." She worked her way through the crowded room, between tables and bookshelves. "Shore'll be nice to have the new room, huh?"

Josie nodded, tiredly, and returned the goodbye wave at the door. Food. Quiet. No hungry men to deal with, and no appetite. Have to eat. Have to take Flip for a walk.

A stiff breeze from the southeast was pushing clouds across the sky. Flip barked at a bold crow trying to scratch up crumbs from the children's lunch sandwiches. Digby sat on a stone beside his tiny home. "Breeze blowin' up some weather. South wind stirs up the north wind and the weather changes."

"Really?"

"That's what folks say, only they don't say what kind'a weather that's comin'. That way they don't make no mistake. You 'bout used up all yourself, haven't you? Have you give thought to slippin' into them new soft quilts for a early night?"

Josie felt her shoulders slump as she thought of the softness so near to her weary muscles. But, really, she should....

Digby again. "Miss Josie, child, forgive my boldness, but I got two fat rabbits skinned and hangin' in my house. Thought to toss 'em in a kettle for a stew, but I'd rather fire up your tiny fireplace and roast 'em over mesquite deadwood. Be leftovers enough for your breakfast. What say?"

Josie's tired smile gave him his answer. Digby nodded, "So you just take that snip of a dog and walk up to the Corner to check your mail, and by the time you get back, the juice'll be drippin' on the logs." With that, he stepped into his house and out again with two huge skinned cottontails.

Josie headed toward the Corners with the pup running circles and flipping in the air around her. The breeze ruffled her hair and whipped her skirt about her calves and knees. Deep breaths filled her lungs, driving out weariness. She'd ask old Miz Carlile if they kept oil for a lamp, or would she need to get it at Argyle. Long evenings were ahead, and the new cut-glass lamp was so cheerful.

As she returned, she sniffed the fragrant smoke from her own chimney, blended with the aroma of roasted meat. Her un-hungryness brisked away on the breeze and a fierce appetite took its place. The pup sniffed every weed and fence post for messages from other four-legged residents of the prairie, only to come dashing to catch up to her.

Sitting across from each other at her tiny table, the man and the girl ate in companionable silence. Restful and undemanding. Meat and toasted left-over biscuits. Fall apples slices pierced with a stick, now leaning over the blaze creating an aroma better than the best perfume. Soft light flowed down from the cut-glass oil lamp.

Josie felt so relaxed that she might just melt out of her clothes and flow into her high-topped, lace-up boots.

Digby's soft voice. "Noticed somebody brought you turnips."

Josie nodded. "And I have no idea what to do with them."

"Figured as much. Folks got their own ways, and likely turnips are a taste you gotta be born with. They make a good fall and winter change of taste. Some folks cut 'em and fry 'em in bacon grease till they turn soft and brownish. Not bad tastin'. I've knowed folks to make 'em into pickles. You got a taste for pickles?"

Josie nodded. "How can I make pickles?"

Digby shook his sadly. "Can't help you there. Never done it, myself." After a moment, "Think you might ask that dark haired girl. Her folks come from where that'd be a thing they'd make, I'm thinkin'."

Silence again. Soft golden, silence, broken only by the pup growling as he tussled with a slipper. Josie gathered a handful of bones and took the dog out.

Digby slid the apple slices onto a plate and drizzled honey over them. The two sat in silence, eating the crisply browned fruit with their fingers, dredging them into the honey in the bottom of the shared plate. The old man sighed with happiness. Wouldn't any lucky father (or grandfather) sit quietly like this of an evening with his daughter? Who needed words at a time like this, and the girl had battled words all day.

At the last slice of apple on the plate, he rose, waved a hand toward her, and walked away. Silence, restful and comforting.

Josie cleared the table and called the pup into the crowded house. How did the seven Sutter residents survive, especially in winter weather?

The fleecy, warm nightie hugged her tiredness, and the softness of the bed enveloped her. A fleeting thought teased her as she thought of the many, many new books she could look at, but before the thought could take feet, her eyes closed. It was hardly dark outside, but the pup willingly leaped onto the bed and circled himself beside her. Nose to tail in a furry donut, he sighed into sleep.

* * *

She was out of her house, and a dark cloud moved down the road toward her. She watched in fascination as it moved along, but as it came nearer, she turned to run. She ran and ran, and the faster she went, the closer the cloud came. In fear, she glanced behind her and there were two clouds instead of one. Then three.

Next there were many dark and menacing shapes and they passed her on both sides, moving with her. Then they were ahead and had her surrounded. Closer and closer. She stopped and they moved in on her until she was totally enclosed. They breathed on her, and she felt their cool breath from every direction. Fear bumps broke out on her arms and she flailed them to shoo away the clouds but they wouldn't go... and there were no more places for her to run.

Terror arose in her throat and she screamed with no sound. Louder, still no sound. Finally, she heard her own voice screaming, "Help me! Someone help me!"

She opened her mouth again and the sound was a woof and a bark. More barks! Startling her eyes open, she felt the pup standing on her chest, barking into her face.

Her trembling arms hugged the furry beast, comforting him and herself. A dream of flames would not have surprised her, though there had been none of them since she moved into her stone house. The globs of blackness, however, were a thing of terror. Where did they come from?

Slipped from the bed, donned the fur boots against the night chill, and wrapped her new robe abound her shoulders. Fireplace coals cast a pale glow around the room. Sitting cross-legged on the bed, she searched her thoughts, as the pup squirmed into her lap and licked her chin. Surely, she had never been as frightened in her life. Flames she knew, and even animals she knew, but black globs of nothing that moved without legs... how could her mind invent something she had never seen?

Her small table held a bowl containing the rear legs of one of the rabbits, napkin covered and waiting for her breakfast. She had gone to bed so early, it seemed like breakfast time now, so she settled onto a stool and stripped the succulent meat from the bone. Cold, now, but still tender. Breakfast could take care of itself, she decided as she chewed. The pup lay on the bed, chin over paws, waiting for a bite.

Josie drank a cup of water and stripped the last bite from the bone for the dog. Crawling back under the covers, she nestled down and shut her eyes. Asleep in minutes.

The dark globs had been waiting, and again surrounded her. Now they had a voice. A long sounding, whining wail pierced her ears and her screams did not drive them away. More screams and she forced her numb feet and legs that refused to move. They must move. She summoned every ounce of strength, and finally the legs consented to carry her... but where? There was no place to go, so she screamed again. Snarles, growls and barks came out of her own mouth, and she felt a creature attack her face.

She flailed her arms again and they contacted a glob. She pushed it away, and an injured yelp woke her. Flip scurried, whining across the room. NOT AGAIN! But, yes, it was the nightmare again.

Crossing the room and gathering the pup in her arms, she returned to the bed and sat hugging him while he nosed and licked her, apologizing for whatever misdemeanor he had committed. Well, one thing was for sure. She must not go to sleep again, so she sat listening to the wail and whine of the coyote the natives called "song dogs". Tonight, she could do without their singing.

Nodding and jerking herself awake, she spent the night. The crowing of the roosters had never been more welcome. She must get dressed and do... what? She must go... where? She'd think of something.

It finally became seven o'clock. She looked out toward the Corners and saw a soft light filling the window. Miz Carlile was awake and there might be coffee. Slipping into her jacket, she called to the dog and headed north.

It was Saturday, but that was a workday on the prairie if there was something to be done that was pressing. At any rate, there were always animals requiring care, so the Corners was open for business.

Josie's nickel clinked into the collection jar and she helped herself to the steaming bitterness of the coffee. All coffee, this time. No hay or grass seeds.

Pumpkin flavored cookies. She had never heard of them in New York, but here they found a use for everything edible, inventing something tasty and interesting. Spicy, chewy, sweet and... comforting. The cup of coffee warmed and steadied her hands.

The door opened and a man she had seen but did not know walked in and clinked his coin in the jar. Greeting the owner of the Mason jar cash register and nodding in Josie's direction, he commented, "Coyotes settin' it up made a short night's sleep. Could'a done without them varmints."

So the howling had been real, and not something her mind dreamed up. A tiny comfort, actually. At least the black globs had no voice. Silence, except for the sniffing pup that had learned he could often find crumbs of biscuit on the floor, or maybe a raisin that had escaped a cookie. The man left.

"Bad night?" Miz Carlile commented.

Josie nodded. "Couldn't wait for the water to heat to make coffee. Hadn't built a fire in my potbelly yet."

The old woman nodded, her multitude of wrinkles settling in the hollow of her cheeks. "Early coffee drinker like you always finds herself a welcome here. 'Course, you could get yourself a coal oil burner. Makes coffee in no time. Don't keep the little stoves for sale here, but they'd send me out one from Argyle."

"Would you get me one, please?" Josie's voice begged.

The old head under the faded hair nodded, then settled restfully into her collar, closed eyes and she awaited her next customer. Josie drained her cup and eased out the door, the pup wriggling between her legs. Southeast breeze was now from the northwest, bringing some kind of weather. As promised.

* * *

Josie's stove tongs arranged a few cow pats and struck a go-fer match. It was time to take stock of her life as it had been so far. The Blaines tried to anticipate her every need, and she was so grateful. Tears formed in her eyes. She had everything she needed but something was missing. Dad... Mom... She hadn't let herself think on them because she needed all her energy to survive. She had to be strong and hold herself together or she would fly apart. Exploding in all directions. Splinters and shards. More tears.

New York. Friends, and winter fun. Lessons from her tutor. How she missed the lessons. Would he still be teaching when she had to send Josh back east? Would Josh like him as well as she had? Tears streamed, and a weakness came over her, lowering her head down onto her arms. Sobs built up within her, and she pushed them down. They came again, and they were stronger now. Much stronger than she was.

The frightened pup was tugging at her skirt so she lifted him to her lap and wept tears into his shaggy coat as he licked her face, her ears, her hands... whatever he could reach. Racking sobs shook her, strangling her with their depth. Bitterness gagging her! Arms desperately hugged the pup until he yipped from pain.

The cow pats in the potbelly finally caught and spread their warmth into the metal of the expensive stove. Soft heat radiated into the room. Josie's sobs reduced to hiccoughs and snubs and the tears eased away. Wiping her face on her sleeve, she moved closer to the comforting stove.

She poured milk into a small saucepan on the stove and spooned cocoa and honey into a thick mug. One couldn't let self pity take over. One must exercise control. Her father always had control. He thought of everything and took care of everything. As Aunt Nettie had said, Josie was her father's daughter, in every way. Enough of this whimpering.

Vapor arose from the milk and she poured it, stirring, into the mug. Flip watched every move, seeming to access her mood. She sipped the warm liquid and the dog sighed, curling into her lap with chin on paws ready to give her whatever comfort he could. All seemed to be well again, so he closed his eyes.

Duties nagged at Josie, but still she sat... sipping and dreaming. A small tap at the door. Flip jerked up his head, ready for whatever came. Josie alert. Another tapping, more insistent and demanding. Putting the dog on the bed, she went to the door. Surely, one of the children had just gotten the days mixed up, and had come to school.

Opening her door a crack, she peeked out, ready to send the eager scholar home, but she drew back, startled, at what she saw. Tiny, stooped and topped with scraggly smoke-gray hair, decorated by a few strands of deep charcoal. The frisky wind whipped a fringe of loose strands around her face.

Wrinkle upon wrinkle, and set within them were two bright, black eyes, squinting against the wind. Faded dress with a fur shawl above and moccasins strapped to her feet and legs, laced up to the knees. A gnarled hand reached out as if to keep the door from being closed and a crackled but firm voice uttered, "Miss?"

Momentarily speechless, Josie found enough voice to ask, "Can I help you... ma'am?"

Considering that an invitation, the wrinkled hand pushed the door open and stepped inside. The hand pointed a bony finger toward her chest and announced, "I... Gray Owl."

"Uh..." the girl uttered, helplessly.

"I come about black cloud." A hesitation between each word indicated a lack of confidence with the language.

Still the girl stared, wordlessly. Did she say 'black cloud'?

"Black cloud at night... in sleep...?" She seemed begging to be understood. "Scare... fear... try to run...? I say talk for you on cloud. Not to run... Bad thing is run."

Josie drew in a breath. Easy for her to say not to run. She wasn't being chased! And is she talking about my dream? If so, how did she know?

The wrinkled face nodded with assurance. "Good is to stop and do hand? To fight?" She demonstrated with a closed fist punching forward like a prizefighter. "Black cloud full of fears. You... Miss... all alone. That is fear. Things to do... hard things... with... little?" The hand indicated a low height, like a child. "Mind strong but fear makes... forget...to be strong? Make hand kill black cloud of fear. Make go away. Shut eyes and sleep. Fear gone." With a series of firm nods, she concluded, "Need sleep to stay strong. Do things. School things."

The old woman stood by the door. Should Josie offer her something to drink, maybe? What was she supposed to do? Aunt Nettie had never told her of the possibility of sudden visitors who were strangers.

The old woman called Gray Owl began again. "We... trade? I say to you black cloud. You say to me school word. School name...? I want word for 'White Flower'. School name."

The old woman sensed she was not being understood, so she struggled on. "Son," and she lifted her hand tall, "woman..." and the hand swept down as though she had a round belly. Pregnant?

"Woman get boy... son... Want son. Not want girl."

Josie nodded. What was she supposed to do about the problem? Lots of people didn't get what they wanted, but it seemed her son was happy enough, but not his woman.

"Girl, White Flower, get no name. Girl... sister... to boy." The wrinkled head shook with such vigor that more smoke and charcoal hair strands were tossed about. Shoving the loose hair from her face with an impatient hand, she drew in a deep breath and started again.

"White Flower need school name. She not... throw away...? She stay..." The woman pointed to her chest with a bony finger. "You tell school name for White Flower."

Still Josie stared in puzzlement. The old woman edged herself onto a school bench and, pointing to herself, said, "White Flower, NO! Want school name for white flower." She smiled and nodded. "New name for girl, not White Flower."

"You want a name that means White Flower?"

The old face wreathed in smiles and nodded with excitement. "We trade. I tell black cloud. You tell school name."

Still puzzling in her mind, Josie reached for a book she had noticed on the shelf, remembering its subject. Thumbing past the pink roses, the yellow sunflowers and the purple lilacs, she located the snow-white lily in the book meant to teach young children the names of colors.

"White flower like this one?"

Vigorous nods. The bony finger jabbed at the picture of a lily. "You tell school name for... that...?

Somewhat relieved, Josie decided they had made a bit of progress. "The name for that white flower is LILY."

"Lay... Lay..."

With a shake of the head, Josie corrected, "Li – Lee"

"Lilee." Without a further word, the woman stepped out the door. Josie watched her depart around Digby's house and return with a child who was hugging a huge armful of fur. Pushing the child before her, the woman came back in the room.

"Her name Lilee." Pushing the child onto the school bench, she continued, "We trade. Lilee come and use school name. I bring... present...? Gift...? To trade...?" Taking the fur bundle from the child, the woman fluffed it with a shake and, with a flourish, spread it before Josie's feet.

The puzzled Josie stared at the creation before her. It was put together with various shaped patches of fur, seemingly dyed in soft colors of pink, lilac, yellow and green, also the natural tan of the local jack rabbit.

"For feet... by bed. Not...?" She pantomimed a shiver. "By sleep... for feel good?" Nodding with confidence, she restated, "Is trade. You give girl school, I bring... gift?"

"Mrs. Gray Owl, do you mean that you want the girl, Lily, to come to my school?" The woman nodded with understanding. "Where is her father, your son?"

A firm shake of the gray head. "Son will get son. No name girl to be sister. I take girl." The old arms surrounded the girl, leaving no doubt about her feelings toward the child. A crackly but firm voice affirmed, "My girl. Lily not sister. Lily girl, learn to say school words." Grabbing up a book, she moved her fingers along the line of printed words. "She say school words." Then pointing to the picture, she told the small girl, "Lily. You Lily. You say 'my name... Lily'."

With a hesitant smile, the girl looked up toward Josie, the black eyes shining with intelligence. "My name Lily".

Nodding, the old woman continued, "Say more words. I stay with... new mama. I laugh smile and not cry. New mama say school good for girl. More girl here..." With that, her hand patted the bench beside where she sat. Touching each finger of her spread hand, she continued, "Girl... girl... boy... girl... girl. New mama say no sister, be Lily."

During this recitation, the old grandmother nodded deeply and smiled with pride. To Josie she summed up the matter. "Trade good. I bring..." She extended two fingers. "Day... day... I bring."

"Bring her Monday," Josie instructed.

Lily patted the wrinkled hand, nodding. "Monday. I here Monday. I say to new mama, is Monday."

With nods, smiles and waves, the two departed, leaving Josie still puzzled. It was clearly a time to go see Aunt Nettie.

The older woman listened with interest and understanding. "I'm thinking you had a visit from Old Gray Owl who lives back in the timber to the south. Folks say she's a medicine woman, the best there is for a doctor out here. Makes medicine from leaves and such. Her man seems to be gone, but she and a son she named Robert Gray Owl came here, hoping to help him fit in with the people who were taking over their lands.

"It sounds like the son was not happy with the girl when he knew he would have a son, and reduced her to servant status. Grandma must have rescued her and wanted her educated. That makes sense from what I hear of the old woman. Seems like she understood the need to trade for services. Looks like you may have made a friend that may come in handy. I just hope there'll be no trouble from the girl's dad."

Josie sipped the peppermint tea and nibbled cookies. "There's more. When she first came in, she told me not to be afraid of the black cloud, that it was made out of fear and that I could kill it." She continued to explain the entire 'trade'.

Nettie waited. Josie shook her puzzled head, "But, Aunt Nettie, I only had the dream last night and she was at my door hardly before the sun was up. It's spooky. How did she know what I dreamed... let alone what it meant?"

Her aunt was silent, shaking her head slowly. There were some things that just had no answer for the question.

Then later, "Josie, these fears. Tell me about them."

"But I didn't think they were fears. I just thought I had a lot to do. The house fire was no one's fault, just something that happened. Teaching was my choice because I didn't want to let Joshua go away. I just have to do what has to be done." Another cookie did its duty to her nervous appetite.

With a grin, "But, Aunt Nettie, it IS a beautiful bedroom rug. The colors almost look like a sunset sky. I wonder how she did it. Maybe she'll tell me, sometime... or maybe a trade. She understands trading, for a fact. Digby told me the coarse wolf fur on the back is for padding and to keep the cold of a stone or dirt floor from coming through. It's like what they put their babies down on for exercise."

A warm-up for the tea. "I'm wondering how it'll go with Lily and the other kids when she starts classes. She's a bit behind, but I'm thinking she'll hold her own... or grandma will see that she does. She seems to have more English words than her grandma. Wonder where she learned them?"

Aunt Nettie contemplated. "Maybe from her mother. I haven't heard where she came from, or maybe her dad works for someone and needed to learn some English. It seems like grandma is firm about the girl learning. Actually, White Flower would not be an unexpected name for a native girl. And the other girls might just call her "White", the way we tend to shorten names. Indians might not like that."

Heading back home to get on with next week's lesson plans, she stopped in at the Corner. "Got your little coffee stove here. You didn't say order it, but I figgered it was somethin' you'd need, at least next summer when you don't want to heat up your house."

Josie figured the old woman had gone to sleep and forgotten about the stove. Anyway, she knew she would be grateful for its speed, liking coffee the way she did. With Flip skipping joyfully around her, anointing every handy weed and rock, she reached the stone room. The walls were completed and a bridge of rafters rose up to the sky. Like the bones of a massive skeleton.

The neighbor, Brad, had conferred with her as to the roof shape. "Now, you'd save a few nickels by makin' the room peak more flat. Take less dimension lumber. On the other hand, that peak'll give you a space up there for pallet bed if you was to need it. I'll need to know 'afore I order the lumber."

Josie opted for the pointed roof. A fleeting thought passed through her mind that it might make a place for children's activity in bad winter weather. Anyway, the nickels to be saved were not a consideration.

Brad again. "Now there's one other thing. We can have the boards planed, that means smoothed, on both sides or one side or on neither side. One sided, that'd be good if you was to want to leave it rough, but if you was to paint it, it'd be a ragged job and never look good. 'Course, your ceiling, now, that'll show from below, that has to be planed on one side at least."

"Two sides, I think. I'm not sure just what I'll do. I was thinkin' it'd be cottonwood poles until you came, so I'll just take what you think'd be best." That took care of that, and now the rafters, planed silky smooth, lifted themselves high over the new room.

"Quick as I get a roof, I'll have to have the 14-year-old boy in two bodies bring Aunt Nettie down to see the new rug and other stuff. Right now, I don't think she'd be able to squeeze through and between the bed, desk, wardrobes and the new study tables." Josie had black and blue bruises from her knees down from bumping their edges.

* * *

Jefferson Wilson could still hardly believe the sight of the fillies and the little colt. The dream had come true so suddenly, that sometimes he thought he was still dreaming. There was the scar (healed now) where the coyote tried to bring down one of the fillies... Lilac, he remembered. When faced with a need for names, he resorted with a gross lack of imagination to flowers. There was Rosie, Sunflower, Lilac and Daisy, and the frisky little guy was Blizzard. He was white as the snow blowing over the prairie except for the trademark of charcoal on feet and face. He would darken in another year or so to the signature shades Jefferson sought.

Jeff examined the new weapon Josie's uncle Blaine had sent, his fingers caressing the satiny steel of the barrels. "Digby gonna teach you how to use this thing? It'll be different from the snake shooter."

Josie shrugged. "Maybe when the house gets finished. He's got no time, right now."

Young Jeff, never slow mentally when he had something to gain, offered, "You let me keep this here gun out in the barn with me at night and I'll teach you how you have to hold it. You're gonna get a sore arm, anyways, no matter who teaches you."

So Josie got a sore arm, and Jeff had reliable nighttime protection for his charges. He insisted on spending every night in the shed with the young animals, also watching out for his brother's Angus cattle. Mama cows were protective of their babies against varmints, but a wolf pack would be more than even a mean mama Angus could handle. The gun on the premises was just a little extra. And the miniature horses had no protection but him.

A rotting coyote carcass on the fence deterred any further attacks from that score for a time, but Jeff Wilson was taking no chances with his high-dollar investment.

Digby wandered over to see how the fancy horseflesh made it through the first bout of freezing rain to find their red-haired keeper sniffling and sneezing, and a bit red-nosed.

"You keepin' warm out here at night?"

After a hesitation, the boy answered, "Tryin' to."

A long minute passed as Blizzard sniffed and tried to nibble the older man's fingers. Then, "Son, mind takin' advice from an old man?"

Jeff grinned. "Why not? Been doin' it all my life."

Digby pointed to the rear of the covered shed. "If you was to close in that end and make the little fellers stay over there at night, and if you was to build a shelf up over 'em, big enough for a bed, you'd find horseflesh puts off a fair amount'a heat. Loose, like this paddock is with them a'millin' around, all that heat is lost when you could have it come up to your bed. Seein' you don't seem to mind the smell."

Jeff stroked his chin. "Hmmmnm."

"'Nother thing. One of them big furry dogs from your dad's house, if they could spare 'im. Makin' a ladder that the dog could climb, and getting' him up there with you, he'd help with the cold. Speck the dog'd like it, too. Make 'im feel important."

It took a bit of hammering and a few pieces of Josie's lumber but Jeff had no more bouts with the cold and sniffles. Before the winter was out, his brothers also appreciated the perch up out of the wind as they took their turn to "watch" their pair of investments.

Josie liked the fact of her cousins being around most of the time, but Digby was her standby. He insisted on it, attempting to anticipate her needs, also wants, before she did.

Strange how the flat floor stones took twice as long as the upright walls, but they were finally completed. High windows, with the sill about even with her chin and two feet wide. One to the north, one to the south and two across the wider side to the east. Mrs. O'Day requested the pleasure of making the curtains.

The whole west side of the room was attached to the cave room.

The new desk would now be against the south end with the three bench tables lined up in front. Book cases against the north wall leaving space in between for other activities, and to spread lunches in bad weather. Digby had built into the wall, a stone ledge that extended out into the room. Each ledge being the size for a cut-glass oil lamp. A pair... for the one she had and the ones to be ordered later. Actually, he had made three ledges, and Josie had requested two more of the darling lamps.

Small bedroom against the north wall. Two wardrobes, bed with canopy and sunset rug, night stand (containing the snake shooter) and a stool. Perfect. Fancy divider was now free to be used for tacking up training material in the schoolroom. Triangular shaped attic if Josh and Darrel ever wanted to stay over.

Of course, it wasn't there, yet, but Josie could see it all in her mind. Already, rolls of tarpaper were being hoisted onto the peaked roof, and the last of the expensive dimension boards, not cottonwood poles, were being nailed into place. Neighbor Brad and his father had worked together, paying for Tray's education. Josie felt she got the best of that bargain, which had included Janine.

Digby surveyed the overhead work with as much pride as if he had done it himself. So much better than the poles, he said. It was not a job he could have done and he was grateful for the neighbors. His Josie deserved the best, the way she worked so hard.

He had shoveled up persimmon trees and created a windbreak row where he planned to spade up a garden, come spring. The blackberry vines were so close to the house that he decided to leave them where they were. Peach and plum seeds were on a shelf in his room, safe from chewing rodents. He'd soak them for several days before putting them in the ground. It had worked in Colorado, and how could the territory be different?

Thank you, little prairie rattler that had to give up your life so rudely. Without the little reptile... what? A crippled foot was a small price to pay for his current blessings.

It was early Monday that Josie asked the question of Janine. “PICKLES! Do I know about pickles, she says! You find yourself lookin’ at the girl who could’a wrote the recipe book. Where I come from, anything that could be pickled, got pickled. Sour, bitter, salty, sweet, or peppery... I’ve made ‘em all. Jars and jars, settin’ in the cellar. Full of all colors, white, green, yellow and red. You say it and I’ve made it. What’re you wantin’ to pickle?”

Laughing at Janine’s response, Josie managed to say, “Turnips. I get turnips and I don’t know what to do with them. I heard the word but I never saw one until I got here. Digby said maybe you’d know.”

“Law sakes, he was right! Thing is, though, they don’t have to be pickled. They’re sort of a strange thing, and have a right sharp taste some folks never get to like. A lotta folks like ‘em peeled and chopped up with onions, fresh green beans and other raw stuff, sprinkled with vinegar. Some youngens like to eat ‘em out of the garden, like an apple. They last all winter under straw, and can be dug out to make a different taste. Some folks slice and fry ‘em with onions and bacon. Turnip pickles are cut raw with onions and peppers, and covered with boiling hot vinegar and spices and let to set. Fellows mostly like ‘em that way to eat with fried pork and such.” Janine paused for breath.

“Hmmm, well I...”

“What I like best is to leave ‘em in the ground and in early spring rake off the straw. Ground starts to warm, and the turnips sprout up and make tender, light green leaves. Taste a little bit peppery. Good to eat raw or heat in a skillet with bacon grease and sliced onions. You know, I don’t know what I’d’a done without pickles. Come spring, workin’ folks get tired of corn, beans, potatoes and fried meat. Why, I’ve seen women eat mustard with a spoon, tryin’ to take care of a spring appetite. I can’t even keep mustard in the house. A quart don’t last us more’n a week. We even put mustard seeds in a lot of the pickles we make."

She paused and grinned, "'Speck I've been tellin' a bit more'n you ever wanted to know. Next time you get turnips, peel one and taste it and if you can stand it, I'll show you all kind of things to do with it."

That just about took care of the question of turnip pickles. Interesting, anyway.

A timid knock, and the door was pushed open. Old Gray Owl gently pushed Lily through the door and eased it closed afterward. Huge black eyes looked expectantly up toward Josie from a face that seemed to want to smile.

"Good morning, Lily. You can come and sit here beside Tray. Boys and girls who come early get to look at books. Tray, will you select a book for Lily? She's going to study with us."

Josie and Janine watched from the corner of their eyes to see how it went. Tray, after a moment's consideration to digest the trust put on him, selected three books from the shelf. Spreading them before the silent girl, he said, "We got lots'a books. You'll like these."

Sitting beside her on the bench, he opened the book showing a girl with a red cape, carrying a basket. A wolf hid behind a tree. "See that wolf? He's gonna cause trouble." The boy turned the pages, synopsizing the story. As the picture showed the girl nearing a house surrounded by flowers, the little girl jabbed an excited finger at the page. "Lily! White Flower means Lily. That's my school name."

"What's a school name?"

"My name Lily..." she explained.

The puzzled boy frowned and studied the girl beside him. "I ain't got no school name."

Janine had been watching and listening and thought it was time to step in. "Tray, you just don't remember. You have a school name and it's Tray. You have other names, though. Sometimes I call you sweetie pie, or honey, or sometimes meanie, or bad boy. Those are not school names. When you're at school, I just call you Tray."

"Oh," nodding with tentative understanding. "Lily, you can sit by me and I can tell you everything. I've been to school for a long time."

Clearly impressed, Lily smiled and ducked her head shyly. Then began to turn pages of the book. Relieved, the older girls resumed their conversation. Seemingly, all was well.

Josie began, "Well, Janine, a bit of good news. This is the last week we'll be cramped up. Digby wants to put something on the flagstones to make them easier to clean, and it had to be ordered from Argyle. Says it isn't always used because it kind'a costs a lot, but he said you and I had better things to do than clean floors, and what if some kid got sick and upchucked. Euuuuh!"

Janine responded, "I can't imagine how good that'll be to have room. Almost like my house. I never in my life had so much room. I scooted all the fellows into one bedroom, and took the other one just for me. I'm plannin' on sewing new dresses and I hate putting everything away when I'm not workin' on 'em."

"You make your dresses?"

"Yeah. I'm all I got so if I want somethin' new, I gotta make it."

Time to start the day. Josie stood up in the crowded room. "Everyone get seated. Level 3 will help Level 1 to make their letters better. Kristie, will you sit by Lily Gray Owl, and show her how to make marks on the slate. Print her first name at the top and let her copy. Level 2, work the equations on page 37.

"Level 4 girls, move to my bed and we're going to practice the way to make full sentences. You won't need your books. We don't want the others to listen to us and forget to do their work."

Shaggy little Flip considered Josie's bed to be his own special domain. He did not object to the girls, only wanted to join them.

"Girls, you may pet Flip if he insists but if he keeps you from listening to me or thinking what I'm saying, you will leave him alone."

Janine, seeing she was not otherwise needed, opened the last two book boxes and tenderly removed the contents. Examining each one, she made a decision as to the correct reading level, though she knew she was likely making miscalculations. Later, she would have time to examine them more fully.

That afternoon when the children were dismissed, Mrs. Gray Owl appeared at the door, as if by magic. Josie took Lily aside and, using a full sheet of paper, wrote 'LILY GRAY OWL' at the top, and handed the child a black crayon.

"Now, Lily, I want you to use the crayon and practice printing your name. The other children your age have already done this, and I want you to catch up. You've done a very good job today and tomorrow will be even better. Good bye, now."

With a 'thank you' smile, the grandmother shepherded her charge to the door, closing it softly behind her.

Turning to Janine, Josie wondered aloud. "I'd really like to know how much of the day's conversation got through to her. I hardly know how to talk to her and was hoping the other children would do better. Her grandmother is most anxious for her to be here."

Janine nodded. "Yeah, but I'm thinkin' it'll be better than you think. Remember how babies learn to talk so fast, and that little girl is very smart, I'm thinkin'. And brave. She didn't cry, and she let Tray sit by her. There's lots of little girls who'd be scared'a him, the way he moves so fast." Holding the boy's coat, she told him, "Come on, Tray. Let's go make a kettle of soup."

There were, however, even greater problems brewing for small Lily. Much harder to solve than writing her name.

* * *

The paddock just north of Josie's house was alive with snorting, kicking, squealing, and dust rolling as five small animals made their presence known.

Jefferson Wilson, their keeper, had difficulty setting his mind in any other direction. He lived and breathed his small charges... his investment... and he could hardly pull himself away to perform his half-day of duties at his father's house.

His new shelf bedroom built into their shed was more home than his bed at the house up the road, and the smell of the lantern and the light it made were as normal as breathing. He had placed an order for two more lanterns that he planned to station at the corners of the paddock to further discourage any four-legged, fur-bearing nighttime visitors.

The removal of two coyotes and the injuring of another had served to keep them at bay, but the snuffing and growling of a wolf-pack now had him concerned. With snow on the ground and many of their food animals in hibernation, the wolves were feeling hunger. Nothing would satisfy them better than a young and tender filly, Conamara or otherwise. Their territory was on the southern edge of their natural range and large elk and moose were no longer available.

It had been past midnight that the pack passed through the homesteads around Carlile Corners. Their whining and snarling had raised the hackles on more than one domesticated farm animal and cost their human owners a fair amount of sleep. Jeff Wilson was one of them.

Huddled on his shelf bed, wrapped in quilts with boots strapped firmly on, he kept the night watch. The horses were not the only bait drawing the gray-furred hunters. Adjoining the paddock was the barn sheltering the Angus cattle. One difference was that the black calves had vicious and protective mothers, not to say the huge bull, also with wicked horns. It would be a brave wolf that would dare to attack the array of horns presented by a circle of irate bovine specimen. The only thing was, wolves came in packs. Multiple forces.

No such protection of horns for the small horses. Only red-haired Jeff, now sixteen-years-old, fighting sleep and shivers. Armed with Josie's new gun, he felt more confident, but a wolf pack was formidable and no one could be certain how many animals were involved in the snarling and whining. Hardly a group of men were gathered that the subject of the wolves was not discussed.

Jeff's dad worried about his son's safety, but what could a father do when his son insisted on becoming a man with responsibilities? Good shot with a six shooter, he was. That eased dad's fears somewhat. Still....

And Jeff heard the howling... so different from the coyote's wail. The voice of the 'song dog' was conversational, where the wolf's cry always sounded argumentive. Enough to raise fear bumps on the hide of the toughest frontiersman.

The sound in the night brought Jeff instantly awake, gun in hand and eyes searching the darkness for reflecting eyes. The single lantern shed enough light to walk by, but the beams did not extend to the outer fence. Also, a fence hardly existed that would keep out a hungry wolf.

Digby also heard the wolves, and reflex action had him instantly awake and slipping his feet into his trousers before his eyes were clearly open.

The animals circled the corral and the paddock, accessing the strength of their prey. Passing by the threatening 'moo' of the cattle, they returned to the tantalizing aroma from the horse paddock.

Jeff lowered himself from his shelf and peered through the gate of the enclosure containing the young animals. Behind him, Blizzard snorted, squealed and tossed his head with concern. Rosie, Daisy, Sunflower and Lilac squirmed past each other in the close quarters, creating a commotion behind the boy with the gun.

When to shoot? Always the problem. Too soon and miss the target... too late and permit bloodshed... likely his own. The faint light of the lantern shone against the gray fur as its owner leaped the fence. With a menacing victory howl, another animal followed.

NOW! Now or never. Leveling the firearm he aimed as best he could. BANG! His arms trembled as he again attempted to sight against the light of the lantern.

B O O M!!

Jeff startled and jerked back the gun. What had he done!

Then again, B O O M! The sound came from another direction. Jeff gathered his courage and pointed the gun again.

A shout from the darkness. "Hold your fire! I'm coming." The graveled voice of the older man was never more welcome. A few steps more and the man was within the enclosure with Jeff, hugging his shotgun.

"Moved 'em off for a minute, we did. They'll be around agin. You got one and I got one. If we got the leader they may leave here for tonight. We got carcasses, though, and that'll be good. Some say it makes 'em stay away, but I wouldn't count on it for long."

Finally, Jeff had breath enough to utter words. "Did I shoot one... really? This is the first I had to use this gun in the dark, and I didn't think on the lantern light bein' right in the way. Gonna change that."

The two stood silent with their guns, listening. The menacing sound seemed to fade into the distance. Good news.

"Seems we might'a got the leader, and it'll be a day or two 'afore the next one is elected."

"Elected?"

"Yeah, there'll be a few scuffles and maybe a bit of blood till they decide on a new leader. It'll depend partly on the head female, she gets a strong vote 'cause the new leader'll be her mate. Some say the alpha female is the real leader."

"Well, I ain't in no hurry for 'em to decide," the younger man stated, firmly.

Consequently, Jeff ordered two more lanterns and persuaded Josie that she also need a couple of them. Lamps were good inside, but there was nothing like the outdoor lanterns to withstand wind, rain and being bumped around.

* * *

Old Mrs. Gray Owl and her granddaughter had left the school and neared their cabin in the woodland, the girl possessively clutching her paper and crayon. Grandma extended a restraining hand, and they stopped instantly. Someone was at the cabin, sitting on the porch.

Lily watched her grandmother's face. Finger to her lips and a small shake of the head, the older woman pointed to a nearby stone. Lily sat down on the rock, and grandma nodded approval, turned and walked on through the trees.

When she reached her cabin, she stopped. The man said, "I come for White Flower. Her ma needs her."

"She is not here."

"Where?"

"Away. She spend night there."

"Get her."

"No. She is mine. I say."

"Get her. I wait. You go get her."

Gray Owl eyed her son up and down. What had gone wrong with him? She had given him her name, calling him Robert Gray Owl instead of a descriptive native name. It was to help him survive around the new people. But she did not make him stubborn headed and unthinking.

"Go get her. I wait."

Making a fast decision, Gray Owl nodded and turned to go the way she came. Silently entering the woodland, she motioned to the girl to come with her, and the two walked back toward the road, the way they had come. With hardly a word, the two traveled far into the night, finally tapping on the window of another woodland cabin. The door opened for her, and a stooped and gray haired man greeted her. The man waited for her words.

"Trouble. Robert came for Lily."

The man shook his head. "There was trade."

"He changed. Said woman wants her. Woman wants help the son."

The man looked at the girl. She smiled and held up the paper for him to see. The black marks meant nothing to him.

The girl smiled and explained. "School name. Word say Lily. Lily is White Flower."

The man looked at the woman who nodded, and told him. "Lily goes in school."

The man motioned to the floor and the three of them sat on the fur pad. A wrinkled old woman joined them with a basket of fried bread and chunks of roasted meat. Silence, except for quiet chewing. The man sat with a bowed head, obviously thinking.

He nodded. "This is it. Robert like a son to me after his father gone. He listen to me. Or he wish he listen to me."

Gray Owl was not convinced. "Robert stubborn."

"I have plan. He will listen." He motioned for the woman to bring a pallet bed for the visitors. "Then I will go with you." His words were sad and hesitant. It was his duty to help his sister with her fatherless son, but as he agreed, the boy had always been stubborn.

So that was why the old man came to the school the next day with Gray Owl and Lily. Lily carried her paper with every scrap of space filled with her printing.

Old Gray Owl explained. "Miss Teacher. Man wants to see school. My... uh, he son of mother... He brother. See Lily in school."

The old man stationed himself just inside the door and sat silent as a statue, legs crossed and hands folded in his lap for the entire day.

Perhaps his presence might have been more noticeable if there had been room, but in the tightly packed crowd, what was one more body? Except for a couple of brief forays outside, he was silent as a stone. He refused food but accepted a drink of water.

Josie was apprehensive, and Janine was actively nervous, burying herself into the new books and not hazarding a glance toward the wrinkled, fierce looking man with the straggling black tail of hair tied at the back of his neck.

When class was dismissed, the old man stood, took Lily's hand and departed without a glance or a sound. He had spent the day thinking and deciding, and now he had work to do.

Depositing the girl with her grandmother, he disappeared into the trees and walked to his nephew's house. When Robert appeared at the door, the old man began, "I help with cabin. Where to put it?"

"What cabin?"

"Your ma. Son takes care of ma, when she is old. Your duty. Good son will do this for ma. Needs help. You will help."

"No. She needs no help. My woman wants White Flower. Ma won't let her go."

The old man nodded, knowingly. "I bring White Flower Lily and your ma to you. Where we put cabin?"

"No. Just bring White Flower."

"White Flower takes care of ma. Your right to take White Flower. Your duty to take ma. Where we put cabin?"

"No. Just White Flower."

"I say, you take ma. Your duty. I know many men to help me make you do your duty. Only son will care for ma. You are only son. Where we put the cabin for her?"

"What's wrong she needs help?"

"White Flower Lily help her. Good help. Your ma likes White Flower to help. You take her away, ma comes with her. Ma needs her so she can help. My duty to help my sister. She has strong son so I help her tell son she need help. My duty to help son take care of ma. You see? If I cannot help you see, I know tribe men. They help me help you see."

Robert knew when he was beaten and he knew the methods tribal men used to guarantee their traditions continued, and that their elders were cared for by their children.

With a slump of the shoulders, Robert knew it was over and muttered, "Leave White Flower with ma." With that, he turned and disappeared into his cabin.

With as near a smile as the old man ever had, he turned and walked back to his sister's house. To Lily he said, "You will stay with Gray Owl. She need you." The girl listened and spread a wide grin across her face. Hugging the new well-marked up sheet of paper to her chest, she hugged her grandmother. The old brother and sister stared into each other's eyes with a love and a knowing born of many years, and the man turned silently and walked away. Maybe tonight he would get sleep instead of solving problems. But then again, he might occasionally stop into the school to sit and listen. After all, he now had the right because of his responsibility for his sister and her granddaughter. And anywhere they chose to go.

It was, of course, his duty as the oldest male member of the family to attempt to settle family problems. But even so, he would always have attempted to comfort his sister, his childhood playmate, in her difficulties.

At times very wise... his sister. It was she who saw good in the newcomers ways. Tying the same name to family members helped to keep them together. It was difficult for young ones to know their father's father when heroic deeds were attributed to him, and when they did not recognize the name. It was she who had added a newcomer name to her only son.

The name, Robert Gray Owl, had a good sound to the ears, but he, Gray Eagle, had not thought so at the time. He had given the picture name to his own children, but they, in their own time, had seen the value of adding the parent's name, and Johnny Black Bear and his brother, Elmer Black Bear were the result. As was William Running Elk, their cousin.

His nephew, Robert, was hardheaded and stubborn, at times, and was not always a happiness to the family. He was pleased enough with White Flower as his first attempt at children, but when he knew his woman would have a son, he changed. Or maybe his woman changed him. The girl would become a caretaker for the boy to make his life easy. No thought was given to her life because she would sometime belong to some other family.

Robert had chosen a woman of lighter skin, or perhaps the woman had chosen him, for Robert was truly a handsome sight. His woman was heavy minded in her thoughts, and her many words wore away anything that was in her way. The son was what she had wanted. White Flower, named for her lighter skin, had only the picture name until her grandmother had insisted on the change and Gray Owl was added. Lily Gray Owl was the result.

Change was not always bad. Robert's father had been like a stubborn tree, resisting the south wind until it broke him apart. Better to bend before the wind, and live, than to be too strong, and become part of the ground.

Change happened. The newcomers knew that, and they learned

from his people. But the newcomers brought new thoughts that they shared. They brought common words so everyone would know the words of everyone else. Even now small Lily was learning the newcomer words, and she was even learning the way to make word pictures on paper that others could know. It was his duty to see that she had the chance to sit with the small ones of the newcomers and learn from them as they learned from her.

It had taken a day and a night of thinking, but he had finally thought up the plan to give his sister and Lily what they wanted. It also told others that he, Gray Eagle, was still wise and looked up to. Stooped shoulders and gray hair were nothing, if he could pass on his wise thought to his family.

It had been done, now, and his thoughts were at peace so he could return to his woman.

Lily sat on the floor by her grandmother and continued her work. 1 2 3 4 5 again and again, her numbers becoming more and more neatly shaped. When the page was full, she and the old woman sat and ate their bread and soup made with tender squirrel meat and vegetables. Together they talked using only the "school" words they knew, refusing to use any of the other words that they knew that were not school words. It was a day to learn new sounds and leave the others behind. It was a gift to be given to Lily by the elders of her family.

* * *

It was after school on a Friday that Digby had banished Josie from her house because of the covering to be spread on flagstones of the floor. It had a smell... one that could make eyes sting and thoughts blurry, and he could not risk damage to his Josie so he sent her away.

Several times he had to put a cover on the can of liquid and step out into the air to clear his own head. He had told Josie she must sleep at her uncle's house tonight, and possible tomorrow night. He would let her know. Part of that was because he did not know if he would have to coat the floor twice to get the effect he wanted, but he wanted to do the best job while he was at it.

Spreading with his brush gave him reason to admire his handiwork. He had never, actually, done anything just like this, but his mind had told him it was possible. The flagstones, naturally flat, had been scraped and filed with a steel rasp, and they were carefully chipped to fit as closely together as the bark on a tree. The small cracks between some of the stones were packed full of sliver chips and stone dust, and now the smelly liquid was binding the stones and the dust into a flat, shiny surface that would be easy to clean. He was so pleased, he thought he might give his own room the same treatment.

The forced overnight visit to her uncle's house gave Josie time to chat with her aunt. It was amazing how much the ladies of the community, who had almost no time to visit, knew everything that went on.

The incident with Gray Owl provided a lot of conversation. It seemed that most of the community had occasion to go to the old woman for cures for this and that. They knew her 'man' had been killed in one of the many skirmishes that had occurred before and during the time of the land run, but that the woman had still brought her son here and built a cabin in the woods as close to the newcomers as she could. It was anyone's guess who actually now owned the land under her house, but apparently her cabin was not a problem to the current owner, if he even knew of her presence. In later years it would change, but likely not during the life of the woman.

It was said that her son had occasionally caused minor trouble, and the children were warned to stay clear of 'that Robert fellow'. Now the little daughter of 'that Robert' sat in a classroom being taught by an eastern newcomer with the education that would be the envy of most of the men in the territory. It made one scratch his head and think of how things worked out.

The thing concerning her aunt and uncle was that Lily's father could cause trouble for Josie, though the old woman had promised that the problem was taken care of. The older relatives had further reason to be glad of old Digby and his appearance at that particular time. Another head scratcher about the way things worked.

Also the Scottish girl, Janine, showing up to fill a need they hadn't known they had. And the brother who could fix just about anything. And him a blacksmith! Every community needed a skilled smithy and in a few years there'd be more work than he could handle alone.

As it turned out, Josie spent two nights away from her home, and was almost homesick to be back. She had brought her dog with her, of course, and he had consented to bed down in a box beside her. If, in later hours of the night, he might have decided to leap companionably in beside her, who would be the wiser in a bed that was already crowded? He could always be pushed out when the first rooster crowed.

At the breakfast table, she confided, "I have a problem to decide on. I know I was the one who wanted to keep Joshua with me here, but I know my dad had no idea what was going to happen to us. I find myself wondering if I'm teaching Josh everything he needs to know to qualify for the higher classes when he goes east. I'm just thinking I should order the books from the school there, and maybe I can tell what I might be missing. I hate it when I don't know what I'm doing."

"Well, Josie darling," her aunt began, "you're not alone. Most everything we've done in the last few years was something we did not know about. Sometimes the neighbors knew, and sometimes we figured it out together."

Joshua, who had just turned nine, stared into his plate at the chopped up hotcake swimming in honey. Somehow the conversation had taken a turn for the worse, and it seemed that it would affect him. As a teacher, she was bossy enough, checking everything he did and telling him where he was wrong. Something about it seemed not quite right. A sister for a teacher... for goodness sake!

None of the other students had a sister who ruled over them... except, of course, there was Tray.

Darrel, almost nine, chewed in silence, casting an apprehensive glance in his cousin's direction. There was reason for concern. Whatever befell Josh seemed to have a fallout in his direction. Cousin Josie was almost like another mother who could boss him around, making him do what she said.

The boys were certain they had spent enough time with their elbows on the table and a book open. They didn't need something else to keep them from having fun.

Uncle Matthew pushed back his plate and nodded his head. That niece of theirs always seemed to be one step ahead of a problem. It had not occurred to him that Josie's teaching could possibly be deficient in any way. All he heard was praise of her, but, of course, that praise came from men who had hardly learned to read and write.

Yes, it would be good to know if there was something else to know. They had already discussed that the boys would be together in whatever they did. Josh had lost enough and it would not do to separate him from his new 'brother'. Darrel, the youngest boy in a busy family had the short end of the stick as well.

"You're thinkin' there'd be a way to keep the boys caught up?"

Josh heard the word, boys, and cheered up slightly. He would not be alone. Darrell heard the same word and bowed his head lower into his plate. His fate was evidently already sealed.

Josie again. "Just thinking. Maybe Uncle Blaine would have thoughts about it, and maybe help me if he knew what I was thinking. He knows my dad wanted Josh to be like him. Or maybe, at least, to have a choice on what to do. I'm thinking I'll send a letter. At least by next summer I should have answers or information."

At the words "next summer" the boys locked their glances. They smiled slightly, kicked each other meaningfully under the table, shoveled the last of the hotcakes into their mouths and grabbed a crisp slice of bacon from the almost empty plate. Like the whirling wisp of a prairie 'dirt devil' they disappeared through the door.

Next summer was a lifetime away. There was too much snow right now to have to gather cow pats, and knocking down hay into the mangers was a fun job. If they could just stay out of sight after that, maybe the grownups would forget about them.

Flip, sensing from the quieter sounds, that the people had finished eating, bumped his nose against Josie's leg as a gentle reminder that someone had not yet been fed. A leftover hotcake dredged in the grease in the bacon dish was more than he had expected. After gobbling it down, he dashed off in search of the two boys.

Aunt Nettie grinned and winked at Josie. "I think our boys were hoping not to be noticed and put to work. I'd already decided to let 'em off today. We get little enough of good snow out here in the territory that a day of play would help to give 'em memories. They'll have even more fun with that little dog to follow 'em."

On Sunday, Josie was permitted to return home. While she was gone, neighbor Bradley Cullen had passed by and been engulfed by the vile smell. Thinking there might be trouble, which was actually what he told himself, he decided to check it out. He found the door open, and stepped in just in time to face Digby stepping out.

"Got 'er finished up and the girl can come home quick as the smell dies down. Step inside and see how you like it." Smell arose from the shiny flagstones like a solid wall, but holding their noses the two men surveyed the new room.

Brad clicked his tongue in appreciative admiration. "That sure is one good lookin' piece'a work. Floor purty as a picture. Girl that lives here is purty as a picture, too," he added with a grin.

Digby frowned in his direction. "Ain't hardly more'n a girl, and that's a fact. Stays busy enough for two girls, though."

Brad nodded. "Yeah, and that's all our Janine talks about. That school excites her more'n a dozen new dresses would. She can't stop talkin' about all the books they have, and how Josie plans on gettin' more. Though where she'll put 'em is more'n I can figger."

Digby shrugged away the thought. "She'll find a way. Girl like her, she don't hardly need no help. Works herself down to a cob and don't hardly want to fix food to eat." He paused, thinking. "Good thing I know about plain cookin', and all. She's good with eatin' roast rabbit or squirrel dumplin's, things as I can make. Folks're good to bring anything they think she'll like. Seems they enjoy doin' things for her."

Brad agreed. "Yeah, and I sure know I do. And I'm just standin' here thinkin' on something else. This here skinny little door 'tween the cave room and that shiny floor... its sort'a trashy lookin' now, don't ya think? All that new stuff from back east and that smooth floor, sort'a shows up the messed up door." He paused and glanced at the older man.

Digby, not a great one for appearances, focused on the door and the new floor. Even he was forced to agree.

"Thinkin' a bit here," the younger man continued. "If I was to take out that door and cut back on each side to make a wide space... with youngens runnin' back and forth... ? What'd ya think?"

Digby nodded. "Have to check with Miss Josie, 'course. Could be she'd like that. I'm thinking she'll want that fancy potbelly in the school room, but that'd be for her to decide."

Brad nodded, but he had already made up his mind, widened the door and let his sister think of a drape of something or other as a closure. It wouldn't do to have a couple of swinging doors for youngens to bump into, or for boys to swing on.

He did comment, however, "I'm figgerin' on sayin' somethin' about that when I come to spread paint on that ceilin'." The fact that Josie had said nothing about painting to be done to the planed boards of the ceiling had nothing to do with his plans. Besides, what else did he have to do?

Digby trained serious eyes on the ambitious young man. “You’d be knowin’, a ’course, that girl’s only seventeen.”

“Yeah, I know”, he responded, but added, cheerfully, “Almost eighteen, though.”

The older man stared at him, meaningfully, with hooded eyes that almost appeared to be a warning... or almost a threat. Turning toward the door, “Speck we’d better step out and get some air, else there’s no guessin’ what all we’d say that didn’t need being said.”

Home

It was Sunday afternoon that Josie had permission to come home as the smell was finally almost gone. It was handy that the cousins were tending their livestock just when there was heavy furniture to be moved. Interesting, too, that Bradley Cullen also just happened to be passing by, and was drafted to help.

Josie's heart pounded dangerously as she directed the placement of her desk (southeast corner – bringing window light over left shoulder) and the bench tables (slanting to the southeast so there would be no backs totally toward her).

The fancy Sutter marriage bed would be east of the outside door of her bedroom (there had to be an outside door, according to Digby, as the high window would be too difficult to exit in case of fire. When asked if rocks could burn, he chose to ignore the question). The two wardrobes were a bit of a squeeze, but they made it. Nightstand (with snake shooter) and slipper stool (placed firmly on the edge of the furry sunset rug).

Bookshelves lined against the north wall. Bradley noted with pleasure that the shelves were practically full, so there would surely be a need for more bookcases. (He'd need crating to make sure they matched).

Josie, herself, placed the cut-glass oil lamps on the three stone ledges designed for them, taking extra care not to drop them due to the nervous, excited tremble of her hands. Space. A way to move about without bumping anyone. Unbelieveable luxury! Standing in the cave room, she thought she detected a faint echo from the extra space. (Likely just her imagination.)

It would now be possible to open the pantry door without moving the table. The small cabinet could be slid just a little to get it away from the fireplace and make a bit of room for the sturdy cow pat basket woven for her by Mrs. Gray Owl. Such a riches of space!

Matt Jr. and Douglas returned to their duties, while Jeff and Bradley leaned against the wall watching Josie go from one item of furniture to another, patting them with satisfaction. A wink and a small smile passed between them as they shared the pleasure of watching the happiness of another, while the pup sniffed everything thoroughly and finally gave his approval.

Then Jeff returned to his galloping herd and Brad shuffled his reluctant way home. "Gonna be a lot'a blank space in the classroom. Seems like everything fits like a glove," he informed his sister.

"How'd you know so much?" she retorted.

"Helped with the movin' in, that's why."

"How come ya to be right there at hand?"

"Aw, just passin' by. Saw it goin' on... Bein' neighborly, that's all."

Janine turned her face toward him, not hiding her mischievous smirk. "Yeah, I believe that, and a few other impossible things!"

While he thought on a plausible response, she continued. "I'm be willin' to say you noticed she'll need more bookcases. Bet you're thinkin' she'll order somethin' that'll give you more packin' boards that match."

Brad lifted his chin and stated, "'Speck some folks are smarter than they oughtta be, too. Likely got a smashed nose from puttin' it other folk's business." With that he departed the kitchen, slamming the door behind him.

Janine grinned at the closed door. It had been easy to see the looks that girls had begun turning toward her brother, so it was clearly amusing to see the same look on his face, for a change, and Josie seeming to give it no notice. This could turn out to be lots of fun to watch!

It seemed rather strange to Josie to slip into a bed that had a proper room and was not so close to the eating table that she could touch it. The polished wood of the wardrobes blended with the colors in the stone of her north wall. The door needed paint, also did the south wall and the ceilings but that was a concern for later.

She slid closed the bolt lock on her north door as Digby had instructed (who would there be wanting to come in?) and blew out the candle. Flip stared at the new arrangement, seemed to approve, and leaped into his place.

And that was the night the black clouds returned. Charcoal lumps of moving non-substances. Rolling wads of...? What was it she should remember? Some one had... said...? There seemed to be an answer somewhere. Fists... ? Punching... ? Don't run!

Turning toward the dark mass, she doubled her fist. The sight of her tightly closed fingers seemed so inadequate against the mass of black. Fight. That was what she needed to do. Drawing back her arm she shot it forward with all her strength. Right through the blackness it jabbed and gave contact to something. The something moved!

Then a howl and a yip and the pup scampered off the bed and back to the cave room and safety... but there was no longer a bed to leap on, or to scuttle under. Pointing his stubby nose toward the stone-ledge ceiling, he expressed his fear and anguish in an agonized howl of echoing intensity.

Josie sat bolt upright at the sound and realized instantly what had happened. Well, one thing was for sure. The black cloud of fear was gone from her, but apparently not from the dog. Reaching her way in the dark, she felt around for the furry animal, finally locating him by his terrified yip.

Gathering him in her arms, she worked her way back to the bed and under the covers, shivering from her head to her icy feet. Hugging and talking softly she finally had her bed partner trembling only slightly and trying to lick her face.

Eventually, a small smile worked its way to her lips as she thought perhaps what happened was likely not what even Gray Owl would have expected, but it worked. At least for now. But, as it happened, the fear cloud had actually departed forever. From now on she would let herself deal with her pain of loneliness and inadequacy in the daylight. Pain could be dealt with when it was seen for what it was. As Aunt Nettie had said, it happened at sometime to everyone who ever did anything.

* * *

On Monday, the children began to filter in, wide eyed and excited. Raymond, for want of suitable ways of expression, took a playful punch at Jacob, who stomped on the toe of his heavy lace-up Brogans, ordered in from the Montgomery Ward Catalog. While Raymond hopped off, laughing and holding up his injured foot, Tray leaped out of the way and onto the bench of the nearest study table. With eyes sparkling with mischief, Isaac took a shove at Raymond, sending him reeling toward Tray, who hopped on up to the tabletop to escape.

Failing to keep his balance, arms flailing, the six-year-old miss-stepped and slipped from the table, bypassing the attached bench and slithering down to the floor... but not before his chin took an audible crack on the board seat of the bench.

Silence everywhere. Stares at the small boy under the table as he moved his lips hesitantly and spit out a mouthful of blood onto the bench. Two small white pebble-looking objects were visible in the spreading stain. As the blood moved itself over the board, the white objects turned unmistakably into teeth.

Tray wallered his tongue around in the new roomy part of his mouth and spit another glob of blood.

Staring wide eyed and open mouthed, Lily gave vent to a scream, and throwing herself under the bench, scooted toward her hero and looped her arms around his neck. His sister, Janine, who was accustomed to emergencies caused by her active charge, had grabbed up a towel, determined to stanch the crimson flow before it descended into the precious stone floor.

Lily loosed one arm from the neck of the boy to lift a hand and pat him lovingly on the cheek. The injured victim looked around at his audience and produced a wide grin, giving a view of the blank and bloody space just under his upper lip. Such an audience! It was truly one of the best days he had ever experienced, and there was more to come.

After his sister swabbed up the crimson pond, she turned the cloth to a clean spot proceeding to clean his face, whereupon he thrust out his tongue, itself dripping more blood. Plain to see was the chunk of tongue that had been loosened by the teeth that had remained stuck in his mouth.

As the boy savored the full attention of a roomful of his peers, his sister crammed a corner of the wadded towel into his mouth, and seizing one arm, pulled him from under the table, Lily still attached to his neck.

With a firm grasp born of experience, Janine withdrew the little girl and sat her on the bench, whispering words in her ear. Only those very close heard the words, “Thank You”. Pulling the boy by the attached arm, she stepped through the door.

Carmelita, age 12 and also being a veteran at handling crises, grabbed up the jug of drinking water and followed. All messes eventually required water.

Josie finally found her voice. “Children, you know how to find your seats. We’ll be storing our lunch buckets on the bookcases for now, and you will go, one at a time, starting with Level Four girls. Rosalie, you may go first.”

In due time, the rescuers and the injured returned. Tray smiled broadly before he noted the difficulty of speaking clearly without his two front teeth. The teeth were not totally lost, however, because in an amazing trick of eye and hand, the small white objects appeared on the left palm of Lily. With great dignity and aplomb, she handed them to her hero, who bestowed them to his shirt pocket.

Josie drew in a deep breath and let it out. "Level One will follow Miss Janine outside to see the white ponies. They're having fun in the snow. Everyone wear your coats."

A shuffle and a door slam, and quiet reined. "Level Two go across the room and sit in front of the bookcases to have a number drill. The rest of you busy yourself for a while."

Order was restored. Level Four girls were folded over their slates, competing in a friendly way, rechecking the accuracy of their assignment. Even while calling numbers to the seven year olds, Josie smiled to herself at the idea that had passed through her mind.

Her small round table! If she had another stool to add to her three, she could set the bigger girls to work in the quiet, and almost empty room at a seating arrangement more suited to their size. Except when they were required to assist younger ones, they could be honored to have that special place at the small round, full-height adult table.

Her pride in the four girls, aged only ten, eleven and twelve, manifested itself in an array of bumps up and down her arm. (Were fear bumps and pride bumps just alike?) No matter how much work she gave the girls, it was always finished to the extent of their ability.

She made herself remember what these girls did at home on weekends and before school, and the sacrifice to their family for them to even get to come. There was the time that Francine, age ten, had brought the sack of socks, yarn and darning egg, proceeding to mend the holes in the heels and toes of the family socks. So many times she had done that in her short life, now her fingers knew what to do without even a glance. Eyes trained on her teacher, the socks became whole again.

Janine had brought her charges back and settled them at their tables. On a slate, she drew a very large "Z". "All right, fellows and ladies, let's see if we can think of a "Z" sound in any word. Remember, we'll have to be careful to remember the "S" sounds. Sometimes they sound like "Z". I'll start you out. When you have pancakes, you can drizzle honey on them. Do you hear the "Z". Can you think of a word? Let's try to think of five words with "Z" sound."

Small tongues pushed against teeth testing the sound, all except Tray. They sounded like small bees on a flower bush.

Bettina's hand went up. "Buzz?"

"Very good, Bettina. Who's next?"

"Fuzz?"

"Good! Let's have two more."

"Da... dozen?"

"Very good! Now one more."

Silence. Young minds searched their limited knowledge. Then Tray's hand shot up, as Lily gazed at him with admiration.

"Yes, Tray..."

"Sipper."

Isaac's hand waved like a flag. "That sounds like "S"

"No!" Tray shouted. "See...?" His fingers pumped up and down on the metal closure of his new jacket. "My jacket has a sipper that goes up and down!"

At a smile and chuckle from Janine, they felt free to laugh loudly, as Janine reminded them, "If it hasn't happened to you yet, it will. When your front teeth are gone, some words don't sound the same. David, what was Tray trying to say?"

David ducked his head and giggled, muttering, "Zipper!"

* * *

The day passed and Brad just happened to be passing by as the students scattered like a flock of starlings. As Janine gathered lunch pail and boots, she suggested, "Brad, go look at the stools at the table. We got four girls and three stools, and we need a quiet place where they can study. You got the kind'a boards you need?"

Lifting a ruler from his pocket, he took a few measurements. Then the three left, heading south to the Cullen house. Ahead, down the road were two small figures bundled in fur. Miz Gray Owl proudly shepherding her student home, and Lily protecting the slate and chalk under her fur coat. She was aware that the others in her class knew more than she did, but she also knew that she would take care of that.

* * *

It was four days later that a fourth stool appeared to complete the set. It was that day that another object also appeared. A long, flat board with a row of hooks extending below was attached to the wall between the rooms.

"A place for the lunches away from the dog so they don't have to be put on the book cases. Hooks for their coats below."

Josie nodded slowly... impressed that before she realized a need, it was filled.

Brad had more to say. "You know, bein' me, I'd take off this door 'tween the two rooms and make the opening a lot wider. You could have a fancy quilt or somethin' hangin' here, if you wanted. Be a lot quieter than a slammin' door and you could see the girls at the table, then." He paused. "What ya say? I got a little job startin' next week, but I could have this out for you by then."

And he did.

Later he brought a bucket of wooden blocks, sanded smooth. "Scrap ends. Worth nothin'. Thought they'd work like the rocks for addin'." Also with the blocks were four thin sticks, one foot long with inches marked. "Could be, you'd find a use for 'em."

And, could be, she did.

When the children were out for Christmas holiday, the ceiling and the bedroom partition became painted. Sky blue. Bucket of paint ordered out of Oklahoma City.

Digby was attempting to dig a channel for the pipe to bring water near the house, and Brad grabbed a shovel and helped. A hand pump appeared, and she had water just outside the door.

After the next snowstorm, a shiny, shellacked quilt chest appeared. Josie placed it in the northeast corner of the classroom with a cushion on it, giving it a second duty as a quiet place for someone wanting to read.

Janine watched with interest as thing after thing appeared... things that Josie had not requested. She forced herself to hide the small smile. It would have been easy for her to tell him it would save time if he would speak up, so the object of his attention could either smile at him occasionally, or tell him to get lost. Either way would make his life less painful.

She could have told him but she would not. It was much more fun seeing him to go through what he had put certain young ladies through. Janine, herself, knew that Josie, the object of his interest, had neither pleasure or pain from his attention and gifts. She was bent on attacking, with singleness of purpose and total tunnel vision, what she thought was her duty. Not knowing whether her efforts were adequate. Worrying that her brother would not have the same advantages as she, and the fault would... somehow... be hers.

Janine, more adult than expected for sixteen, knew that time would even it out. In the meantime, her brother provided her with a certain amusement. One took amusement where they could.

Taking shovel to her kitchen garden, she pushed aside heaps of straw over the turnip row. Fresh turnips fried with onions and bacon sounded good with the three rabbits that had the misfortune to cross the yard in daylight.

Remembering Josie's question about the turnips that were

brought to her, and homemade pickles, she sliced a pint Mason jar full of the crisp, white vegetable interspersed with onion, and filled the jar with boiling spiced vinegar. Sealing with a tight lid, she set it aside. A week should be enough time.

* * *

Old Gray Owl spent hours observing the children of the newcomers. She was determined that her Lily should fit in. With her almost invisible stitches, she had put together colorful dresses made from fabric purchased at Argyle. She was not, however, happy with the result.

Speaking to Josie, she asked. “How to make dress look good, with puffs on the arm.”

Puzzled, Josie asked, “Puffs...?”

“Arm holes. Like...” and she smoothed her gnarled hand around the delicate shoulder of her Lily, patting and caressing and shaking her head. “How is the puffs...” With her other hand, she patted the gathers where Josie’s sleeve was set in.

“You need to... ? I don’t understand. Lily’s dress is very pretty.” It had a style all its own. Being cut flat like a dress for a paper doll, it molded softly to the slight frame of the girl, slender as a cattail reed. Miz Gray Owl frowned and shook her head with dismay. “How is arm to be puffy?”

Janine, skilled at listening two ways, left her list of books and came. “Josie, I think she wants to know how to put in a sleeve with gathers. Lily’s dress is perfect for little girls, but later... when they get a shape... ?”

Old Gray Owl stared at Janine, eyes twinkling and head nodding. Jabbing her finger against her chest, “I need... help?”

“Sure, I can help you. I’ve been making small patterns bigger all my life. If you bring the fabric,” and she fingered the checked cotton of her own dress, “and some paper if you can, I can make you a pattern.”

"Pattern... You can help me do... puffs?"

The dark haired girl smiled. "Puffs are called gathers. It's easy. You can do it."

Gray Owl picked up Janine's hand and patted her face against it. "I'll learn. Easy, no. I'll learn hard." Nodding rapidly, she let herself out the door and disappeared.

Josie grinned and shrugged. "Looks like you have yourself a job."

"Yeah, imagine not knowing how to put in a sleeve."

"I can't."

Janine stared with interest, and nodded. "Yeah, and I can't do all that figurin' and plannin' you do, and I don't have to worry about what my little brother learns in school. His daddy and big brother are thrilled about what he's doing. And you're scared spitless yours ain't doin' enough. I'd rather be me... most times."

* * *

It had been over a month since she had written Mr. Blaine for information. Since that time she had received the stockings and underwear and softening lotion she had asked for, and now looked forward to the new books the book supplier had promised.

She had about decided Uncle Blaine was not going to tell her what she asked when she got a fat letter in a fat, brown envelope that appeared at her mail hook at the Corner. The return address made her catch her breath and have fear her heart had stopped. BARNABAS MASTERBY

Her New York tutor! Her friend of a large part of her life. She had spent most of the last four years with him, leaving books behind and doing the fun exercises he dreamed up. Her fingers trembled so violently she could not lift the flap. Fumbling the pack into her bag, she let herself out the door of the little shop, completely forgetting the bar of lye soap she had come for.

Her feet hardly touched the ground, and she forced herself to remember to breathe. Why had he written to her? Putting the packet on her table, she removed her coat, poked up the fire in the potbelly and filled the water jug from the pump. Setting her small kettle on the potbelly, and adding cocoa and honey to her mug, she watched the water until it arose in steam. Stirring the hot drink, she set it on the small table.

Josie, you can do it. Just pick it up and see what it says. Don't be such a ditz. Just reach out and pick it up.

Taking a deep breath and letting it out slowly. Seating herself on a stool she took a calming sip from the cup. Slitting the flap, she removed the sheaf of papers.

Dear Josephine,

I'm so glad to hear about you. I've wondered how things were going. I've spent the last year in the old country, attending school myself. Didn't learn a great lot, but now I can charge more for what I do know!

Your father's partner forwarded me the letter with your request, thinking I could advise you better than he. Possibly he's right, considering the time you and I spent together. I feel that I knew your father very well, and felt sorely what a loss it was to his children and to the world that he was taken so young.

Your father was an unusual man. I had tutored a number of young men, but never a young woman. I had mostly prepared the young men to learn at whatever they were designed for. Some learned well, and others just did what they could.

Your father was different from their fathers. I would not have agreed to accept an 8 year old girl if he had been the usual sort of man. He had an idea of exactly what he wanted done for you, and he made it VERY clear to me. I'll admit, it made me curious as to what could be done and I was eager to try.

He did not want you given the reasons why you should learn a certain thing. He wanted you to DO a thing, and analyze why and how you did it, and what it did to you to make you different than you were before you did it. He did not want you to be given a problem. He wanted you to be challenged to find a problem and solve it, then analyze the steps you took. He wanted you to determine, within yourself, if you had proceeded efficiently, and done what you had set out to do... or if you would do it differently if you had a similar situation before you. Are you following me so far?

I did not explain this to you before, because you were too young to understand, did not need to know and would have been too concerned that he would be displeased with you if you didn't do as he would have done. He never asked that you be taught the RIGHT way to do anything. He wanted only for you to do what YOU thought needed to be done, be willing to accept the outcome, and that you could have a bit of fun at it.

We talked many times, your father and I, during the several years we worked together. Not at any time was he less than pleased with the report and with the way you were maturing. I can tell you this, now, because I believe you can understand everything I say due to what you have been through. I feel certain, after talking with Mr. Blaine, that your father would be very happy with the way you've taken care of yourself and planned for your brother. I agree that the cousin should be kept with your brother as long as they understand each other and have no serious disagreements. Family is a good thing to have.

Now, about what you wanted to know. I know Sharon is sending you a set of the required books, one through five, though I think you'll find very little good in them. They may serve to reassure you that what you're doing is the best thing for the boys just now. Also, attending your school with neighbors may also be good, as that is surely where he will choose to spend his life. It will help him know how the frontier people think, which will be different from New York, as I'm sure you now know.

What I will say, though, is that there is a lot you can do, and much of it is what I learned working with you. I wouldn't advise spending time on such things as book equations... that is what he'll learn when he comes here at age 12 or so. When he comes, I will be glad to work with Mr. Blaine to find the best place for his board and assist with his training, so the boys, both, will have the best access to facts and algorithms. Here's what I would advise to you, if you can find the time in your busy life.

Actually it might be easier and more interesting for the both of them, letting them work together for a common answer. I feel that you would have enjoyed a fellow student, but that is not how things worked out for you.

I would begin with simple things to give the boys a pattern of success, a history of finding a solution.

Avoid frustration. It just takes energy that is better used in succeeding.

Have them measure around the wheel of a wagon and ride to a place where you know the mileage. You can mark one spoke of the wheel so they can count the revolutions. They may need to walk beside the vehicle to count revolutions, and a bit of weariness has never hurt anyone!

Use common things they see around them. Check the limbs on a tree to see if there are more (or less) on the windward side. Take them to a hardware store with list of items to find and price. Let them determine what could be done with the tools they priced, and the value of the item made. Is the item produced with the tool worth the price of the tool and the time spent using it? But if a dozen different items could be made from the same tool, what should be the price, then? Could they devise ANY tool that would do better than one they priced, and NEVER tell them they are wrong. If they actually ARE wrong, let it go, and come back to it later.

Take them to well drilling equipment to see the effect of the pound-feet of the spudder as it falls. Learn sun/shadow volume as you did. Assign each boy to make a situation to be solved by the other one, and then work together on them. If they succeed, let them explain on paper. If they fail, do they have a better way? Put away the problems and let them try again, later... or use the symbols of their own problems and devise one in which they can succeed.

Summer will be a good time, if it works out that way at their house. This activity should never take the place of work assigned by the other boy's father. Knowing the way your mind works, problem/solutions will come to you in your sleep. I am CERTAIN you will KNOW exactly what will be best for them. The age eight to twelve is ideal for them to create a history of success so they can plunge with confidence into the prep school. At sixteen they will be well ready to be placed in a legal office (or possible a place of merchandise) to observe and learn what can often be more valuable than classroom instruction.

You may likely wish to place them in Oklahoma City, near where they will spend their lives. I don't see them wanting to stay in New York, away from family. When the time comes, you will KNOW what to do, so I don't want you thinking about it now. I'm only mentioning it now to relieve you of worry. You have NOTHING to worry about, because you have your own HISTORY OF SUCCESS. Don't be concerned about what your father would have done... he is not here and you are. He did, however, wish to make certain you would be capable of succeeding in your world.

I'm going to sign off now, with just one other thing. You learned from me, but I also learned a lot from you that will make me a better tutor. But now, you must plan to HAVE SOME FUN! That is what I KNOW your father wanted. He told me so. Make her learning fun... he told me, and I hoped I had succeeded.

Now, you have my address, or your Uncle Blaine will be able to find me if there is something I can do or say that will help you. And first of all, HAVE SOME FUN!

Thoughtfully yours,

Barnabas Masterby, Ph.D

New York City, New York

Once... twice... She read slowly the second time. Prepared herself another cup of warming drink and began again. Yes, there was one last assignment from her tutor. A message from her father. Have some fun.

How does one decide to have fun? Shouldn't that be something that just happens? Seemingly not. Well, she'd just have to set her mind to it.

When the other package arrived from New York, it was evident that Uncle Blaine knew what he was talking about. The books seemed to be based on the curriculum she already used. Still, something might be gained, she decided as she set them aside for later.

Small note from Sharon:

I raised your domino order up to 15 sets because they sounded like such fun, and they now have colored spots! Then the supplier (the one who sent the extra books) advised that they came in packs of two dozen for practically the same price. So you're getting 24 sets! Oh, well....

Josie smiled as she examined the blocks. Sure enough, the ones were white, twos were blue and threes were green... and so on. Josie wasn't sure that was a plus over having all the numbers white, but that is what she got. (She thought of this again when Tray insisted that white and yellow equaled red.)

They did, however, have great fun using them as building blocks.

So, to start having fun... Being with Janine... did that count? A quiet meal with Digby, that he had cooked for her after she had completed an exhausting day... what about that? Probably not fun, actually. Fun should make people laugh, shouldn't it? Maybe tell jokes with friends... ?

It was clearly a question for tomorrow, as she had lesson plans to create this evening. And tomorrow was another day.

Janine came to school early carrying a wrapped package and a jar of something white... maybe tan. In addition to her neatly cared for dress and coat, she wore a bright smile.

Depositing the package on a study table, she brought the jar to the round kitchen table. Opening it, she jabbed a fork into a slice of something and handed it to Josie. "You asked about turnips, and wondered about pickles. Well, here's your answer. Take a small bite at first. It's got kind of a wake-up taste."

Josie eyed the gift apprehensively and sniffed, drawing back in surprise at the sharp and spicy aroma. Touched it with her tongue, then took a nibble. Serious expression. Larger nibble and a bit of chewing. Suddenly, an open-mouthed gasp and widened eyes.

Janine, grinning, "Has a bit of a bite, huh? I didn't put in as many spices as I would for my fellows. I was thinkin' it might just crack your New York head wide open, and then how would I explain that to your brother?"

Josie, nodding, inserted the rest of the slice carefully into her mouth. "You know, I'm thinking vegetable pickles could have a place. You mentioned the winter hunger that happens even with a full stomach and I'm thinking I might be getting it. Is this jar for me?"

Janine nodded, pleased beyond her best expectations. "I promise, if you like that, I can introduce you to another world of taste. Peppered okra pods, maybe, or there's the sweet/sour three bean salad that's put together with whipped sour cream. That was one of the last things my mom made for me so I would learn. Before she had to leave. The fellows like that salad with anything, no matter what else I make."

Josie smiled over her friend's reaction. Janine was so definitely pleased that they shared something, even if it was pickled vegetables. Was enjoying Janine's reaction a way to have fun? Nice, but... No, probably not exactly fun.

"What's in the package or is it none of my business?"

"It IS your business." With that, she tore open the package and slid out a number of flat bags made of some heavy tan material. They were about a foot square and had a small cluster of flowers embroidered on each one.

"Book bags," she explained with a grin. "I thought we'd be wantin' to let the youngens take a book home, and I didn't want anything to happen that would hurt the books. If they put the book in a bag, and if they were told to keep it in the bag every minute they weren't looking at it, I thought they'd take good care of it. Even if it was raining, the book would stay dry because of the flap that lays over... see? This here canvas sheds water like a duck."

"Hmmm. Such a clever idea. I'd never have thought of it. Or had this fabric if I did think of it. Where did you get it?"

Another pleased grin. "That, I'm glad to tell you, is what happened to the floor cover of my sleeping tent on the way here. I'm never gonna leave here, so I'll never need it again."

"Floor cover?"

"Yeah, to keep bugs from crawling in your clothes while you slept, or even a grass snake from looking for a warmer place to sleep. The fellows just flaked out on the grass at night, day clothes and all. Except when I made Tray sleep with me. He didn't like it, but he can disappear so fast, I didn't want to give him a chance. I done put too much time and energy into him to risk loosin' him now when it looks like he might amount to somethin'."

Josie spread the cloth bags into a fan, examining the different flower clusters on each bag. Six of them.

"I know there's only six but I got six more waitin' for the trimmin'. I just got excited to show you, and the big girls are already askin' about gettin' to take one home. It'll be good for 'em 'cause they can look at the books with lamp light of a evenin' after they got their chores done."

Impressed, Josie continued to stare at the bags. As much has she had always valued books, she had never been fearful of wear and tear. There were always more, but apparently not for Janine and probably not for these girls. They had no New York address and unlimited coins to turn to.

Later, as she was monitoring the copying of spelling words by Level Two, she heard Janine say to Level One, "Now you see how purty these domino's are with their colors, but don't be sayin' a color when you need to say a number. These colors are just to save time so you don't have to count the spots every time you want a special number. Tray, did you hear me?"

No answer.

Persistently, "Tray...?"

A grin and an answer. "Yes, Miss Janine."

A burst of spontaneous laughter broke out with Level Four at the answer he gave his sister. Janine made no response. "I want each of you to find three dominos that have two spots. Then you count them and tell me how much is three twos?"

A duck of the head and a shyly lifted hand.

"Yes, Lily?"

"Six, Miss Janine."

"Very good. Now find me two fours."

Even Josie was amazed when later several of them remembered, without looking, what was 2 X 4 and 3 X 2. Janine was a master at dealing with every situation that arose.Later, she heard Janine explaining the purpose of the canvas bags, and that no book could go home with any person unless it had a bag. Also, that when a book was put down, even for a minute, it must be put into the bag with a bookmark to hold the place. Also, they would be making bookmarks tomorrow, and a bookmark must be shown before a take-home book could happen. A book must come back the next day even if they wanted to take it home again.

With a small smile and a shake of the head, Josie noted how possessive Janine was over every action that involved the precious books.

Josie was finally at her desk, alone, at the end of the day and warming her hands on a mug of hot coffee. Bradley Cullen tapped on the door, and pushed it open. Advancing with a pleased smile and a box, he seated himself at a study table, dwarfing the table by his size. Emptying the box, he displayed a pile of shaped wood pieces, all sanded smooth and made shiny with shellac.

"States of the Union," he announced. "Took a pattern off a book Janine brought home. Made 'em bigger for youngen's hands, and they fit together like a puzzle."

Leaving the comfort of the warm mug, Josie joined him at the table. In silence, they fitted the pieces together creating a nation easily measuring two and a half feet wide and a foot or so high.

"I'm thinkin' I might'a got off the line on some state borders, 'cause the picture was so little. With a better picture, I could try again."

Josie stared, amazed. Janine had clipped out a sleeve pattern for Miz Gray Owl, just as though it was nothing. Just a thing to be done for a sudden need. And here her brother had a map of the states as they were this year, and it was made of wood that would not tear up like cardboard. Surely there was nothing else they could do, but there was.

"Nuther thing. See this box? It's like what I made for Tray when he was a little feller, so he could reach the table and other things.

Called it a 'Stand-On Box'. Made him a good carryin' box, too. See, it's 8 inches wide and 15 inches long. The other side is ten inches high. It's nailed so solid that even a big feller could stand on it if he need to be taller to reach somethin'. One more thing, they make a good holdin' box for the puzzle or the blocks, or even the domino blocks."

Josie stared, speechless, but Brad inserted, "I know there's only one, but that was 'cause this was all the scraps I had of this material. Next trip to the mill, I'll pick up more. Bein' the same size, they stack to take up less room. I thought to make another 5 or 6 of them, or however many you could use."

Josie finally found her tongue, to rescue her from a rude, stunned silence. "This is absolutely fantasic! I truly never thought of needing the boxes until I saw this one. Certainly, I never thought of a wooden puzzle of the states. You and Janine... I just don't know what to think."

Later, as he headed south, he was whistling. Perhaps it was just a small step, but he was now included with his sister who ranked high in Josie's favor, and right now he'd be glad for what he could get. To be included anywhere was an encouragement.

It was in the middle of the dark night, with Tray tossing and turning in his nervous energy, and his father snoring with manly vigor, the next step of Brad's plan entered his head, complete and set about with every element of success built in. Now, the only thing left to be determined was the way to go about it.

Three days later, he stood with elbows resting on the rail fence of the paddock watching his red-haired neighbor work his lively charges. Tossing a small pad on the back of Blizzard, he stepped back to watch while the young stallion bared his teeth and bent his neck into a perfect "U". Grabbing the edge of the pad with his teeth, he flung it in the direction of his trainer.

Brad commented, "Not havin' much luck, huh?"

Jeff joined him at the fence. “Yep. He’s doin’ what I wanted, havin’ fun with his game. I want him to think he has control of the game so he can enjoy it. He don’t know the game’s gonna change a few times till he thinks it’s still part of the game to have a saddle and bridal strapped on. Have him comin’ along, then the girls’ll follow.”

Brad showed his admiration. “Bein’ sneaky, huh?”

“Yeah. Gonna make a good trained carriage horse. Even if there ain’t no carriages inside’a twenty miles, I’m thinkin’ there might be. Someday.”

“You know, Jeff, I had me a thought. I know it takes time to run over to Argyle, but I find myself needin’ to make a trip soon. I was wonderin’ if maybe there’d be thing or two you be needin’, and we could make the trip together. I’m havin’ to take the buggy anyway, to bring stuff back.”

“Don’t know. Hadn’t thought on it.”

Meaningful pause. “Noticed last time I was there that the Sweet Shop got ‘em a generator to freeze store-bought ice cream. They make it on Fridays and Saturdays. My sister has an uncommon likin’ for store bought ice cream, especially chocolate. Thought next trip over with the buggy, I’d take her along if I went on a Saturday. ‘Course, she works of a Friday so that day’d be out.”

Calculated silence as the two young men leaned against the fence watching the young animals cavort and playfully nip at each other. Such fortunate animals! Never having to scrounge for food or seek shelter in a storm.

Jeff made a move to return to his work, so Brad interjected. “I don’t know if your cousin has a taste for ice cream, or not. Never talked with her about it, but I’m thinking Janine would have more fun with her along. Thinkin’ about askin’ her.”

Jeff made no response.

Brad again. He needed to press the matter now while he still had the courage. “I know it’s sudden, and things a body needs don’t just jump up and remind 'im. I gotta head on back, but I'll stop in a day or two to see if you thought of somethin'."

Jeff, now sixteen, was thoroughly wrapped up in his training. Picking up his saddle pad, he dismissed Brad with the words, "I'll do that."

Walking away, Brad sighed. Not as good as he'd hoped, but it was not all bad. He'd sort of put the younger fellow on the spot while he was working, but then again, he hadn't said he didn't have time. Two days should give him time to think about it. Only bad way it could go, would be for Jeff to say that, yes, he needed something and would Brad pick it up for him. That'd put the cabache on his whole plan.

Now, all he had to do was to think up something he needed that could be carried only by the two-seated buggy. But he had two days to do it in. He was encouraged.

It was clearly time for Brad to have a bit of luck, and he did. As it turned out, that was the day that the sole of Jeff's boot purely left the rest of the shoe, the threads being worn bare from the rocky soil of the paddock. Needed to get it sewed up, and look at the chances of getting another pair. Montgomery Ward Catalog, for certain, but the tack store in Argyle might have work boots by now.

Brad finally settled on the need for a new spade, hoe and shovel. Maybe if they had a hand sickle... but if not, he'd need a scythe for harvesting summer hay. Janine warned him that the handle of the current shovel was pretty well rotted through, and she could not exist without a shovel for her kitchen garden. Furthermore, she didn't intend to try. A lady had to stand up for her rights.

She complained that the previous owner of the shovel that had come with the house had seemingly neglected to oil the handle sufficiently when it was new, or it wouldn't have rotted. That'd not happen to a new one, with her in charge.

The mere mention of the store-bought ice cream was enough to keep her singing for days. She was almost about ice cream like ladies who were "carrying" were about pickles.

Things moved slowly. Janine greatly enjoyed the ice cream, and Josie greatly enjoyed Janine's enjoyment. The conversational current was revved up occasionally by Brad, as he figured he had the most to gain... or loose. He had collected and stored up a few bits of community interest, and had let the girls take off on their own whenever possibly.

Enough fun was had that they actually discussed when they would come again. In her analytic mind, Josie sought to determine if it was fun, and decided it must be. At least it was a lot different from her usual day, and that had its own possibilities.

The second outing left the girls at the catalog store looking at new styles and other new inventions. Conversation in the Sweet Shop became more animated, and so many things seemed funny but, later, could not be remembered why. Josie nodded to herself with satisfaction. This could, actually, become fun, and she just needed to readjust her life enough to accommodate it.

Then the Sweet Shop installed the machine that made liquid fizzy, and gave flavor to the ice cream. Something new and fun. As she stepped back through the door of her beautiful new room after a satisfying couple of hours in which she had experienced not one thought of lesson preparation, Josie smiled to herself. Yes, Papa, I think I may have discovered fun.

Then she actually giggled to herself at the audacity of having to analyze the act of having fun!

A Note From The Narrator

(Researched and written by historian
Merytaten Franchesca Angelique Evengeline Cullen Carpenter)

For those of you who have followed this historical saga so far, don't you hate it when you get left with a bundle of loose ends? Well, I do, too. So don't you fret none, because there's more to come. A body can get only so much stuff in one little book.

So I started checking around, and there's definitely more to Carlile Corners than you know so far. What's more, Miss Josie will insist on it all being documented and archived for posterity. So it will be my assignment to get it done.

You've been left just after a successful visit to the Sweet Shop in Argyle on the second leg of a serious COURTSHIP ATTEMPT as engineered by Mr. Bradley Cullen, who possesses very little skill in that area. Well, now that I have the horses hitched to the wagon of this Chronicle, hang on for the ride! You, of course, will be staying on for the second leg of the trip called ***Blossoms in the Grass***.

Being that a Chronology is an unwieldy thing, as several incidents happen at the same time, causing overlaps to occur. The next three books cover some of the same time periods from different areas of the community. This method was the only way to satisfy Miss Josie's demand for completeness.

Meanwhile, I'll tell you right off that Brad was successful. For anyone who spent the time and energy in the chase, such as he has, you will understand that he would have to win. It was not an easy chase, but a stubborn Scotsman sometimes doesn't know when to quit, and certainly doesn't realize when he's been beaten.

It is not surprising that it would take almost two years of trying to think of something a girl likes when she steadfastly refuses to furnish clues. It was clear, however, that seated at that round table at Argyle's Sweet Shop, flanked by a friend (in Janine) and a chaperone (in her cousin), that an important step had occurred, though Brad was unaware at the time.

It so happened that Josephine Eleanor Wheeler, formerly from New York City, learned that it was possible to have FUN. Even if you had to work at it. She also learned exactly what it was because her analytical mind came to her aid. Having fun was friends laughing at nonsense while being separated, geographically, from responsibilities. Still true, though, that except for the command from her deceased father (through her former tutor) she might never have figured it out. But it happened.

Skipping a few pages to be filled in later. The two were married a few months after Josie's nineteenth birthday on the same day she moved into the spacious four roomed house Brad had constructed just south of the stone cabin built by Digby. More about that later.

The path of the other two of the foursome, Janine and Jefferson, was somewhat different. Janine had always enjoyed the view across the paddock fence and on past the expensive horseflesh, but with the singleness of mind of the Wilson family (so much like the Wheeler family, actually) the red-haired Scottish Viking saw only the challenge of his five four-footed investments.

It took the small round table in Argyle, the maturing of his inter-workings, the sight of a pale, but rosy tinted complexion across the table from him without a cloud of corral dust in between, and a moment when his companions had heard everything (twice) about his animals... to get his attention.

What followed was almost three years of house parties with popcorn and fudge, rides in the new, high-wheeled carriage behind the muscular rear of Blizzard... and occasional Sunday dinners at this place and that. It took a lot of conversation to learn that they, too, seemed to talk pretty much the same language. It took the feminine skill of handling family situations and the staunch, singleness of purpose of a man to succeed. On that, they could agree.

After that, there seemed to be no place to go where it would not be better for them to go together.

Jeff took a lease on one half of Josie's quarter section with an option to buy at some future date if she wanted to sell. He acquired a barn, cross-fencing and plowed acres with the deal, as his brothers were then elsewhere with their black, sickle-horned charges. The Angus cattle were an expanding investment, and they have their own story.

Jefferson traded his services for a specified number of days of hauling flagstone building material to the house Brad was putting together in the time he spared from the smithy.

More about those two couples as time goes on.

So with that taken care of, let's plunge ahead to Josephine's pride and joy, her Level Four class of girls. Because of the satisfaction and pleasure of their parents, the girls were permitted time (almost two whole extra years) to spend at the school, at the price of sacrificed time at their homes.

Their help as assistant tutors gave Josie time to expose them to a higher degree of math and literature than they would likely ever need, and to the novels composed of what went on the outside world. These were valued as well as the graceful, musical words of the English poets.In addition, some of the American writers were now gaining their own prominence.

By contacting the authorities in the educational field, Josie was able to procure a copy of the requirements for school teaching in the Territory of Oklahoma. Seated at the round table in the stone cave, she coached them into the depth of detail required by the grammar, tables of weight, measurement and the abstract details of math as well as the elements of geography up to that period.

When Brad, at length, took them aboard his double buggy (that was Josie, Carmelita, age almost 14, Rosalie, almost 14, and Carlotta and Francine, both barely 13) and made the trip to Oklahoma City. Two nights were spent in a boarding house for the test that took no less than six hours.

During this time, Brad and Josie wandered around the new city, wondering with amazement at the improvements that happened almost daily.

Where most states and cities grew at an even rate, with housing and conveniences, as well as entertainment, being provided as the need acquired, such did not happen in the territory. The settling of the central nugget of land of central Oklahoma, the part settled by the sound of a gunshot, the situation was entirely different.

Cities were born in a day. Landowners, from three states distance and beyond, who never expected to farm their own acres, found themselves owners of a quarter section of fertile land. Eager families flowed in like a flood in the spring rains, and one important activity lagged behind. The school system was totally inadequate to handle the influx of the children. The addition of four new teachers from the outlying prairie was heralded with joy. Four more teachers to place in communities begging for their services.

Such a disappointment, however, for the authorities to learn the facts. These four young ladies had no idea of submitting themselves to the rigors of a ten-hour day and the other requirements of a regimented system. The Teaching Certificate they earned and received, was desired and valued, but only as a stepping stone and a validation as they went down a path of their choosing. They were enlightened and they knew they would create their space where and when they wanted it... and they did.

Josie relaxed and enjoyed her day as her charges took their test. She had not an iota of a doubt as to whether the girls would qualify for a certificate. After the almost three years she had spent with them, she knew them well, and knew there was no way that the girls could do anything else but sail through with flying colors. So to say.

After that, their future was up to them, as hers had been with her.

Josie was right.

Now I think it's only fair that I introduce myself and my part of this chronicle. Josie Wheeler Cullen moved into the new house and one year later produced a strapping pair of twin sons. The next year... the same. Then after four boys in three years. there came a little girl.

All the pent up desire for a daughter came out when Josie named her tow-headed girl child Merytaten (after the Egyptian relative of Joseph), Franchetta, Angelique, Evangeline Cullen. That girl child was me, and despite the vast variety of names and nicknames available, I was never called anything by my father but Mutt. Except by my husband, but more about that, later.

Josie produced one more son, and thought she'd done enough toward populating Carlile Corners. She named him Barnabas after guess who?

I was barely walking when Digby passed on to his duties in the next life. An attractive corner of Josie's land was dedicated as a place to honor the town's people who required a burying place. Old Gray Owl, her brother, Gray Eagle, and Miz Carlile were to follow during the next years.

The loss of Digby had sent Josie into a period of depression. He had become more of an integral part of her life than her blood parents whom she lost in the fire. There was a lot of talk about the value of the crippled man to the orphaned girl and how his own life was wrapped around pleasing her and anticipating her needs. He was a combined protective father and indulgent grandfather... and she was the precious treasure he had never expected to have.

She greatly desired a daughter but first produced four sons. There were those who speculated at Digby's death and seemed to agree that he had refused to go on to his reward until Josie got her girl. When that happened, then the worn-out old man could pass on and rest in peace.

Josie performed her duty with the education of her brother and cousin, opening their mind and challenging their skills. Joshua was twelve and Darrel was not far behind when Jefferson took them to Oklahoma City and saw them onto the noisy Santa Fe headed for New York City and their future.

At the other end of the line, they were deposited into the care of Josh's guardian and placed in the school chosen by Barnabas Masterby, PhD.

As the dust of their departure from the Corners settled, and Josie and Aunt Nettie had wept sufficiently on each other's shoulders, the two ladies dried their tears, firmed their chins and waited for the letters the boys had promised to write. Just as they had been expected to do.

Young Trayler Cullen blossomed. He could not do otherwise under the able tutoring of Josie and the firm sisterly hand of Janine. From a very early age he began so show talent at dealing with other people. He moved with utmost confidence through restless helpfulness (whether his help was desired or not), through bouts of growth-induced clumsiness and periods of being accident-prone.

It seemed that so many young males were intent on destroying themselves, but the truth is that few of them succeed (as evidenced by the number of grown men still living.) Everyone for miles in every direction knew of the young man from his brother's blacksmith shop. In truth, though, he might have been less than he was if it had not been for Lily Gray Owl, who insisted on being his third hand. She was his shadow and, when necessary, his prop. It was her adoration that plunged him ahead. Lily was his everything, and seemingly all he needed.

Young Henry Hastings, a disciplined and favored only child stepped into luck at the Prairie Academy. So happy and pleased were his parents that they felt he could benefit by further education and moved themselves to Oklahoma City. Their quarter section, the one they had acquired in the Run of 1889, was put up for two year lease with the stipulation that the house be kept in good repair and certain areas cross-fenced.

The offer of the lease was snapped up by the brothers, Matt and Doug Wilson, who were ready to move off Josie's section for more space. They were also convinced that the land would be eventually for sale at a time when they would be able to acquire it, and it was.

Raymond Canfield managed, with the help of his father, to acquire a Lease to Buy to the quarter section just west of Carlile Corners. The "lease to buy" provided that he would develop a graveled road midway north and south, also east and west creating an + that cut the fourth of a square mile containing his land into its four quarters. This activity assured the increased value of the land in the event Raymond was not able to raise the price after two years.

The strong young man managed for a dirt slip, also a strong wagon and a deal to scrape gravel and broken chips of stone from Josie's stone ledge. The creation of the school, Digby's cabin, as well as paved areas and the new house that Brad built while waiting for Josie to set the day, had created an impressive pile of stone chips.

Watching his progress, Miss Josie smiled and nodded to herself with a noticeable pride as the chips were spread on the dirt road for strength. The teacher, who was not a teacher, could almost imagine the Academy was like a bird's nest containing baby birds. It was as though she had fed and nurtured them and then the moment came that they were lifted up and tossed in the air... ready to fly on their own wings

Josie was not surprised as she watched her former student. Raymond's work had always been neat and thought out, and his sketches and illustrations were above average. Though he pretended that school was a snap and that his instant answers had not been the result of effort on his part, the truth was far different. Josie had it on good authority that the boy had spent lamp-lit hours, the same as his sisters, elbows on the kitchen table and head bent over the assignments.

Gwinnie and Kristy McLaughlin, the sisters who started in Level Three at ages 8 and 9, had influenced their father to buy for them the strip of land where Carlile Corners was located. The owner of the land was actually Matt Wilson, Senior, who had willingly allowed the Corners to squat on his land without cost. What was the worth of a small corner out of a quarter section?

So he sold a 100 foot strip bordering on the road to Argyle, and across the road from Raymond Canfield's purchase. He could plainly see that development of this strip would raise the value of all surrounding land.

The two girls (now young ladies) had dreams of a shop offering sweets and sandwiches, rather an updated version on the one operated by old Miz Carlile. The Cookie Jar was the current name of the future shop. More details about it in ***Cookies, Hats and Hankies***, the fourth book of the Chronology. ***Cookies, Hats and Hankies*** contains a lot that has nothing to do with food and clothing. You'll be surprised... really.

Josie thought the cookie shop had a good chance of being a success. The morning coffee and lunch sandwiches had been popular, and if the girls could turn out food like their mother had sent to her when she first arrived, their success was certain. Mrs. McLaughlin's desserts were lauded for miles around.

Matthew Wilson bought a lot of good will with the sale of that strip of land, and with his children going their separate ways, who needed the whole tract, anyway? And if it turned out that his last son, Darrell, was interested (though not likely) there was still a lot of land left. He had, as yet, not shown the same interests his brothers had, so likely his future was turned in another direction. Possibly with his cousin. Maybe reading the law out on the prairie.

The O'Day brothers, Isaac and David, worked with their father growing hay for animal feed. The demand was increasing as the land became more closely populated. Not everyone had access to the space to produce the food for animals. Such was the problem of the United States Cavalry, commissioned to protect the area to the west. Small skirmishes arose with regularity, and the transportation animals involved in the skirmishes, required hay. The government became a valued customer.

Load after load of the horse feed was delivered by the O'Day brothers, until the day came that Isaac, weary of hay cutting and entranced by the uniform of the Cavalry, did not return to the farm with Jacob.

That was all right with his brother. Jacob quickly saw that it would mean more money for him, and he now had squatter's rights to his father's farmstead. It was difficult not to notice the young ladies who came with their parents from farther east. The right one was bound to come along, and his father would let him build wherever he wanted to. He knew the hay business would not progress without him, and it didn't.

Already he had seen the flyers on the new grass seed that would better withstand the unique weather of the territory. Fact is, he'd just stop over at Argyle next chance he got, and see about ordering some of that seed.

Isaac, the Cavalryman, also performed a service to the Corners community. With his family so close, he came home often for visits and a home-cooked meal. It was natural he would bring friends with him, and they were always welcome. Especially were they welcome to some of the girls whose families were filling in the population of the Corners, Shady Ridge, Pigeon Creek, Enterprise, Sentinel Rock and other small settlements.

The occasional weddings were major social occasions that were well attended by Isaac's fellow Cavalrymen as well as friends of the bride. This had been one of the things that the settlement had missed. An important bond to any community is its social life, and now that vacancy was seemingly being filled.

The situation with Carlotta was unusual. The only daughter of Carl Owen was the youngest of the Level Four girls. When she was barely thirteen, actually while the girl was in Oklahoma City taking her test for her Teaching Certificate, it happened. Her parents were scouting the backside of their quarter section, combining the outing with a picnic. The picnic lunch was consumed and while her mother relaxed on the quilt beside the spread lunch, her father strolled over to the stream to check the quantity of water.

He knew his beloved wife was napping, and would not need him for a while, so he became involved in his plan. There was a place where a small dam could be built, and the water that accumulated would be a perfect pond for fish. He was thinking of the pleasure of showing the pond to his daughter when the scream of pain occurred.

Running, terrified toward the scream, he had the fear of being too late. She was not given to hysterics, but sound she was making was tearing out his heart.

For years afterward, he berated himself for leaving her, though if he had stayed, he might also have been napping. Neither of them would have seen the prairie rattler as it moved onto the softness of the spread quilt, its forked tongue waving in inquiry. The warmth of the human enticed the reptile forward, and it slipped unnoticed into the folds of her petticoat.

The smooth flesh of her thigh had the aroma of food, so he sunk his bare fangs into the warmth, just to check it out. The venom-coated fangs of the reptile cut into a network of capillaries that sent their blood back to the beating heart.

The unbearably fiery pain was instantaneous. Grabbing up his precious wife and sprinting back to the cabin accomplished nothing. The venom had filled her body, and the pain had thrown her into unconsciousness... into blessed relief from the pain that nothing could alleviate.

Carlotta Owen returned, proudly in possession of a Teaching Certificate earned by her own effort, to a house full of neighbors and a father in a state of delirium.

She put away her crisp new Certificate and joined a father who could not comfort her, and who was unable to accept comfort.

Thinking back, she appreciated the neighbors who dropped whatever necessary duty they were engaged in and came. A friend and neighbor could not be let to agonize alone. Food to be brought. Words to be said. An attempt to gain a normal feeling in an abnormal day.

The sound of the construction of the pine box was put together out of the hearing of the bereaved. The fertile soil of the cemetery was moved aside to accept the final result of the tragedy.

Neighbors stayed as long as they could afford the time. Ladies sought to comfort the girl who sought to comfort her father. Carlotta determined that she could grieve later and learn to survive but she was only thirteen and her efforts were in vain. Her father was not able to accept what had happened.

There's a lot more that should go in here, but I must let it go for now. There will be room for that in the next book of this chronicle. ***Blossoms in the Grass*** was created for that purposes.

Enough to say that, as my Aunt Nettie Wilson says, "its an ill wind that blows nobody good". Out of this horrible incident a healing occurred, and one outcome was that Carlotta, in later years, became my own beloved mother-in-law.

Can something good ever outweigh something bad? That is probably a job for the philosopher to decide, but it has its value. Mrs.

Gray Owl's healing salve cannot keep the dirt-dobber wasp from stinging the inquisitive child, but it can relieve the pain and reduce the red whelp. So we have the right to be grateful for the salve.

When I hear my mom and Aunt Janine talking of that time in the life of Carlotta, one of the precious Level Four girls, it is just too painful for my mind to engage.

I haven't yet mentioned my Aunt Esther, one of the very important people to my life, and I wish I could have met her. She was five when Josie came to the territory. She was too young and delicate to come to the Prairie Academy, but she came anyway so she wouldn't be left out.

She sat at the table with Tray Cullen, and he protected her as he did Lily Gray Owl. They tell me there was something about Esther that just made people want to take care of her. Slight built and slender as a wheat stalk, she grew up with those friends and neighbors who possessed sturdy and hearty bodies. She could only stay and watch her friends who were active as monkeys.

But Esther was beautiful. Beautiful as an angel is beautiful and seeming that she might just float away if she were not lovingly held. At sixteen, she was to meet a Cavalry officer who was smitten at first sight.

Nothing could keep him from Esther if there was a way, and he risked military discipline as a result. He was young for the assignments given him, but he was perfectly set up for an enviable career in uniform.

One look at Esther erased all his hopes and dreams of a military career, and he *would have* her as his own. With reluctance, Uncle Matthew gave consent and they were married, though on the condition that he would let them build a cabin for her near her parents. They reasoned that an officer would be forced to be away on many occasions, and this way she would be kept safely close and have help if needed.

Young Jeremiah Day would have agreed to anything, and routinely risked dismissal from the force just to be with her. In practically no time, it happened that she was carrying the next generation under her delicate ribs. It was not good news to those who knew and loved her, but that did not change facts. Life *would* go on.

The excited future parents could talk of almost nothing else, and as though enough had not already happened, Mrs. Gray Owl sadly told Aunt Nettie that Esther was carrying twins, and that there would be trouble. What kind of trouble? The old Kiowa doctor woman would not say. She insisted some things did not deserve to be put into words.

At eight months, the old woman came in the night and pounded on Uncle Matthew's door. It was time. She was right. It was clearly time for the trouble.

Hurrying to Esther's cabin, they found her alone and in labor. Young Jeremiah was on duty at the outpost. Esther's small delicate bones just would not readily spread, and the two undersized girls barely slid into the world, gasping their first breath.

A quick examination by the old Kiowa doctor, and she turned away from the babies to the mother. Silently she worked with her, though she knew it was useless. Too much blood gone! Too much strength... also gone. Her breath came in faint vapors, then it, too, was gone.

When the distraught officer was notified, he came at breakneck speed and threw himself at her as if he could force her back to life. Hysterical with grief, he was totally incoherent.

The two little girls were fed milk spooned into their mouths drop by drop.

Names for them? He shook his head and turned away. My great aunt Nettie, grandmother to the twins, asked him, is Catherine and Carolyn all right? A nod was all she got. The papers had to be filled out. And that was the way they were named.

A nod of acceptance with tears streaming down his face. How did he have so many tears in one body? Mrs. Gray Owl heated a cup of liquid and insisted he drink it. He did, and in a short time he leaned over in exhausted, and medicated, sleep. In the morning he awoke and stared about him as though he remembered nothing.

At the burial he stood by the pine box and watched the birds in the trees. Returning to the house, he picked up the two babies, burying his face into their delicate sweetness. His tears flowed onto their faces... down their necks. Then, kissing them both, he walked away.

Before the day was out, a message came that he had walked into the line of fire on the practice range and three bullets caught him in the head and back.

The loose dirt in the cemetery was again scooped out to hold the additional box. If he had living people to mourn him, it was never known.

Like Mrs. Gray Owl predicted... trouble. When life hands more to humans than they can bear, they just politely excuse themselves from participating in life. And that was what he did.

For a pair of identical twins, there was a surprising difference. From the very first, one was laughing and one was sober. One was mischievous and one was serious. They were as different as... well, Aunt Nettie (who insisted they were hers and she would care for them), said we could just forget their legal names. They were Sunny Day and Rainy Day. The same way I was Mutt.

I was two years old at the time, and the girls became my best friends. Like I said, I would like to have known my Aunt Esther, as she was a great part of my life through the two girls she left. I often thought she left them as play-toys... just for me.

Fascinating, though...the concern over their health due to their early arrival was wasted effort. They inherited the stocky, solid body of most of the Wilson family, and were as healthy as the tumble weeds that heaped themselves against fences and houses. Angelic faces and red-blond curls.

We grew up in a wonderful world of our own. What does a child need but food, loving parents and a protective community?

It years later after many activities when Miss Josie assigned me to writing a history of the Corners. How's it going so far?

Life on the prairie had its own flavor and had to be enjoyed fast as it was a continuously moving panorama of humans and scenery. After the statehood party held at the Cookie Jar, there was no stopping the progress of these hardy pioneers.

What comes next? Well, here are my notes.

Miss Josie's assignment for me was to detail life at Carlile Corners as it was central and typical of the magical saga of America. When Miss Josie assigned a project, it was meant to be accomplished.

Dear to her heart was her "Level Four Girls" and also, those of her "Level Three". They are all in their late thirties, now, and there is no more guessing about their future.

Miss Josie thought the assignment of the second book should be titled ***First Teachers of Oklahoma***, but she was not a writer. Who would be interested in reading anything with a title like that? Just tell me that!

I can accept the assignment, but not that title. I could think of one much better, and I plan to use the title of a poem written by one of the Level Four Girls. It will be called, ***Blossoms in the Grass***, and I will begin it right away.

If you liked this one, you'll love the next one!

Selected Excerpts from the Next Four Books in the Carlile Corners Series

Excerpt One:

It was while they ate breakfast in the diner that he dared to bring up the subject again. "Shall it be today that we get on with killing you? We don't have to be in a hurry. We can look for the willin' fellow. What do you think?"

A napkin delicately touched her mouth. A sign passed her lips. "I always thought there'd be a white dress and veil and music. And that I'd be happy. It's all gone. I've got no place to go to get away from what happened. I know you're just tryin' to help, but there's no help to be had."

Ralph watched. Things were definitely looking up. "Listen to this. We don't have to go straight home. I can send a note and tell 'em we found a lotta things to see here, and that way we could wait around and see if what you are scared of is really going to happen."

Long moment of thought, "Maybe..."

Silence as Ralph forced himself to wait.

Then, "You say that even after what I did there'd be a fellow to marry me no matter what happened?"

"Carlotta, you did NOT do anything. Plenty was done to you, but you did nothing. Remember that. And, yes, there are fellows who'd jump at the chance, even knowin'..." He watched her face.

"Of course, we're just talkin'. Nothin' we say'll make a bit of difference when you're dead. I'm gonna sure hate tellin' your Papa that you decided not to live. Here he lost his own folks and he had babies die before they were born," and Ralph paused to let the words sink in.

"All those babies he wanted, but what he got was only you, and you were more than he ever expected in a daughter. Obedient, beautiful, hardworking. Earning a teaching Certificate in only two years was special and he was proud of you. But all of that will be gone. He lost your Mama who he loved more than his own life, and now he'll loose his daughter. I KNOW he would want you to come home NO MATTER WHAT happened, and he will try to help you forget.

"Of course, all of that means nothing, because I promised to let you drown. At least, he'll get to have another look at you before we bury you. That way, he'll have a picture in his mind of how beautiful you are."

"I'm not beautiful," she responded, stubbornly.

"Depends on who's lookin', wouldn't you say?"

He watched her hand as it moved toward the breadbasket. Would a girl wanting to die bother with another jam and biscuit?

She sighed. "Where would you look?"

"Where would I look for what?"

"The fellow... the one that didn't care... no matter... even..."

Then later...........

"I said I'd do what I could, and this is something I can do. White dress and all."

"NO! No white dress! I don't deserve that. You don't know what happened to me!"

"Now, that'd be up to you. The thing is, I thought girls couldn't wear white dresses because'a what they did. You didn't do a thing. That means you qualify to wear a white dress. That is, if you want to."

"Well, I...."

Another excerpt:

"Is there someone I could leave the baby with for a few hours? I have to make a trip back to where we were ambushed. I didn't see much in the dark and I speck they got all six horses. I have to look around, though, because everything I had was there but the baby. Miz Lizzie was with the other wagon that got burned. I don't know her at all, but she seems to have developed an idea of who I am. She's calling me James, and acts like she may have cared for a baby."

"Couldn't say who her folks were?"

"No. She was wanderin' through the brush. But the fact is, I'm gonna take her with me. I'm thinkin' the law won't say its kidnappin' and it may turn out we need each other. Anyway, I need to go back."

It was a slow journey and the young man was torn between wishing to get this mission completed, and dread for what he might see. The lone horse trotting between the double-tree poles of the small wagon seemed to be enjoying the day.

Compass in hand, Stanley guided himself directly to the scene of the damage. Three piles of ashes and chunks of burned debris. A quick glance revealed no slain bodies. A guilty sigh of relief. Nature's clean-up committees a work.

Another guilty sigh. No bodies to bury that would compound his agony.

There were tools without handles. Hammer, ax, hatchet. Rake, spade and shovel with the grubbing picks.

Anger ground its way through his brain. The thieving demons had taken a half a dozen animals. He trembled from head to bended knees with hatred.

A few glass dishes. Smoked, but not broken. A necklace and two rings. He put them in his pocket. A present for the baby. It was all that was left of her parents. Something to save. He swallowed hard to remove the lump in his throat, but was not successful. Dragged his sleeve roughly across his blurry eyes. Time, now, for tears.

His soot-blackened face became tear-streaked as he made his way back to the baby and the old woman, neither of whom belonged to him.

Another except:

Miss Francine had just set her students to light work. It was much too hot for them to concentrate and the blank paper and crayons were saved for such a time as this. Fanning herself with a card from the math game, she stepped to the front door for a breath. Along with the breath of air came the smoke. Fear like an iron-fingered hand clutched her lungs and heart.

PRAIRIE FIRE! And here she had a room full of children she was responsible for! She looked around outside and saw no one. She drew in a breath and braced herself for attack.

"Students, listen. This is not a game, and I want you to stay in your seat unless I call your name. Eddie Brown, you run to your house and ring the dinner bell until someone comes. Keep yelling 'Fire, Fire' until you see someone, and then start drawing water into the water trough.

Mary Kate, run as fast as you can to your house and ring the bell. Be careful not to fall. Richie, go draw water and pour it in the stock tank until Eddie can help. Then you carry it here in buckets."

Grabbing up her bonnet, a pillow and the bath towels that were handy, she went to the yard to watch for sparks.

The flames were now visible across the road. The fire had passed the nearest farmhouse, and the noisy group was still trying to save the barn. Sparks flew.

"Troy, go in the schoolroom and get help to bring out a study table. You've got to get on the roof. I see sparks landing."

Darlene was there first with the water, lifting it up to Troy on the table. Troy handed it on to the man on the roof. The man scrambled to the gable and splashed a stream of water on the flame. A shout from the young lady, and a wet towel came hurdling through the air toward him.

The teacher felt heat on her arm, and glanced down to see the flames climbing up the lace of her skirt.........................

Another except:

Old Miz Carlilie was dead.

It was practically impossible for anyone to believe that she was no longer to be found on her rocker in the shack located at the corner of State Highway and the road to Argyle.

It was inconceivable that she no longer sat there... where every curve of the rocker was shaped to fit her lumpy body while she dispensed coffee, or something similar. She no longer sat with her pleasant wrinkled-face smile while customers (neighbors) helped themselves before checking their own particular mail hook.

Not much was known about Miz Carlile except that she was possibly older than the prairie itself, and was certainly here before the great Land Run in 1889. Her establishment was originally located where a small stream of water crossed a buffalo migration route, or so it was said. But things, as well as stories, had to start somewhere.

Old Miz Carlile was dead. Unbelievable, actually. There had seemed to be thought that she might live forever.

Her death was to effect great changes at Carlile Corners. The first thing was that two young sisters would start their own business. Were they not graduates of the Prairie Academy where that sort of thing was taught? They had worked hard and done well, and now they could come into their own.

Putting their knowledge to work, they created that which became the first of several landmarks.

Years later, young America Forrester happened in at the Cookie Jar. She was the official caretaker of the massive Clydesdale horses used for road work. What had she been doing... why, mucking out, of course.

"What is 'mucking out?"

"Oh, that's when... well, it's really... what it is... is poop! It has to be taken out of the stalls and piled up to start it decaying. Raymond says I can't operate the spreader, but I'll convince him I can. It's part of my job. Oh, say! We just had a baby! Our Lucy, she's just old enough and this is her first foal. A little girl and I named her Katie. I just love babies! She follows me and tries to suck on my clothes or my fingers. Oh, please excuse me. I just rattle on and on..."

Just one more excerpt:

Merytaten stood by, watching and wondering, knowing within herself that a MOMENT had happened. The inspiration and drive to complete the Chronology... the fierce urgency, had lasted with her for almost twenty years... sometimes more pressing and other times taking a back seat to necessary events in her life. It had now served out its time.

She had known it would happen. She was no longer Miss Josie's only daughter with an assignment, nor was she Merytaten, armed with her Composition book and a purpose.

The Chronology of the Corners might continue. There were grumbling in Europe. Germany was restless... France was apprehensive... and England was still war-weary, but that would not matter. So what!

There had been an Armistice (whatever that was) but it was of no consequence. The matter had not been settled, only kicked forward as a small boy kicks a stone down the road. The war would continue and another group of young men would attempt to settle it.

But now she stood in the Cemetery as one of Carlile Corners first residents passed on, leaving his land to the next generation.

But for me... Miss Josie's only daughter... the MOMENT has happened. The writer has gone, and the wife, daughter and mother remain.

While I stand here... empty... my oldest daughter, my bright star of happiness and joy, works her way toward me with a note. I glance at the familiar hand and then at the figure moving away from me into the crowd of mourners.

The note read, "Would you like to be a Grandmother?"

I glance toward my second daughter, my lovely, long-burning candle of a girl... my solid and unshakeable lady who quietly and steadily becomes important in the lives of others. She is my rock and she senses my thought as no one else has.

Her soft and delicate fingers withdraw the note and when I see it again, it is placed within the pages of her father's Bible, the one left to him as an inheritance. With it are other notes of importance to my life. With it is the white feather that was placed on her father's head as an infant.

It was to bring him peace, and it did after the long struggle of the war. His dedication and talents were brought home, and the white feather remains in his favorite Book.

I feel a flooding sense of completion of a chapter of our lives. As the sound of the shovels fill in the grave of one who has gone to his eternal home, I return to the parsonage. I have done my part.

I have given the prairie a bright and shining star...a shimmering curtain of northern lights... and also I have given it a steady long-burning candle to illuminate the family supper table... a lantern to light the way to the barn for the early milking or a lamp beside the bedside of a sick child.

Two girls I have given to Carlile Corners. The prairie needs both kinds of girls, and I was the fortunate one to be chosen to provide them. Thank you, God.

These excerpts were from the next books in the Carlile Corners series:

Blossoms in the Grass

The Shaping of Shady Ridge

Cookies, Hats, and Hankies

Under the Haystack

Joann Sisco was born in the beautiful mountains of northwestern Arkansas, and grew up as the daughter of the preacher. She later moved to Oklahoma where she lives near her daughters and grandchildren.

We hope you enjoyed reading ***Prairie Academy*** by Joann Ellen Sisco, the first book in the ***Carlile Corners*** series.

For further reading including novels and non-fiction titles by this author and others, please go to our online catalog at
http://www.signalmanpublishing.com

34969825R00141

Made in the USA
Lexington, KY
31 August 2014